David Brainerd Williamson

Life and Public Services of Abraham Lincoln

Sixteenth President of the United States

David Brainerd Williamson

Life and Public Services of Abraham Lincoln
Sixteenth President of the United States

ISBN/EAN: 9783337425739

Printed in Europe, USA, Canada, Australia, Japan

Cover: Foto ©Raphael Reischuk / pixelio.de

More available books at **www.hansebooks.com**

LIFE AND PUBLIC SERVICES

OF

ABRAHAM LINCOLN,

SIXTEENTH

PRESIDENT OF THE UNITED STATES;

AND

COMMANDER-IN-CHIEF OF THE ARMY AND NAVY OF THE UNITED STATES.

With a full history of his Life; his career as a Lawyer and
Politician; his services in Congress; with a full account of his
Speeches, Proclamations, Acts, and services as President of the
United States, and Commander-in-Chief of the Army and Navy
of the United States, up to the present time.

.

PHILADELPHIA:

T. B. PETERSON & BROTHERS,
306 CHESTNUT STREET.

CONTENTS.

18   CONTENTS.

PAGE

LIFE AND PUBLIC SERVICES

OF

ABRAHAM LINCOLN.

HIS BIRTH AND ANCESTORS.

ABRAHAM LINCOLN, the sixteenth President of the
United States, and the skilful ruler under whose wise administration the country in its hour of peril has been enabled to combat successfully with the traitors who have
attempted its destruction, was born on the twelfth of
February, 1809, in that part of Hardin county, Kentucky,
which is now known as Larue. His father, Thomas Lincoln, and his grandfather, Abraham, were born in Rock-
ingham county, Virginia, a section of the "Old Dominion"
to which their ancestors had migrated from Berks county,
Pennsylvania. In the year 1780, the grandfather removed
his family to Kentucky, where, taking possession of a
small tract of land in the wilderness, he erected a rude
cabin, and proceeded to make his new home comfortable
and productive. His daily labors were attended in their
prosecution with great personal danger. There was no
other resident within two or three miles, and the country
was infested with Indians, who allowed no opportunity to
pass to slaughter the white settlers. His gun was carried

21

as regularly to his work as was his axe or any other implement necessary to the successful clearing of the land, and at night when he retired to the bosom of his little flock, the faithful weapon was placed in a convenient corner, where it could be quickly grasped in the event of an attack from the wily enemy.

Individuals and whole families living in the vicinity were murdered by the Indians, but Abraham Lincoln for four years escaped their bloodthirsty characteristics; but at the end of that period, while clearing a piece of land about four miles from home, he was suddenly attacked, and killed, and his scalped remains were found the next morning. The loss was a severe one to the widow, who now found herself alone in the wilderness with her three sons and two daughters, and with but little money with which to provide even the necessities of life for the young members of her household. Poverty made it necessary that the family should separate; and all the children but Thomas bade adieu to their remaining parent, and left the county, the second son removing to Indiana, and the others to other sections of Kentucky.

DESCRIPTION OF HIS PARENTS.

Thomas also left home before he was twelve years old, but subsequently returned to Kentucky, and in the year 1806, married Miss Nancy Hanks, who was also a native of Virginia; so that it will be observed nearly all of the immediate ancestors of the President were born upon Southern soil. Thomas Lincoln and his wife were a plain, unassuming couple, conscientious members of the Baptist Church, and almost entirely uneducated. Mrs. Lincoln could read, but not write, while her husband could do neither, save so far as to scribble his own name in a style of caligraphy which a few of his more intimate friends could decipher. He, however, appreciated the advantages of education, and honored and respected the superior learning of others. His kindness of heart was proverbial, and he was always industrious and persevering. His wife, although uneducated, was blessed with much natural talent, excellent judgment, and good sense, and these qualifications, with her great piety, made her a suitable partner for a man of Thomas Lincoln's attributes, and a mother whose precepts and teachings could not fail to be of vast benefit in the formation of her children's characters. This estimable couple had three children—a daughter, a son who had died in infancy, and Abraham. The sister attained the years of womanhood, and married, but subsequently died without issue.

ABE" GOES TO SCHOOL.

When Abraham, or "Abe," as he was already called at home and by his companions, was seven years of age, his name was entered for the first time on the roll of an educational institution—an academy which had but little pretension in outward appearance, and the presiding genius of which had neither ambition nor ability to impart greater instruction than that which would enable his pupils to read and write. His term of schooling was, however, to be of short duration.

THE LINCOLN FAMILY REMOVE TO INDIANA.

Mr. Lincoln, although a Southerner by birth and residence, had become early imbued with a disgust for slavery. He witnessed the evils of the "peculiar institution," and longed to be free from the disagreeable effects of a condition of society which made a poor white man even more degraded than the unfortunate negro, whose energies and labors were controlled by an unprincipled and lazy master. With these sentiments he naturally desired to change his place of residence, and early in October, 1816, finding a purchaser for his farm, he made arrangements for the transfer of the property and for his removal. The price paid by the purchaser was ten barrels of whiskey, of forty gallons each, valued at two hundred and eighty dollars, and twenty dollars in money. Mr. Lincoln was a temperate man, and acceded to the terms, not because he desired the liquor, but because such transactions in real estate were common, and recognized as perfectly proper.

The homestead was within a mile or two of the Rolling Fork river, and as soon as the sale was effected, Mr. Lincoln, with such slight assistance as little Abe could give him, hewed out a flat-boat, and launching it, filled it with his household articles and tools and the barrels of whiskey, and bidding adieu to his son who stood upon the bank, pushed off, and was soon floating down the stream on his way to Indiana, to select a new home. His journey down the Rolling Fork and into the Ohio river was successfully accomplished, but soon afterwards his boat was unfortunately upset, and its cargo thrown into the water. Some men standing on the bank witnessed the accident and saved the boat and its owner, but all the contents of the craft were lost except a few carpenter's tools, axes, three barrels of whiskey and some other articles. He again started, and proceeded to a well-known ferry on the river, from whence he was guided into the interior by a resident of the section of country in which he had landed, and to whom he had given his boat in payment for his services. After several days of difficult travelling, much of the time employed in cutting a road through the forest wide enough for a team, eighteen miles were accomplished, and Spencer county, Indiana, was reached. The site for his new home having been determined upon, Mr. Lincoln left his goods under the care of a person who lived a few miles distant, and returning to Kentucky on foot, made preparations to remove his family. In a few days the party bade farewell to their old home and slavery; Mrs. Lincoln and her daughter riding one horse, Abe another, and the father a third. After a seven days' journey through an uninhabited country, their resting-place at night being a blanket spread upon the ground, they arrived at the spot selected for their future residence, and no unnecessary delays were permitted to interfere with the immediate and successful clearing of a site for a cabin. An axe was placed in Abe's hands, and with the additional assistance of a neighbor, in two or three days Mr. Lincoln had a neat house of about eighteen feet square, the logs composing which being fastened together in the usual manner by notches, and the cracks between them filled with mud. It had only one room, but some slabs laid across logs overhead gave additional accommodations which were obtained by climbing a rough ladder in one corner. A bed, table and four stools were then made by the two settlers, father and son, and the building was ready for occupancy. The loft was Abe's bedroom, and there night after night for many years, he who now occupies the most exalted position in the gift of the American people, and who dwells in the "White House" at Washington, surrounded by all the comforts that wealth and power can give, slumbered with one coarse blanket for his mattress and another for his covering. Although busy during the ensuing winter with his axe, he did not neglect his reading and spelling, and also practised frequently with a rifle, the first evidence of his skill as a marksman being manifested, much to the delight of his parents, in the killing of a wild turkey, which had approached too near the cabin. The knowledge of the use of the rifle was indispensable in the border settlements at that time, as the greater portion of the food required for the settlers was procured by it, and the family which had not among its male members one or more who could discharge it with accuracy, was very apt to suffer from a scarcity of comestibles.

DEATH OF MRS. LINCOLN—"ABE" LEARNS TO WRITE.

A little more than a year after removing to Spencer county, Mrs. Lincoln died, an event which brought desolation to the hearts of her husband and children, but to none so much as to Abe. He had been a dutiful son, and she one of the most devoted of mothers, and to her instruction may be traced many of those traits and characteristics for which even now he is remarkable. Soon after her death, the bereaved lad had an offer which promised to afford him other employment during the long, monotonous evenings, than the reading of books, a young man who had removed into the neighborhood having offered to teach him how to write. The opportunity was too fraught with benefit to be rejected, and after a few weeks of practice under the eye of his instructor, and also out of doors with a piece of chalk or charred stick, he was able to write his name, and in less than twelve months could and did write a letter.

HIS FATHER MARRIES AGAIN—ABE FINISHES HIS EDUCATION.

During the next year Mr. Lincoln married Mrs. Sally Johnston, of Elizabethtown, Kentucky, a widow-lady with three children, and who was admirably adapted to supply the vacancy which existed in the Lincoln family; and a superior woman, between whom and Abe a most devoted attachment sprung up, which ever afterwards continued. About the same time a person named Crawford moved into the neighborhood, and understanding how to read and write and the rudiments of arithmetic, was induced to open a school, to which Abe was sent, and in which he greatly improved his knowledge of the first two branches, and soon mastered the second. His school-garb comprised a suit of dressed buckskin and a cap made from a raccoon skin. His memory was retentive, and as he took an unusual pride in his studies, his close application made him a favorite scholar with his teacher, while his superior knowledge, limited though it was, caused him to be used by the more ignorant settlers as their scribe whenever they had letters to be written. A brief period at this school, and to use a fashionable phrase, his education was finished. Six months of instruction within the walls of an insignificant school-house is all the education that Abraham Lincoln has received during a long lifetime, a greater portion of which has been spent in public positions, where ability and talent were indispensable requisites.

BECOMES A HIRED HAND ON A FLATBOAT.

For four or five years after leaving school, or until he was eighteen, he constantly labored in the woods with his axe, cutting down trees and splitting rails, and during the evenings, read such works as he could borrow from the other settlers. A year later, he was hired by a man living near by, at ten dollars a month, to go to New Orleans on a flatboat loaded with stores, which were destined for sale at the plantations on the Mississippi river, near the Crescent City, and with but one companion started on his rather dangerous journey. At night they tied up alongside of the bank, and rested upon the hard deck with a blanket for a covering, and during the hours of light, whether their lonely trip was cheered by a bright sun or made disagreeable in the extreme by violent storms, their craft floated down the stream, its helmsmen never for a moment losing their spirits, or regretting their acceptance of the positions they occupied. Nothing occurred to mar the success of the trip, nor the excitement naturally incident to a flatboat expedition of some eighteen hundred miles, save a midnight attack by a party of negroes, who, after a severe conflict, were whipped by Abe and his comrade and compelled to flee, and after selling their goods at a handsome profit, the young merchants returned to Indiana.

THE FAMILY REMOVE TO ILLINOIS—ABE SEEKS HIS FORTUNE AMONG STRANGERS.

In March, 1830, Mr. Thomas Lincoln removed his family to Illinois, their household articles being transported thither in large wagons drawn by oxen, Abe himself driving one of the teams. Upon the journey, and while crossing the bottom lands of the Kaskaskia river, the males of the family were compelled to wade through water up to their waists. In two weeks they reached Decatur, Macon county, Illinois, near the centre of that State, and in another day were at the tract of land (ten acres) on the north side of the Sangamon river, and about ten miles west of Decatur. A log cabin was immediately erected, and Abe proceeded to split the rails for the fence with which the lot was to be enclosed. As a rail-splitter, as a tiller of the soil, or as a huntsman, to whose accuracy of aim the family depended in a great measure for their daily food, young Abraham Lincoln was active, earnest and laborious, and when in the following spring he signified his intention to leave his home to seek his fortune among strangers, the tidings were received by his parents and friends with the most profound sorrow.

Confident that a more extended field of observation and action would be more suitable to his tastes and disposition, he packed up what little clothing he possessed, and went westward into Menard county. He worked on a farm in the vicinity of Petersburg, during the ensuing summer and winter, at the same time improving himself, in reading, writing, grammar, and arithmetic.

HE TAKES ANOTHER TRIP TO NEW ORLEANS—
BECOMES MILLER AND SALESMAN.

Early in the following spring he was hired by a man named Offutt, to assist in taking a flatboat to New Orleans; and, as it was found impossible to purchase a suitable boat, Abe lent a willing and industrious hand in building one at Sangamon, from whence, when completed, it was floated into the Mississippi river. The trip was made, and his employer was so much gratified with the industry and tact of his hired hand, that he engaged him to take charge of his mill and store in the village of New Salem. In this position, "Honest Abe," as he was now called, won the respect and confidence of all with whom he had business dealings, while socially, he was much beloved by the residents—young and old—of the place. He was affable, generous, ever ready to assist the needy or to sympathize with the distressed, and never was known to be guilty of a dishonorable act.

HIS SERVICES IN THE BLACK HAWK WAR.

Early in the following year the Black Hawk War broke out, and the Governor of Illinois calling for troops, Abe determined to offer his services; and a recruiting station being opened in New Salem, he placed his name the first on the roll; and by his influence inducing many of his friends and companions to do likewise, a company was soon organized, and Abe was unanimously elected captain. The company marched to Beardstown, and from there to the seat of war; but during their term of enlistment— thirty days—were not called into active service. A new levy was then called for, and he re-enlisted as a private, and at the end of thirty days again re-enlisted, and re- mained with his regiment until the war ended.

IS NOMINATED FOR THE LEGISLATURE AND IS DEFEATED.

Soon after his return from this campaign, in the progress of which he proved himself an efficient and zealous soldier, although his regiment was not brought in conflict with the enemy, or as he subsequently expressed it, he "did not see any live fighting Indians, but had a good many bloody struggles with the mosquitoes," he was waited upon by several of the influential citizens of New Salem, who asked his consent to nominate him for the Legislature. He had only been a resident of the county for nine months, but as a thorough-going "Henry Clay man" was needed, he was deemed the most suitable person to run, particularly as it was believed that his popularity would ensure success in a county which had, the year before, given General Jackson a large majority for President. There were eight aspirants for the legislative position; but, although Abraham received two hundred and seventy-seven votes out of two hundred and eighty-four, cast in New Salem, he was not elected, the successful candidate leading him a few votes.

BECOMES A MERCHANT AND SURVEYOR.

Soon after his political defeat he engaged in the mercantile business, but in a few months sold out, and under the tuition of John Calhoun (in later years President of the Lecompton Constitutional Convention) became proficient in surveying, an occupation which for more than a year he found very remunerative for a novice. He was also for a time Postmaster of New Salem.

IS ELECTED TO THE LEGISLATURE—STUDIES LAW.

In August, 1834, he was again nominated for the Legislature, and was elected by a large majority; and in 1836,

1838, and 1840, was re-elected. While attending the proceedings of the first session, he determined to become a lawyer, and being placed in possession of the necessary books
through the kindness of the Hon. John T. Stuart, applied
himself to study, and in 1836 was admitted to practice at
the bar. In April, 1837, he removed to Springfield, and
became a partner of Mr. Stuart.

A THRILLING INCIDENT IN HIS LEGAL CAREER.

One instance which occurred during his early legal
practice is worthy of extended publication. At a camp
meeting held in Menard county, a fight took place which
ended in the murder of one of the participants in the
quarrel. A young man named Armstrong, a son of the
aged couple for whom many years before Abraham Lincoln had worked, was charged with the deed, and being
arrested and examined, a true bill was found against him,
and he was lodged in jail to await his trial. As soon as
Mr. Lincoln received intelligence of the affair, he addressed
a kind letter to Mrs. Armstrong, stating his anxiety that
her son should have a fair trial, and offering in return for
her kindness to him while in adverse circumstances some
years before, his services gratuitously. Investigation convinced the volunteer attorney that the young man was the
victim of a conspiracy, and he determined to postpone the
case until the excitement had subsided. The day of trial
however finally arrived, and the accuser testified positively
that he saw the accused plunge the knife into the heart of
the murdered man. He remembered all the circumstances
perfectly; the murder was committed about half-past nine
o'clock at night, and the moon was shining brightly.
Mr. Lincoln reviewed all the testimony carefully, and
then proved conclusively that the moon which the accuser
had sworn was shining brightly, did not rise until an hour

or more after the murder was committed. Other dis-
crepancies were exposed, and in thirty minutes after the
jury retired they returned with a verdict of " Not Guilty "

A PROTEST AGAINST SLAVERY.

On the third of March, 1837, a protest was presented
to the House of Representatives of Illinois and signed by
"Daniel Stone and Abraham Lincoln, Representatives
from Sangamon county," which is the first record that we
have of the sentiments of the subject of our sketch on the
slavery question. It was in opposition to a series of resolutions which had been adopted, taking an extreme Southern view of slavery, for which Mr. Lincoln refused to vote,
and subsequently handed in the protest.

IS A CANDIDATE FOR PRESIDENTIAL ELECTOR.

In every campaign from 1836 to 1852, he was a Whig
candidate for Presidential Elector, and in 1844, he stumped
the entire State of Illinois for Henry Clay; and then
crossing the line into Indiana, spoke daily to immense
gatherings, until the day of election. His style of speaking was pleasing to the masses of the people, and his
earnest appeals were not only well received, but were
productive of much benefit to his favorite candidate.
Accustomed from early childhood to the habits and pecu-
liarities of all kinds and conditions of men—the refined
and the vulgar, the intelligent and the illiterate, the rich
and the poor—he knew exactly what particular style of
language best suited his hearers, and the result was that
he was always listened to with a degree of attention and
interest which few political speakers receive.

MR. LINCOLN ELECTED TO CONGRESS—HIS VOTES AND SPEECHES DURING HIS CONGRESSIONAL TERM.

In 1846, Mr. Lincoln was elected to Congress from the

Central District of Illinois, by a majority of over fifteen hundred votes, the largest ever given in that District to any candidate opposed to the Democratic party. Illinois elected seven Representatives that year; and all were Democrats but Mr. Lincoln. He took his seat on the first Monday of December, 1847, and during the exciting session that followed, cast his vote *pro* or *con* on every important question, and on more than one occasion displayed his eloquence and superior argumentative ability. One of his first votes was given on the twentieth of December in favor of the following resolution :

"*Resolved*, That if, in the judgment of Congress, it be necessary to improve the navigation of a river to expedite and render secure the movements of our army, and save from delay and loss our arms and munitions of war, that Congress has the power to improve such river.
"*Resolved*, That if it be necessary for the preservation of the lives of our seamen, repairs, safety, or maintenance of our vessels-of-war, to improve a harbor or inlet, either on our Atlantic or Lake coast, Congress has the power to make such improvement."

On the twenty-second of the same month, he voted in favor of a similar resolution, and on the same day offered the following series of resolutions, which he introduced with one of his characteristic speeches, humorous at one moment and logical at the next. Although, like the large majority of the Whig party opposed to the declaration of war with Mexico by the President, he never failed to vote for any resolution or bill which had for its object the sending of supplies to our troops who had been ordered to the seat of war. The resolutions read as follows :

" *Whereas*, The President of the United States, in his message of May 11th, 1846, has declared ' that the Mexican Government not only refused to receive him (the envoy of the United States) or listen to his propositions, but, after a long-continued series of menaces, have at last invaded our territory and shed the blood of our fellow-citizens on our own soil.'
"And again, in his message of December 8th, 1846, that ' we

had ample cause of war against Mexico long before the break-ing out of hostilities, but even then we forbore to take redress into our own hands until Mexico herself became the aggressor by invading our soil in hostile array, and shedding the blood of our citizens.'

"And yet again, in the message of December 7th, 1847, that 'the Mexican Government refused even to hear the terms of adjustment which he (our minister of peace) was authorized to propose; and, finally, under wholly unjustifiable pretexts, in-volved the two countries in war by invading the territory of the State of Texas, striking the first blow, and shedding the blood of our citizens on our own soil.'

"*And whereas*, This House is desirous to obtain a full knowl-edge of all the facts which go to establish whether the particu-lar spot on which the blood of our citizens was so shed, was or was not at that time our own soil. Therefore,

"*Resolved, by the House of Representatives*, That the Presi-dent of the United States be respectfully requested to inform this House,

"*1st*. Whether the spot on which the blood of our citizens was shed, as in his messages declared, was or was not within the Territory of Spain, at least after the treaty of 1819, until the Mexican revolution.

"*2nd*. Whether that spot is or is not within the territory which was wrested from Spain by the revolutionary Govern-ment of Mexico.

"*3rd*. Whether that spot is or is not within a settlement of people, which settlement has existed ever since long before the Texas revolution, and until its inhabitants fled before the ap-proach of the United States Army.

"*4th*. Whether that settlement is or is not isolated from any and all other settlements by the Gulf and the Rio Grande on the south and west, and by wide uninhabited regions on the north and east.

"*5th*. Whether the people of that settlement, or a majority of them, or any of them, have ever submitted themselves to the Government or laws of Texas or of the United States, by con-sent or by compulsion, either by accepting office, or voting at elections, or paying tax or serving on juries, or having process served upon them, or in any other way.

"*6th*. Whether the people of that settlement did or did not flee from the approach of the United States Army, leaving un-protected their homes and their growing crops, before the blood was shed, as in the message stated; and whether the first blood, so shed, was or was not shed within the enclosure of one of the people who had thus fled from it.

"*7th*. Whether our citizens, whose blood was shed, as in his messages declared, were or were not, at that time, armed officers and soldiers, sent into that settlement by the military order of the President, through the Secretary of War.

"8th. Whether the military force of the United States was or was not so sent into that settlement after General Taylor had more than once intimated to the War Department that, in his opinion, no such movement was necessary to the defence or protection of Texas."

On several occasions during the session, he voted for the reception of petitions and memorials in favor of the abolition of slavery in the District of Columbia, against the slave-trade, and advocating the prohibition of slavery in the territory that might be acquired from Mexico.

On the seventeenth of February, 1848, Mr. Lincoln voted for a Loan bill reported by the Committee of Ways and Means, authorizing the raising of sixteen millions of dollars to enable the Government to provide for its debts, principally incurred in Mexico.

On the eleventh of May, in moving to reconsider a vote by which a bill having reference to the public lands had passed, he made the following remarks :

"He stated to the House that he had made this motion for the purpose of obtaining an opportunity to say a few words in relation to a point raised in the course of the debate on this bill, which he would now proceed to make, if in order. The point in the case to which he referred, arose on the amendment that was submitted by the gentleman from Vermont (Mr. Collamer), in Committee of the Whole on the State of the Union, and which was afterwards renewed in the House, in relation to the question whether the reserved sections, which, by some bills heretofore passed, by which an appropriation of land had been made to Wisconsin, had been enhanced in value, should be reduced to the minimum price of the public lands. The question of the reduction in value of those sections was, to him, at this time, a matter very nearly of indifference. He was inclined to desire that Wisconsin should be obliged by having it reduced. But the gentleman from Indiana (Mr. C. B. Smith), the Chairman of the Committee on the Territories, associated that question with the general question, which is now, to some extent, agitated in Congress, of making appropriations of alternate sections of land to aid the States in making internal improvements. and enhancing the prices of the section reserved, and the gen·

tleman from Indiana took ground against that policy. He did not make any special argument in favor of Wisconsin ; but he took ground generally against the policy of giving alternate sections of land, and enhancing the price of the reserved sections. Now, he (Mr. L.) did not at this time, take the floor for the purpose of attempting to make an argument on the general sub-·ject. He rose simply to protest against the doctrine which the gentleman from Indiana had avowed in the course of what he (Mr. L.) could not but consider an unsound argument.

"It might however be true, for any thing he knew, that the gentleman from Indiana might convince him that his argument was sound ; but he (Mr. L.) feared that gentleman would not be able to convince a majority in Congress that it was sound. It was true, the question appeared in a different aspect to persons in consequence of a difference in the point from which they looked at it. It did not look to persons residing east of the mountains as it did to those who lived among the public lands. But, for his part, he would state that if Congress would make a donation of alternate sections of public lands for the purpose of internal improvement in his State, and forbid the reserved sections being sold at $1.25, he should be glad to see the appropriation made, though he should prefer it if the reserved sections were not enhanced in price. He repeated, he should be glad to have such appropriations made, even though the reserved sections should be enhanced in price. He did not wish to be understood as concurring in any intimation that they would refuse to receive such an appropriation of alternate sections of land because a condition enhancing the price of the reserved sections should be attached thereto. He believed his position would now be understood, if not, he feared he should not be able to make himself understood.

"But before he took his seat he would remark that the Senate, during the present session, had passed a bill making appropriations of land on that principle for the benefit of the State in which he resided—the State of Illinois. The alternate sections were to be given for the purpose of constructing roads, and the reserved sections were to be enhanced in value in consequence. When the bill came here for the action of this House, it had been received, and was now before the Committee on Public Lands—he desired much to see it passed as it was, if it could be put in a more favorable form for the State of Illinois. When it should be before this House, if any member from a section of the Union in which these lands did not lie, whose interest might be less than that which he felt, should propose a reduction of the price of the reserved sections to $1.25, he should be much obliged ; but he did not think it would be well for those who came from the section of the Union in which the lands lay, to do so. He wished it, then, to be understood, that he did not join in the warfare against the principle which had engaged the minds of some members of Congress who were favorable to improvements in the western country.

"There was a good deal of force, he admitted, in what fell from the Chairman of the Committee on Territories. It might be that there was no precise justice in raising the price of the reserved sections to $2.50 per acre. It might be proper that the price should be enhanced to some extent, though not to double the usual price; but he should be glad to have such an appropriation with the reserved sections at $2.50; he should be better pleased to have the price of those sections at something less; and he should be still better pleased to have them without any enhancement at all.

"There was one portion of the argument of the gentleman from Indiana, the Chairman of the Committee on Territories (Mr. Smith), which he wished to take occasion to say that he did not view as unsound. He alluded to the statement that the General Government was interested in these internal improvements being made, inasmuch as they increased the value of the lands that were unsold, and they enabled the Government to sell lands which could not be sold without them. Thus, then, the Government gained by internal improvements, as well as by the general good which the people derived from them, and it might be, therefore, that the lands should not be sold for more than $1.50, instead of the price being doubled. He, however, merely mentioned this in passing, for he only rose to state, as the principle of giving these lands for the purposes which he had mentioned had been laid hold of and considered favorably, and as there were some gentlemen who had constitutional scruples about giving money for these purposes, who would not hesitate to give land, that he was not willing to have it understood that he was one of those who made war against that principle. This was all he desired to say, and having accomplished the object with which he rose, he withdrew his motion to reconsider."

On the nineteenth of the following month he first had an opportunity to record his views upon the Tariff question, by voting in favor of a resolution instructing the Committee of Ways and Means to inquire into the expediency of reporting a bill increasing the duties on foreign luxuries of all kinds, and on "such foreign manufactures as are now coming into ruinous competition with American labor." He subsequently voted for a resolution instructing the Committee of Ways and Means to inquire into the expediency of reporting a Tariff bill based upon the principles of the Tariff of 1842.

On the 28th of July, 1848, the celebrated bill establishing Territorial governments for Oregon, California and New Mexico, the peculiar feature of which was a provision prohibiting the Legislatures of California and New Mexico from passing laws in favor of or against slavery, and providing that the laws of the Legislatures should be subject to the sanction of Congress, was argued, and after an exciting debate, laid on the table, Mr. Lincoln voting with Mr. Webster, Mr. Corwin, and other illustrious colleagues for this disposition of the bill.

On the sixteenth of January, 1849, Mr. Lincoln offered the following substitute for a resolution which he had voted against, not being satisfied with all its provisions:

" *Resolved*, That the Committee on the District of Columbia be instructed to report a bill in substance, as follows:

" *Sec.* 1. *Be it enacted by the Senate and House of Representatives of the United States in Congress assembled,* That no person not now within the District of Columbia, nor now owned by any person or persons now resident within it, nor hereafter born within it, shall ever be held in slavery within said District.

· *Sec.* 2. That no person now within said District, or now owned by any person or persons now resident within the same, or hereafter born within it, shall ever be held in slavery without the limits of said District: Provided, That officers of the Government of the United States, being citizens of the slaveholding States, coming into said District on public business, and remaining only so long as may be reasonably necessary for that object, may be attended into and out of said District, and while there, by the necessary servants of themselves and their families, without their right to hold such servants in service being impaired.

" *Sec.* 3. That all children born of slave mothers within said District, on or after the 1st day of January, in the year of our Lord 1850, shall be free; but shall be reasonably supported and educated by the respective owners of their mothers, or by their heirs or representatives, and shall serve reasonable service as apprentices to such owners, heirs, or representatives, until they respectively arrive at the age of ———— years, when they shall be entirely free: And the municipal authorities of Washington and Georgetown, within their respective jurisdictional limits, are hereby empowered and required to make all suitable and necessary provision for enforcing obedience to this section, on the part of both masters and apprentices.

" *Sec.* 4. That all persons now within this District, lawfully

held as slaves, or now owned by any person or persons now resident within said District, shall remain such at the will of their
respective owners, their heirs or legal representatives : Provided that such owner, or his legal representatives, may at any
time receive from the Treasury of the United States the full
value of his or her slave, of the class in this section mentioned,
upon which such slave shall be forthwith and forever free : And
provided further, That the President of the United States, the
Secretary of State, and the Secretary of the Treasury, shall be
a board for determining the value of such slaves as their owners
desire to emancipate under this section, and whose duty it shall
be to hold a session for the purpose on the first Monday of each
calendar month, to receive all applications, and, on satisfactory
evidence in each case that the person presented for valuation
is a slave, and of the class in the section mentioned, and is
owned by the applicant, shall value such slave at his or her full
cash value, and give to the applicant an order on the Treasury
for the amount, and also to such slave a certificate of freedom.

"*Sec.* 5. That the municipal authorities of Washington and
Georgetown, within their respective jurisdictional limits, are
hereby empowered and required to provide active and efficient
means to arrest and deliver up to their owners all fugitive slaves
escaping into said District.

"*Sec.* 6. That the elective officers within said District of Columbia are hereby empowered and required to open polls at all
the usual places of holding elections, on the first Monday of
April next, and receive the vote of every free white male citizen above the age of twenty-one years, having resided within
said District for the period of one year or more next preceding
the time of such voting for or against this act, to proceed in
taking said votes in all respects not herein specified, as at elections under the municipal laws, and with as little delay as possible to transmit correct statements of the votes so cast to the
President of the United States ; and it shall be the duty of the
President to count such votes immediately, and if a majority
of them be found to be for this act, to forthwith issue his proclamation giving notice of the fact ; and this act shall only be
in full force and effect on and after the day of such proclamation.

"*Sec.* 7. That involuntary servitude for the punishment of
crime, whereof the party shall have been duly convicted, shall
in nowise be prohibited by this act.

"*Sec.* 8. That for all purposes of this act, the jurisdictional
limits of Washington are extended to all parts of the District
of Columbia not included within the present limits of Georgetown."

We have given a sufficient record of Mr. Lincoln's services as a Representative in Congress, to show that in his

numerous votes and remarks upon the slavery question, he was uniformly consistent, and a determined opponent to that peculiar institution which, Mr. Corwin truly remarked, was an exotic that blights with its shade the soil in which it is planted. He with almost equal determination opposed the annexation of Texas, and voted more than forty different times in favor of the Wilmot Proviso.

BECOMES A DELEGATE TO THE NATIONAL CONVENTION OF 1848.

In the Whig National Convention of 1848, he was an active delegate, and earnestly advocated the selection of General Zachary Taylor as the nominee for the Presidency, and during the canvass which followed, he traversed the States of Indiana and Illinois, speaking in behalf of his favorite candidate and the choice of his party.

HE IS NOMINATED FOR UNITED STATES SENATOR, BUT WITHDRAWS.

In 1849 he was a candidate before the Legislature of Illinois for United States Senator, but his political opponents being in the majority, General Shields was chosen. From that time until 1854, he confined himself almost exclusively to the practice of his profession, but in that year he again entered the political arena, and battled indefatigably in the celebrated campaign which resulted in victory for the first time to the opposition of the Democratic party in Illinois, and gave that State a Republican Legislature, and sent Mr. Trumbull to the United States Senate. During the canvass, Mr. Lincoln was frequently brought into controversy upon the stand with Stephen A. Douglas, one of the discussions, that was held on the fourth of October, 1854, during the progress of the annual State Fair, being particularly remarkable as *the* great discussion of the campaign.

At the election of United States Senator, nine-tenths of the majority were Whigs and in favor of Mr. Lincoln, and the other tenth were Democrats, but not in favor of voting for a Whig, and for the purpose of securing the success of a man whom he knew was opposed to the Nebraska bill, and thus preventing the election of a third person who had little or nothing in common with the Republican party, which was then in its conception, he entreated his friends to vote for Mr. Trumbull. Mr. Lincoln was subsequently offered the nomination for Governor of Illinois, but declined the honor in favor of Mr. Bissell; was also presented, but ineffectually, at the first Republican National Convention for Vice-President; and at the next Presidential election headed the Fremont electoral ticket, and labored industriously in support of that candidate.

AGAIN NOMINATED FOR THE SENATE—HIS SPEECHES IN THE CELEBRATED LINCOLN-DOUGLAS CAMPAIGN.

On the second of June, 1858, the Republican State Convention met at Springfield, and nominated Mr. Lincoln as their candidate for the United States Senate. At the close of their proceedings the honored recipient of their suffrage delivered a speech, which was a forcible exposition of the views and aims of the party of which he was to be the standard-bearer.

The contest which followed was one of the most exciting and remarkable ever witnessed in this country. Mr. Stephen A. Douglas, his opponent, had few superiors as a political debater, and while he had made many enemies by his course upon the Nebraska bill, his personal popularity had been greatly increased by his independence, and by the opposition manifested to him by the Administration. His re-election, however, to the Senate would have been equivalent to an indorsement of his acts and views by his Commonwealth, and at the same time would have promoted his prospects for the Presidential nomination. The Republicans, therefore, determined to defeat him if possible, and to increase the probabilities of success in the movement, selected Mr. Lincoln as the man who was most certain of securing the election. Illinois was stumped throughout its length and breadth by both candidates and their respective advocates, and the people of the entire country watched with interest the struggle. From county to county, township to township, and village to village, the two leaders travelled, frequently in the same car or carriage, and in the presence of immense crowds of men, women and children—for the wives and daughters of the hardy yeomanry were naturally interested—face to face, these two opposing champions argued the important points of their political belief, and contended nobly for the mastery.

During the campaign, Mr. Lincoln paid the following tribute to the Declaration of Independence

"These communities, (the thirteen colonies,) by their representatives in old Independence Hall, said to the world of men, 'We hold these truths to be self-evident, that all men are born equal; that they are endowed by their Creator with inalienable rights; that among these are life, liberty, and the pursuit of happiness.' This was their majestic interpretation of the economy of the universe. This was their lofty, and wise, and noble understanding of the justice of the Creator to His creatures. Yes, gentlemen, to all His creatures, to the whole great family of man. In their enlightened belief, nothing stamped with the Divine image and likeness was sent into the world to be trodden on, and degraded, and imbruted by its fellows. They grasped not only the race of men then living, but they reached forward and seized upon the furthest posterity. They created a beacon to guide their children and their children's children, and the countless myriads who should inhabit the earth in other ages. Wise statesmen as they were, they knew the tendency of prosperity to breed tyrants, and so they established these great self-evident truths that when, in the distant future, some man, some faction, some interest, should set up the doctrine that none but rich men, or none but white men, or none but Anglo-Saxon white men, were entitled to life, liberty, and the pursuit of happiness, their posterity might look up again to the Declaration of Independence, and take courage to renew the battle which their fathers began, so that truth, and justice and mercy, and all the humane and Christian virtues might not be extinguished from the land; so that no man would hereafter dare to limit and circumscribe the great principles on which the temple of liberty was being built.

"Now, my countrymen, if you have been taught doctrines conflicting with the great landmarks of the Declaration of Independence; if you have listened to suggestions which would take away from its grandeur, and mutilate the fair symmetry of its proportions; if you have been inclined to believe that all men are not created equal in those inalienable rights enumerated by our chart of liberty, let me entreat you to come back—return to the fountain whose waters spring close by the blood of the Revolution. Think nothing of me, take no thought for the political fate of any man whomsoever, but come back to the truths that are in the Declaration of Independence.

"You may do any thing with me you choose, if you will but heed these sacred principles. You may not only defeat me for the Senate, but you may take me and put me to death. While pretending no indifference to earthly honors, I *do claim* to be actuated in this contest by something higher than an anxiety for office. I charge you to drop every paltry and insignificant thought for any man's success. It is nothing; I am nothing; Judge Douglas is nothing. *But do not destroy that immortal emblem of humanity—the Declaration of American Independence.*"

PEN-PORTRAITS OF ABRAHAM LINCOLN.

As we have stated, the exciting struggle was watched with intense interest, not only by the members of the respective political parties of which the two orators were recognized leaders and champions, but by that portion of the different communities of the Union who do not generally trouble their minds with political contests. Copious extracts from the speeches of both Mr. Lincoln and Mr. Douglas were published in the journals of the day, and criticisms of the orators and their discussions appeared in the leading magazines and newspapers.

From some of the latter we select the following, for the purpose of showing in what estimation the talents and ability of the honorable subject of our sketch were held at the time of which we now more particularly speak, and to give those readers of this work who have not had the opportunity to see Mr. Lincoln, an idea of his personal appearance :

One writer gives the following pen-portrait :

"Mr. Lincoln stands six feet and four inches high in his stockings. His frame is not muscular, but gaunt and wiry; his arms are long, but not unreasonably so for a person of his height ; his lower limbs are not disproportioned to his body. In walking, his gait, though firm, is never brisk. He steps slowly and deliberately, almost always with his head inclined forward, and his hands clasped behind his back. In matters of dress he is by no means precise. Always clean, he is never fashionable ; he is careless, but not slovenly. In manner he is remarkably cordial, and, at the same time, simple. His politeness is always sincere, but never elaborate and oppressive. A warm shake of the hand, and a warmer smile of recognition, are his methods of greeting his friends. At rest, his features, though those of a man of mark, are not such as belong to a handsome man ; but when his fine dark gray eyes are lighted up by any emotion, and his features begin their play, he would be chosen from among a crowd as one who had in him not only the kindly sentiments which women love, but the heavier metal of which full-grown men and Presidents are made. His hair is black, and though thin is wiry. His head sits well on his shoulders, but beyond that it defies description. It nearer resembles that of Clay than that of Webster; but it is unlike either. It is very large, and, phrenologically, well proportioned, betokening power in all its developments. A slightly Roman nose, a wide-cut mouth, and a dark complexion, with the appearance of having been weather-beaten, complete the description.

"In his personal habits, Mr. Lincoln is as simple as a child. He loves a good dinner, and eats with the appetite which goes with a great brain ; but his food is plain and nutritious. He never drinks intoxicating liquors of any sort, not even a glass of wine. He is not addicted to tobacco in any of its shapes. He never was accused of a licentious act in all his life. He never uses profane language.

"A friend says that once, when in a towering rage, in consequence of the efforts of certain parties to perpetrate a fraud on the State, he was heard to say: 'They sha'n't do it, d—n 'em !' but beyond an expression of that kind, his bitterest feelings never carry him. He never gambles ; we doubt if he ever indulges in any games of chance. He is particularly cautious about incurring pecuniary obligations for any purpose whatever, and in debt, he is never content until the score is discharged. We presume he owes no man a dollar. He never speculates. The rage for the sudden acquisition of wealth never took hold of him. His gains from his profession have been moderate, but sufficient for his purposes. While others have dreamed of gold, he has been in pursuit of knowledge. In all his dealings he has the reputation of being generous but exact, and, above all, religiously honest. He would be a bold man who would say that Abraham Lincoln ever wronged any one out of a cent, or ever spent a dollar that he had not honestly earned. His struggles in early life have made him careful of money; but his generosity with his own is proverbial. He is a regular attendant upon religious worship, and though not a communicant, is a pew-holder and liberal supporter of the Presbyterian Church, in Springfield, to which Mrs. Lincoln belongs. He is a scrupulous teller of the truth—too exact in his notions to suit the atmosphere of Washington, as it now is. His enemies may say that he tells Black Republican lies; but no man ever charged that, in a professional capacity, or as a citizen dealing with his neighbors, he would depart from the Scriptural command. At home, he lives like a gentleman of modest means and simple tastes. A good-sized house of wood, simply but tastefully furnished, surrounded by trees and flowers, is his own, and there he lives, at peace with himself, the idol of his family, and for his honesty, ability, and patriotism, the admiration of his countrymen."

Another person gives the subjoined sketch of him :

"In personal appearance, Mr. Lincoln, or, as he is more familiarly termed among those who know him best, 'Old Uncle Abe,' is long, lean, and wiry. In motion he has a great deal of the elasticity and awkwardness which indicates the rough training of his early life, and his conversation savors strongly of Western idioms and pronunciation. His height is six feet four inches. His complexion is about that of an octoroon ; his face, without being by any means beautiful, is genial-looking, and good humor seems to lurk in every corner of its innumerable angles. He has dark hair tinged with gray, a good forehead, small eyes, a long penetrating nose, with nostrils such as Napoleon always liked to find in his best generals, because they indicated a long head and clear thoughts ; and a mouth, which, aside from being of magnificent proportions, is probably the most expressive feature of his face.

"As a speaker he is ready, precise, and fluent. His manner before a popular assembly is as he pleases to make it, being either superlatively ludicrous, or very impressive. He employs but little gesticulation, but when he desires to make a point, produces a shrug of his shoulders, an elevation of his eyebrows, a

depression of his mouth, and a general malformation of countenance so comically awkward that it never fails to 'bring down
the house.' His enunciation is slow and emphatic, and his voice,
though sharp and powerful, at times has a frequent tendency to
dwindle into a shrill and unpleasant sound ; but as before stated,
the peculiar characteristic of his delivery is the remarkable mo-
bility of his features, the frequent contortions of which excite a
merriment his words could not produce."

A third says :

"In perhaps the severest test that could have been applied
to any man's temper—his political contest with Senator Douglas in 1858—Mr. Lincoln not only proved himself an able speaker
and a good tactician, but demonstrated that it is possible to
carry on the fiercest political warfare without once descending
to rude personality and course denunciation. We have it on
the authority of a gentleman who followed Abraham Lincoln
throughout the whole of that campaign, that, in spite of all the
temptations to an opposite course to which he was continuously
exposed, no personalities against his opponent, no vituperation
or coarseness, ever defiled his lips. His kind and genial nature
lifted him above a resort to any such weapons of political warfare,
and it was the commonly-expressed regret of fiercer natures that
he treated his opponent too courteously and urbanely. Vulgar
personalities and vituperation are the last thing that can be
truthfully charged against Abraham Lincoln. His heart is too
genial, his good sense too strong, and his innate self-respect too
predominant to permit him to indulge in them. His nobility
of nature—and we may use the term advisedly—has been as
manifest throughout his whole career as his temperate habits,
his self-reliance, and his mental and intellectual power."

And a fourth, a distinguished scholar, after listening to
a speech delivered at Galesburgh, thus wrote :

"'The men are entirely dissimilar. Mr. Douglas is a thick-set,
finely-built, courageous man, and has an air of self-confidence
that does not a little to inspire his supporters with hope. Mr.
Lincoln is a tall, lank man, awkward, apparently diffident, and
when not speaking has neither firmness in his countenance nor
fire in his eye.
"Mr. Lincoln has a rich, silvery voice, enunciates with great
distinctness, and has a fine command of language. He commenced by a review of the points Mr. Douglas had made. In
this he showed great tact, and his retorts, though gentlemanly,
were sharp, and reached to the core the subject in dispute.
While he gave but little time to the work of review, we did not
feel that any thing was omitted which deserved attention.

"He then proceeded to defend the Republican party. Here he charged Mr. Douglas with doing nothing for freedom; with disregarding the rights and interests of the colored man: and for about forty minutes he spoke with a power that we have seldom heard equalled. There was a grandeur in his thoughts, a comprehensiveness in his arguments, and a binding force in his conclusions, which were perfectly irresistible. The vast throng were silent as death; every eye was fixed upon the speaker, and all gave him serious attention. He was the tall man eloquent; his countenance glowed with animation, and his eye glistened with an intelligence that made it lustrous. He was no longer awkward and ungainly; but graceful, bold, commanding.

"Mr. Douglas had been quietly smoking up to this time; but here he forgot his cigar and listened with anxious attention. When he rose to reply he appeared excited, disturbed, and his second effort seemed to us vastly inferior to his first. Mr. Lincoln had given him a great task, and Mr. Douglas had not time to answer him, even if he had the ability."

MR. LINCOLN DEFEATED BY MR. DOUGLAS.

The election-day at length arrived, and although the efforts of Mr. Lincoln resulted in an immense increase of the Republican vote, whatever aspirations he had for personal success were frustrated. A vote of 126,084 was cast for the Republican candidates, 121,940 for the Douglas Democrats, and 5,091 for the Lecompton candidates, but Mr. Douglas was elected United States Senator by the Legislature, in which his supporters had a majority of eight on joint ballot.

Although defeated in the hope of securing Mr. Lincoln as their representative in the United States Senate, the Republicans were not discouraged, and from that time determined that their favorite leader should be rewarded with even more exalted honors.

IS NAMED FOR THE PRESIDENCY—EVIDENCE OF HIS SKILL AS A RAIL-SPLITTER.

He was immediately mentioned prominently for the Presidency, and at a meeting of the Illinois State Republican Convention, where he was present as a spectator, a

3

veteran Democrat of Macon county brought in and presented to the Convention two old fence-rails, gayly deco-
rated with flags and ribbons, and upon which the following words were inscribed :

ABRAHAM LINCOLN,

THE RAIL CANDIDATE

FOR PRESIDENT IN 1860.

Two rails from a lot of 3,000 made in 1830, by
Thos. Hanks and Abe Lincoln—whose
father was the first pioneer
of Macon county.

The event occasioned the most unbounded enthusiasm,
and for several minutes the most deafening applause re-
sounded through the building.   Mr. Lincoln was vocifer-
ously called for, and arising from his seat, modestly acknowledged that he had split rails some thirty years previous in Macon county, and he was informed that those
before him were a small portion of the product of his
labor with the axe.

The fame of the able advocate of Republican principles
induced the members of that party in other States to secure his voice and influence in their behalf, and in the fall
of 1859 he made several effective speeches in favor of the
cause.

HIS GREAT SPEECH AT THE COOPER INSTI-
TUTE, NEW YORK.

On the twenty-seventh of February, 1860, he made the
following forcible speech at the Cooper Institute, New
York, before an immense audience :

"MR. PRESIDENT AND FELLOW-CITIZENS OF NEW YORK:
The facts with which I shall deal this evening are mainly old

and familiar; nor is there any thing new in the general use I shall make of them.   If there shall be any novelty, it will be in the mode of presenting the facts, and the inferences and observations following that presentation.

"In his speech last autumn, at Columbus, Ohio, as reported in *The New York Times*, Senator Douglas said:

"'Our fathers, when they framed the Government under which we, live, understood this question just as well, and even better than we do now.'

"I fully indorse this and I adopt it as a text for this discourse. I so adopt it because it furnishes a precise and agreed starting point for the discussion between Republicans and that wing of Democracy headed by Senator Douglas.   It simply leaves the inquiry : 'What was the understanding those fathers had of the questions mentioned ?'

" What is the frame of Government under which we live ?

"The answer must be : 'The Constitution of the United States.'   That Constitution consists of the original, framed in 1787 (and under which the present Government first went into operation), and twelve subsequently framed amendments, the first ten of which were framed in 1789.

" Who were our fathers that framed the Constitution ?   I suppose the 'thirty-nine' who signed the original instrument may be fairly called our fathers who framed that part of the present Government.   It is almost exactly true to say they framed it, and it is altogether true to say they fairly represented the opinion and sentiment of the whole nation at that time.   Their names being familiar to nearly all, and accessible to quite all, need not now be repeated.

" I take these 'thirty-nine,' for the present, as being 'our fathers who framed the Government under which we live.'

" What is the question which according to the text, those fathers understood just as well, and even better than we do now ?

" It is this : Does the proper division of local from federal authority, or any thing in the Constitution, forbid our Federal Government control as to slavery in our Federal Territories ?

" Upon this, Douglas holds the affirmative, and Republicans the negative.   This affirmative and denial form an issue ; and this issue—this question—is precisely what the text declares our fathers understood better than we.

" Let us now inquire whether the 'thirty-nine,' or any of them, ever acted upon this question ; and if they did, how they acted upon it—how they expressed that better understanding.

" In 1784—three years before the Constitution—the United States then owning the Northwestern Territory, and no other— the Congress of the Confederation had before them the question of prohibiting slavery in that Territory; and four of the 'thirty-nine' who afterward framed the Constitution were in that

Congress, and voted on that question. Of these, Roger Sherman, Thomas Mifflin, and Hugh Williamson voted for the prohibition—thus showing that, in their understanding, no line dividing local from federal authority, nor any thing else, properly forbade the Federal Government to control as to slavery in federal territory. The other of the four—James McHenry—voted against the prohibition, showing that, for some cause, he thought it improper to vote for it.

"In 1787, still before the Constitution, but while the Convention was in session framing it, and while the Northwestern Territory still was the only territory owned by the United States —the same question of prohibiting slavery in the territory again came before the Congress of the Confederation; and three more of the 'thirty-nine' who afterward signed the Constitution, were in that Congress, and voted on the question. They were William Blount, William Few and Abraham Baldwin; and they all voted for the prohibition—thus showing that, in their understanding, no line dividing local from federal authority, nor any thing else, properly forbids the Federal Government to control as to slavery in federal territory. This time the prohibition became a law, being part of what is now well known as the Ordinance of '87.

"The question of federal control of slavery in the territories, seems not to have been directly before the Convention which framed the original Constitution; and hence it is not recorded that the 'thirty-nine' or any of them, while engaged on that instrument, expressed any opinion on that precise question.

"In 1789, by the first Congress which sat under the Constitution, an act was passed to enforce the Ordinance of '87 including the prohibition of slavery in the Northwestern Territory. The bill for this act was reported by one of the 'thirty-nine,' Thomas Fitzsimmons, then a member of the House of Representatives from Pennsylvania. It went through all its stages without a word of opposition, and finally passed both branches without yeas and nays, which is equivalent to an unanimous passage. In this Congress there were sixteen of the 'thirty-nine' fathers who framed the original Constitution. They were John Langdon, Nicholas Gilman, Wm. S. Johnson, Roger Sherman, Robert Morris, Thos. Fitzsimmons, William Few, Abraham Baldwin, Rufus King, William Patterson, George Clymer, Richard Bassett, George Read, Pierce Butler, Daniel Carrol, James Madison.

"This shows that, in their understanding, no line dividing local from federal authority, nor any thing in the Constitution, properly forbade Congress to prohibit slavery in the federal territory; else both their fidelity to correct principle, and their oath to support the Constitution, would have constrained them to oppose the prohibition.

"Again, George Washington, another of the 'thirty-nine,'

was then President of the United States, and, as such, approved and signed the bill, thus completing- its validity as a law, and thus showing that, in his understanding, no line dividing local from federal authority, nor any thing in the Constitution, forbade the Federal Government to control as to slavery in federal territory.

" No great while after the adoption of the original Constitution, North Carolina ceded to the Federal Government the country now constituting the State of Tennessee ; and a few years later Georgia ceded that which now constitutes the States of Mississippi and Alabama. In both deeds of cession it was made a condition by the ceding States that the Federal Government should not prohibit slavery in the ceded country. Besides this, slavery was then actually in the ceded country. Under these circumstances, Congress, on taking charge of these countries did not absolutely prohibit slavery within them. But they did interfere with it—take control of it—even there, to a certain extent. In 1798, Congress organized the Territory of Mississippi. In the act of organization they prohibited the bringing of slaves into the Territory, from any place without the United States, by fine and giving freedom to slaves so brought. This act passed both branches of Congress without yeas and nays. In that Congress were three of the ' thirty-nine' who framed the original Constitution. They were John Langdon, George Read, and Abraham Baldwin. They all, probably, voted for it. Certainly they would have placed their opposition to it upon record, if, in their understanding, any line dividing local from federal authority, or any thing in the Constitution, properly forbade the Federal Government to control as to slavery in federal territory.

" In 1803, the Federal Government purchased the Louisiana country. Our former territorial acquisitions came from certain of our own States ; but this Louisiana country was acquired from a foreign nation. In 1804, Congress gave a territorial organization to that part of it which now constitutes the State of Louisiana. New Orleans, lying within that part, was an old and comparatively large city. There were other considerable towns and settlements, and slavery was extensively and thoroughly intermingled with the people. Congress did not, in the Territorial Act, prohibit Slavery ; but they did interfere with it—take control of it—in a more marked and extensive way than they did in the case of Mississippi. The substance of the provision therein made, in relation to slaves, was :

"*First.* That no slave should be imported into the territory from foreign parts.

"*Second.* That no slave should be carried into it who had been imported into the United States since the first day of May, 1798.

"*Third.* That no slave should be carried into it, except by the owner, and for his own use as a settler; the penalty in all the cases being a fine upon the violator of the law, and freedom to the slave.

"This act also was passed without yeas and nays. In the Congress which passed it, there were two of the 'thirty-nine.' They were Abraham Baldwin and Jonathan Dayton. As stated in the case of Mississippi, it is probable they both voted for it. They would not have allowed it to pass without recording their opposition to it, if, in their understanding, it violated either the line proper dividing local from Federal authority or any provision of the Constitution.

"In 1819–20, came and passed the Missouri question. Many votes were taken, by yeas and nays, in both branches of Congress, upon the various phases of the general question. Two of the 'thirty-nine'—Rufus King and Charles Pinckney—were members of that Congress. Mr. King steadily voted for slavery prohibition and against all compromises, while Mr. Pinckney as steadily voted against slavery prohibition and against all compromises. By this Mr. King showed that, in his understanding, no line dividing local from Federal authority, nor any thing in the Constitution, was violated by Congress prohibiting slavery in federal territory; while Mr. Pinckney, by his votes, showed that in his understanding there was some sufficient reason for opposing such prohibition in that case.

"The cases I have mentioned are the only acts of the 'thirty-nine,' or of any of them, upon the direct issue, which I have been able to discover.

"To enumerate the persons who thus acted, as being four in 1784, three in 1787, seventeen in 1789, three in 1798, two in 1804, and two in 1819–20—there would be thirty-one of them. But this would be counting John Langdon, Roger Sherman, William Few, Rufus King, and George Read, each twice, and Abraham Baldwin four times. The true number of those of the 'thirty-nine' whom I have shown to have acted upon the question, which, by the text they understood better than we, is twenty-three, leaving sixteen not shown to have acted upon it in any way.

"Here, then, we have twenty-three out of our 'thirty-nine' fathers who framed the government under which we live, who have, upon their official responsibility and their corporal oaths, acted upon the very question which the text affirms they 'understood just as well, and even better than we do now;' and twenty-one of them—a clear majority of the 'thirty-nine'—so acting upon it as to make them guilty of gross political impropriety, and wilful perjury, if, in their understanding, any proper division between local and Federal authority, or any thing in the Constitution they had made themselves, and sworn to support, forbade the Federal government to control as to slavery in the Federal territories. Thus the twenty-one acted; and, as actions speak louder than words, so actions under such responsibility speak still louder.

"'Two of the twenty-three voted against Congressional prohibition of slavery in the Federal territories, in the instances in which they acted upon the question. But for what reasons they so voted is not known. They may have done so because they thought a proper division of local from Federal authority, or some provision or principle of the Constitution, stood in the way; or they may, without any such question, have voted against the prohibition, on what appeared to them to be sufficient grounds of expediency. No one who has sworn to support the Constitution, can conscientiously vote for what he understands to be an unconstitutional measure, however expedient he may think it; but one may and ought to vote against a measure which he deems constitutional, if, at the same time, he deems it inexpedient. It, therefore, would be unsafe to set down even the two who voted against the prohibition, as having done so because, in their understanding, any proper division of local from Federal authority, or any thing in the Constitution, forbade the Federal government to control as to slavery in Federal territory.

"'The remaining sixteen of the 'thirty-nine,' so far as I have discovered, have left no record of their understanding upon the direct question of Federal control of slavery in the Federal territories. But there is much reason to believe that their understanding upon that question would not have appeared different from that of their twenty-three compeers, had it been manifested at all.

"'For the purpose of adhering rigidly to the text, I have purposely omitted whatever understanding may have been manifested, by any person, however distinguished, other than the 'thirty-nine' fathers who framed the original Constitution; and, for the same reason, I have also omitted whatever understanding may have been manifested by any of the 'thirty-nine' even, on any other phase of the general question of slavery. If we should look into their acts and declarations on those other phases, as the foreign slave-trade, and the morality and policy of slavery generally, it would appear to us that on the direct question of Federal control of slavery in Federal territories, the sixteen, if they had acted at all, would probably have acted just as the twenty-three did. Among that sixteen were several of the most noted anti-slavery men of those times—as Dr. Franklin, Alexander Hamilton, and Governeur Morris—while there was not one now known to have been otherwise, unless it may be John Rutledge, of South Carolina.

"'The sum of the whole is, that of our 'thirty-nine' fathers who framed the original Constitution, twenty-one—a clear majority of the whole—certainly understood that no proper division of local from Federal authority nor any part of the Constitution, forbade the Federal government to control slavery in the Federal territories, while all the rest probably had the same understanding. Such, unquestionably, was the understanding of our fathers who framed the original Constitution; and the text affirms that they understood the question better than we.

"But, so far, I have been considering the understanding of the question manifested by the framers of the original Constitution. In and by the original instrument, a mode was provided for amending it; and, as I have already stated, the present frame of government under which we live consists of that original, and twelve amendatory articles framed and adopted since. Those who now insist that Federal control of slavery in Federal territories violates the Constitution, point us to the provisions which they suppose it thus violates; and, as I understand, they all fix upon provisions in these amendatory articles, and not in the original instrument. The Supreme Court, in the Dred Scott case, plant themselves upon the fifth amendment, which provides that 'no person shall be deprived of property without due process of law;' while Senator Douglas and his peculiar adherents plant themselves upon the tenth amendment, providing that 'the powers not granted by the Constitution are reserved to the States respectively, and to the people.'

"Now, it so happens that these amendments were framed by the first Congress which sat under the Constitution—the identical Congress which passed the act already mentioned, enforcing the prohibition of slavery in the northwestern territory. Not only was it the same Congress, but they were the identical, same individual men who, at the same session, and at the same time within the session, had under consideration, and in progress toward maturity, these Constitutional amendments, and this act prohibiting slavery in all the territory the nation then owned. The Constitutional amendments were introduced before, and passed after the act enforcing the Ordinance of '87; so that during the whole pendency of the act to enforce the Ordinance, the Constitutional amendments were also pending.

"That Congress, consisting in all of seventy-six members, including sixteen of the framers of the original Constitution, as before stated, were pre-eminently our fathers who framed that part of the government under which we live, which is now claimed as forbidding the Federal government to control slavery in the Federal territories.

"Is it not a little presumptuous in any one at this day to affirm that the two things which that Congress deliberately framed, and carried to maturity at the same time, are absolutely inconsistent with each other? And does not such affirmation become impudently absurd when coupled with the other affirmation, from the same mouth, that those who did the two things alleged to be inconsistent understood whether they really were inconsistent better than we—better than he who affirms that they are inconsistent?

"It is surely safe to assume that the 'thirty-nine' framers of the original Constitution, and the seventy-six members of the Congress which framed the amendments thereto, taken together, do certainly include those who may be fairly called 'our fathers who framed the government under which we live.' And so assuming, I defy any man to show that any one of them ever, in his whole life, declared that, in his understanding, any proper division of local from Federal authority, or any part of the Constitution, forbade the Federal government to control as to slavery in the Federal territories. I go a step further. I defy any one to show that any living man in the whole world ever did, prior to the beginning of the present century (and I might almost say prior to the beginning of the last half of the present century), declare that, in his understanding, any proper division of local from Federal authority, or any part of the Constitution, forbade the Federal government to control as to slavery in the Federal territories. To those who now so declare, I give, not only 'our fathers who framed the government under which we live,' but with them all other living men within the century in which it was framed. among whom to search, and they shall not be able to find the evidence of a single man agreeing with them.

"Now, and here, let me guard a little against being misunderstood. I do not mean to say we are bound to follow implicitly in whatever our fathers did. To do so, would be to discard all the lights of current experience—we reject all progress—all improvement. What I do say is, that if we would supplant the opinions and policy of our fathers in any case, we should do so upon evidence so conclusive, and argument so clear, that even their great authority, fairly considered and weighed, cannot stand ; and most surely not in a case whereof we ourselves declare they understood the question better than we.

"If any man, at this day, sincerely believes that a proper division of local from Federal authority, or any part of the Constitution, forbids the Federal government to control as to slavery in the Federal territories, he is right to say so, and to enforce his position by all truthful evidence and fair argument which he can. But he has no right to mislead others, who have less access to history and less leisure to study it, into the false belief that 'our fathers, who framed the government under which we live,' were of the same opinion—thus substituting falsehood and deception for truthful evidence and fair argument. If any man, at this day, sincerely believes 'our fathers, who framed the government under which we live,' used and applied principles, in other cases, which ought to have led them to understand that a proper division of local from Federal authority, or some part of the Constitution, forbids the Federal government to control as to slavery in the Federal territories, he is right to say so. But he should, at the same time, brave the responsibility of declaring that, in his opinion, he understands their principles better than they did themselves; and especially should he not shirk that responsibility by asserting that they 'understood the question just as well, and even better than we do now.'

"But enough. Let all who believe that 'our fathers, who framed the government under which we live, understood this question just as well, and even better than we do now,' speak as they spoke, and act as they acted upon it. This is all Republicans ask, all Republicans desire, in relation to slavery. As those fathers marked it, so let it be again marked, as an evil not to be extended, but to be tolerated and protected only because of and so far as its actual presence among us makes that toleration and protection a necessity. Let all the guaranties those fathers gave it, be, not grudgingly, but fully and fairly maintained. For this Republicans contend, and with this, so far as I know or believe, they will be content.

"And now, if they would listen—as I suppose they will not—I would address a few words to the Southern people.

"I would say to them: You consider yourselves a reasonable and a just people; and I consider that, in the general qualities of reason and justice, you are not inferior to any other people. Still, when you speak of us Republicans, you do so only to denounce us as reptiles, or, at the best, as no better than outlaws. You will grant a hearing to pirates or murderers, but nothing like it to 'Black Republicans.' In all your contentions with one another, each of you deems an unconditional condemnation of 'Black Republicanism' as the first thing to be attended to. Indeed, such condemnation of us seems to be an indispensable prerequisite—license, so to speak—among you to be admitted or permitted to speak at all.

"Now can you, or not, be prevailed upon to pause and to consider whether this is quite just to us, or even to yourselves?

"Bring forward your charges and specifications, and then be patient long enough to hear us deny or justify.

"You say we are sectional. We deny it. That makes an issue; and the burden of proof is upon you. You produce your proof; and what is it? Why, that our party has no existence in your section—gets no votes in your section. The fact is substantially true; but does it prove the issue? If it does, then, in case we should, without change of principle, begin to get votes in your section, we should thereby cease to be sectional. You cannot escape this conclusion; and yet, are you willing to abide by it? If you are, you will probably soon find that we have ceased to be sectional, for we shall get votes in your section this very year. You will then begin to discover, as the truth plainly is, that your proof does not touch the issue. The fact that we get no votes in your section is a fact of your making, and not of ours. And if there be fault in that fact, that fault is primarily yours, and remains so until you show that we repel you by some wrong principle or practice. If we do repel you by any wrong principle or practice, the fault is ours; but this brings us to where you ought to have started—to a discussion of the right or wrong of our principle. If our principle, put in practice, would wrong your section for the benefit of ours, or for any other object, then our principle, and we with it, are sectional, and are justly opposed and denounced as such. Meet us, then, on the question of whether our principle, put in practice, would wrong your section; and so meet it as if it were possible that something may be said on our side. Do you accept the challenge? No? Then you really believe that the principle which our fathers, who framed the government under which we live, thought so clearly right as to adopt it, and indorse it again and again upon their official oaths, is, in fact, so clearly wrong as to demand your condemnation without a moment's consideration.

"Some of you delight to flaunt in our faces the warning against sectional parties given by Washington in his Farewell Address. Less than eight years before Washington gave that warning, he had, as President of the United States, approved and signed an act of Congress enforcing the prohibition of slavery in the Northwestern Territory, which act embodied the policy of the government upon that subject, up to and at the very moment he penned that warning; and about one year after he penned it he wrote Lafayette that he considered that prohibition a wise measure, expressing, in the same connection, his hope that we should some time have a confederacy of free States.

"Bearing this in mind, and seeing that sectionalism has since arisen upon this same subject, is that warning a weapon in your hands against us, or in our hands against you? Could Washington himself speak, would he cast the blame of that sectionalism upon us, who sustain his policy, or upon you, who repudiate it? We respect that warning of Washington, and we commend it to you, together with his example pointing to the right application of it.

"But you say you are conservative—eminently conservative—while we are revolutionary, destructive, or something of the sort. What is conservatism? Is it not adherence to the old and tried against the new and untried? We stick to, contend for, the identical old policy on the point in controversy which was adopted by our fathers who framed the government under which we live; while you, with one accord, reject, and scout, and spit upon that old policy, and insist upon substituting something new. True, you disagree among yourselves as to what that substitute shall be. You have considerable variety of new propositions and plans, but you are unanimous in rejecting and denouncing the old policy of the fathers. Some of you are for reviving the foreign slave-trade; some for a Congressional Slave-Code for the Territories; some for Congress forbidding

the Territories to prohibit slavery within their limits; some for
maintaining slavery in the Territories through the Judiciary;
some for the 'gur-reat pur-rinciple' that, 'if one man would en-
slave another, no third man should object,' fantastically called
'Popular Sovereignty;' but never a man among you in favor of
Federal prohibition of slavery in Federal Territories, according
to the practice of our fathers who framed the government under
which we live. Not one of all your various plans can show a
precedent or an advocate in the century within which our government originated. Consider, then, whether your claim of
conservatism for yourselves, and your charge of destructiveness
against us, are based on the most clear and stable foundations.

"Again, you say we have made the slavery question more
prominent than it formerly was. We deny it. We admit that
it is more prominent, but we deny that we made it so. It was
not we, but you, who discarded the old policy of the fathers.
We resisted, and still resist, your innovation; and thence comes
the greater prominence of the question. Would you have that
question reduced to its former proportions? Go back to that
old policy. What has been will be again, under the same conditions. If you would have the peace of the old times, re-adopt
the precepts and policy of the old times.

" You charge that we stir up insurrections among your slaves.
We deny it. And what is your proof? Harper's Ferry! John
Brown! John Brown was no Republican; and you have failed
to implicate a single Republican in his Harper's Ferry enterprise. If any member of our party is guilty in that matter, you
know it, or you do not know it. If you do know it, you are inexcusable to not designate the man, and prove the fact. If you
do not know it; you are inexcusable to assert it, and especially to persist in the assertion after you have tried and failed to
make the proof. You need not be told that persisting in a
charge which one does not know to be true is simply malicious
slander.

" Some of you admit that no Republican designedly aided or
encouraged the Harper's Ferry affair; but still insist that our
doctrines and declarations necessarily lead to such results. We
do not believe it. We know we hold to no doctrine, and make
no declarations which were not held to and made by our fathers
who framed the government under which we live. You never
deal fairly by us in relation to this affair. When it occurred,
some important State elections were near at hand, and you
were in evident glee with the belief that, by charging the blame
upon us, you could get an advantage of us in those elections.
The elections came, and your expectations were not quite ful-
filled. Every Republican man knew that, as to himself, at least,
your charge was a slander, and he was not much inclined by it
to cast his vote in your favor. Republican doctrines and declarations are accompanied with a continual protest against any

interference whatever with your slaves, or with you about your slaves. Surely, this does not encourage them to revolt. True, we do, in common with our fathers, who framed the government under which we live, declare our belief that slavery is wrong; but the slaves do not hear us declare even this. For any thing we say or do, the slaves would scarcely know there is a Republican party. I believe they would not, in fact, generally know it but for your misrepresentations of us in their hearing. In your political contests among yourselves, each faction charges the other with sympathy with Black Republicanism; and then, to give point to the charge, defines Black Republicanism to simply be insurrection, blood and thunder among the slaves.

" Slave insurrections are no more common now than they were before the Republican party was organized. What induced the Southampton insurrection, twenty-eight years ago, in which, at least, three times as many lives were lost as at Harper's Ferry? You can scarcely stretch your very elastic fancy to the conclusion that Southampton was got up by Black Republicanism. In the present state of things in the United States, I do not think a general, or even a very extensive slave insurrection, is possible. The indispensable concert of action cannot be attained. The slaves have no means of rapid communication; nor can incendiary free men, black or white, supply it. The explosive materials are everywhere in parcels; but there neither are, nor can be supplied, the indispensable connecting trains.

" Much is said by southern people about the affection of slaves for their masters and mistresses; and a part of it, at least, is true. A plot for an uprising could scarcely be devised and communicated to twenty individuals before some one of them, to save the life of a favorite master or mistress, would divulge it. This is the rule; and the slave revolution in Hayti was not an exception to it, but a case occurring under peculiar circumstances. The gunpowder-plot of British history, though not connected with the slaves, was more in point. In that case, only about twenty were admitted to the secret; and yet one of them, in his anxiety to save a friend, betrayed the plot to that friend, and, by consequence, averted the calamity. Occasional poisonings from the kitchen, and open or stealthy assassinations in the field, and local revolts extending to a score or so, will continue to occur as the natural results of slavery; but no general insurrection of slaves, as I think, can happen in this country for a long time. Whoever much fears, or much hopes, for such an event, will be alike disappointed.

" In the language of Mr. Jefferson, uttered many years ago, 'It is still in our power to direct the process of emancipation, and deportation, peaceably, and in such slow degrees, as that the evil will wear off insensibly; and their place be, *pari passu*, filled up by free white laborers. If, on the contrary, it is left to force itself on, human nature must shudder at the prospect held up.'

" Mr. Jefferson did not mean to say, nor do I, that the power of emancipation is in the Federal Government. He spoke of Virginia ; and, as to the power of emancipation, I speak of the slaveholding States only.

" The Federal Government, however, as we insist, has the power of restraining the extension of the institution—the power to insure that a slave insurrection shall never occur on any American soil which is now free from slavery.

" John Brown's effort was peculiar. It was not a slave insurrection. It was an attempt by white men to get up a revolt among slaves, in which the slaves refused to participate. In fact, it was so absurd that the slaves, with all their ignorance, saw plainly enough it could not succeed. That affair, in its philosophy, corresponds with the many attempts, related in history, at the assassination of kings and emperors. An enthusiast broods over the oppression of a people till he fancies himself commissioned by Heaven to liberate them. He ventures the attempt, which ends in little else than in his own execution. Orsini's attempt on Louis Napoleon, and John Brown's attempt at Harper's Ferry were, in their philosophy, precisely the same. The eagerness to cast blame on old England in the one case, and on New England in the other, does not disprove the sameness of the two things.

"And how much would it avail you, if you could, by the use of John Brown, Helper's book, and the like, break up the Republican organization ? Human action can be modified to some extent, but human nature cannot be changed. There is a judgment and a feeling against slavery in this nation, which cast at least a million and a-half of votes. You cannot destroy that judgment and feeling—that sentiment—by breaking up the political organization which rallies around it. You can scarcely scatter and disperse an army which has been formed into order in the face of your heaviest fire ; but if you could, how much would you gain by forcing the sentiment which created it out of the peaceful channel of the ballot-box, into some other channel ? What would that other channel probably be ? Would the number of John Browns be lessened or enlarged by the operation.

" But you will break up the Union rather than submit to a denial of your Constitutional rights.

" That has a somewhat reckless sound ; but it would be palliated, if not fully justified, were we proposing, by the mere force of numbers, to deprive you of some right plainly written down in the Constitution. But we are proposing no such thing.

"When you make these declarations, you have a specific and well-understood allusion to an assumed Constitutional right of yours, to take slaves into the federal territories, and hold them there as property. But no such right is specifically written in the Constitution. That instrument is literally silent about any such right. We, on the contrary, deny that such a right has any existence in the Constitution, even by implication.

" Your purpose, then, plainly stated, is, that you will destroy the Government, unless you be allowed to construe and enforce the Constitution as you please, on all points in dispute between you and us. You will rule or ruin in all events.

" This, plainly stated, is your language to us. Perhaps you will say the Supreme Court has decided the disputed Constitutional question in your favor. Not quite so. But waiving the lawyer's distinction between dictum and decision, the Courts have decided the question for you in a sort of way. The Courts have substantially said, it is your Constitutional right to take slaves into the Federal Territories, and to hold them there as property.

" When I say the decision was made in a sort of way, I mean it was made in a divided Court by a bare majority of the Judges, and they not quite agreeing with one another in the reasons for making it; that it is so made as that its avowed supporters disagree with one another about its meaning, and that it was mainly based upon a mistaken statement of fact—the statement in the opinion that ' the right of property in a slave is distinctly and expressly affirmed in the Constitution.'

" An inspection of the Constitution will show that the right of property in a slave is not distinctly and expressly affirmed in it. Bear in mind the Judges do not pledge their judicial opinion that such right is impliedly affirmed in the Constitution ; but they pledge their veracity that it is distinctly and expressly affirmed there—' distinctly' that is, not mingled with any thing else—' expressly' that is, in words meaning just that, without the aid of any inference, and susceptible of no other meaning.

" If they had only pledged their judicial opinion that such right is affirmed in the instrument by implication, it would be open to others to show that neither the word ' slave' nor ' slavery' is to be found in the Constitution, nor the word ' property' even, in any connection with language alluding to the things slave, or slavery, and that wherever in that instrument the slave is alluded to, he is called a ' person ;' and wherever his master's legal right in relation to him is alluded to, it is spoken of as ' service or labor due,' as a ' debt' payable in service or labor. Also, it would be open to show, by contemporaneous history, that this mode of alluding to slaves and slavery, instead of speaking of them, was employed on purpose to exclude from the Constitution the idea that there could be property in man.

" To show all this is easy and certain.

" When this obvious mistake of the Judges shall be brought to their notice, is it not reasonable to expect that they will withdraw the mistaken statement, and reconsider the conclusion based upon it ?

"And then it is to be remembered that 'our fathers, who framed the Government under which we live'—the men who made the Constitution—decided this same Constitutional question in our favor, long ago—decided it without a division among themselves, when making the decision; without division among themselves about the meaning of it after it was made, and so far as any evidence is left, without basing it upon any mistaken statement of facts.

" Under all these circumstances, do you really feel yourselves justified to break up this Government, unless such a court decision as yours is, shall be at once submitted to, as a conclusive and final rule of political action.

" But you will not abide the election of a Republican President. In that supposed event, you say, you will destroy the Union ; and then, you say, the great crime of having destroyed it will be upon us !

" That is cool. A highwayman holds a pistol to my ear, and mutters through his teeth, 'stand and deliver, or I shall kill you, and then you will be a murderer !'

" To be sure, what the robber demanded of me—my money— was my own ; and I had a clear right to keep it ; but it was no more my own than my vote is my own ; and threat of death to me, to extort my money, and threat of destruction to the Union, to extort my vote, can scarcely be distinguished in principle.

"A few words now to Republicans. It is exceedingly desirable that all parts of this great Confederacy shall be at peace, and in harmony, one with another. Let us Republicans do our part to have it so. Even though much provoked, let us do nothing through passion and ill temper. Even though the southern people will not so much as listen to us, let us calmly consider their demands, and yield to them if, in our deliberate view of our duty, we possibly can. Judging by all they say and do, and by the subject and nature of their controversy with us, let us determine, if we can, what will satisfy them ?

" Will they be satisfied if the Territories be unconditionally surrendered to them? We know they will not. In all their present complaints against us, the Territories are scarcely mentioned. Invasions and insurrections are the rage now. Will it satisfy them if, in the future, we have nothing to do with invasions and insurrections? We know it will not. We so know because we know we never had any thing to do with invasions and insurrections ; and yet this total abstaining does not exempt us from the charge and the denunciation.

" The question recurs, what will satisfy them ? Simply this : We must not only let them alone, but we must, somehow, convince them that we do let them alone. This, we know by experience, is no easy task. We have been so trying to convince them from the very beginning of our organization, but with no success. In all our platforms and speeches we have constantly protested our purpose to let them alone; but this has had no tendency to convince them. Alike unavailing to convince them is the fact that they have never detected a man of us in any attempt to disturb them.

"These natural, and apparently adequate means all failing, what will convince them? This, and this only: cease to call slavery *wrong*, and join them in calling it *right*. And this must be done thoroughly—done in *acts* as well as in *words*. Silence will not be tolerated—we must place ourselves avowedly with them. Douglas's new sedition law must be enacted and enforced, suppressing all declarations that slavery is wrong, whether made in politics, in presses, in pulpits, or in private. We must arrest and return their fugitive slaves with greedy pleasure. We must pull down our Free-State Constitutions. The whole atmosphere must be disinfected from all taint of opposition to slavery, before they will cease to believe that all their troubles proceed from us.

"I am quite aware they do not state their case precisely in this way. Most of them would probably say to us, 'Let us alone, do nothing to us, and say what you please about slavery.' But we do let them alone—have never disturbed them—so that, after all, it is what we say, which dissatisfies them. They will continue to accuse us of doing, until we cease saying.

"I am also aware they have not, as yet, in terms demanded the overthrow of our Free-State Constitutions. Yet those Constitutions declare the wrong of slavery, with more solemn emphasis, than do all other sayings against it; and when all these other sayings shall have been silenced, the overthrow of these Constitutions will be demanded, and nothing be left to resist the demand. It is nothing to the contrary, that they do not demand the whole of this just now. Demanding what they do, and for the reason they do, they can voluntarily stop nowhere short of this consummation. Holding, as they do, that slavery is morally right, and socially elevating, they cannot cease to demand a full national recognition of it, as a legal right, and a social blessing.

"Nor can we justifiably withhold this, on any ground save our conviction that slavery is wrong. If slavery is right, all words, acts, laws, and constitutions against it, are themselves wrong, and should be silenced, and swept away. If it is right, we cannot justly object to its nationality—its universality; if it is wrong, they cannot justly insist upon its extension—its enlargement. All they ask, we could readily grant, if we thought slavery right; all we ask, they could as readily grant, if they thought it wrong. Their thinking it right, and our thinking it wrong, is the precise fact upon which depends the whole controversy. Thinking it right, as they do, they are not to blame for desiring its full recognition, as being right; but,

4

thinking it wrong, as we do, can we yield to them? Can we cast our votes with their view, and against our own? In view of our moral, social, and political responsibilities, can we do this?

"Wrong as we think slavery is, we can yet afford to let it alone where it is, because that much is due to the necessity arising from its actual presence in the nation; but can we, while our votes will prevent it, allow it to spread into the National Territories, and to overrun us here in these Free States?

"If our sense of duty forbids this, then let us stand by our duty, fearlessly and effectively. Let us be diverted by none of those sophistical contrivances wherewith we are so industriously plied and belabored—contrivances such as groping for some middle ground between the right and the wrong, vain as the search for a man who should be neither a living man nor a dead man—such as a policy of 'don't care' on a question about which all true men do care—such as Union appeals beseeching true Union men to yield to Disunionists, reversing the divine rule, and calling, not the sinners, but the righteous to repentance—such as invocations to Washington, imploring men to unsay what Washington said, and undo what Washington did.

"Neither let us be slandered from our duty by false accusations against us, not frightened from it by menaces of destruction to the Government, nor of dungeons to ourselves. Let us have faith that right makes might, and in that faith, let us, to the end, dare to do our duty, as we understand it."

IS NOMINATED FOR PRESIDENT OF THE UNITED STATES BY THE REPUBLICAN CONVENTION.

On the sixteenth of May, 1860, the Republican National Convention assembled in Chicago, for the purpose of nominating candidates for the Presidency and Vice-Presidency. The first day was spent in organizing, and the second, in adopting rules for the government of the Convention and the platform of the party, and on the third, the body proceeded to ballot for the two candidates. Mr. Lincoln was nominated for President by Mr. Judd, of Illinois, and on the first ballot, received 102 votes, Mr. Seward receiving, on the same ballot, 173½ votes, and the balance being divided between the other candidates. On the second ballot, the vote stood: Lincoln, 181; Seward, 184½; and on the third, Mr. Lincoln received 230½ votes, or within one and one-half of a nomination.   One of the delegates then changed four votes of his State, giving them to Mr. Lincoln, thus nominating him, and then, amid a scene of the most intense excitement, vote after vote was changed to the successful candidate, until at length the nomination was made unanimous.   The selection was received by the Republican voters of the country with the most unbounded enthusiasm, and immediate preparations were made for an arduous campaign.   The antecedents of their standard-bearer were of such an honorable and noble character, that they felt convinced the different factions among the opposition—indeed, all who were inspired more by patriotism than party predilections—would support him in the canvass and at the ballot-box.   The architect of his own fortunes, he had raised himself from obscurity to eminence and distinction.   Born in a floorless log-cabin, in a Kentucky wilderness ; the child of humble and uneducated, but Christian parents ; and with no education save that received during six months tuition in an unpretending school-house, and from attentive study at home by the light of a log fire, Abraham Lincoln, by his indefatigable perseverance and energy, rapidly rose from one position of trust and responsibility to another, until he attained the nomination of a great political party for the highest office in the gift of the American people.

IS NOTIFIED OF HIS NOMINATION—THE ADDRESSES ON THE OCCASION.

The committee appointed by the Convention to notify Mr. Lincoln of his nomination, performed their duty without delay, and upon arriving at his residence in Springfield, whither they were escorted by an immense concourse of citizens, the President of the Convention addressed the nominee as follows :

SPEECH OF THE PRESIDENT OF THE CONVENTION.

"I have, sir, the honor, in behalf of the gentlemen who are present, a Committee appointed by the Republican Convention, recently assembled at Chicago, to discharge a most pleasant duty. We have come, sir, under a vote of instructions to that Committee, to notify you that you have been selected by the Convention of the Republicans at Chicago, for President of the United States. They instruct us, sir, to notify you of that selection, and that Committee deem it not only respectful to yourself, but appropriate to the important matter which they have in hand, that they should come in person, and present to you the authentic evidence of the action of that Convention; and, sir, without any phrase which shall either be considered personally plauditory to yourself, or which shall have any reference to the principles involved in the questions which are connected with your nomination, I desire to present to you the letter which has been prepared, and which informs you of the nomination, and with it the platform, resolutions and sentiments, which the Convention adopted. Sir, at your convenience, we shall be glad to receive from you such a response as it may be your pleasure to give us."

REPLY OF MR. LINCOLN.

In response, Mr. Lincoln said:

"*Mr. Chairman and Gentlemen of the Committee:* I tender to you, and through you to the Republican National Convention, and all the people represented in it, my profoundest thanks for the high honor done me, which you now formally announce. Deeply, and even painfully sensible of the great responsibility which is inseparable from this high honor—a responsibility which I could almost wish had fallen upon some one of the far more eminent men and experienced statesmen whose distinguished names were before the Convention, I shall, by your leave, consider more fully the resolutions of the Convention, denominated the platform, and without unnecessary or unreasonable delay, respond to you, Mr. Chairman, in writing, not doubting that the platform will be found satisfactory, and the nomination gratefully accepted. And now I will not longer defer the pleasure of taking you, and each of you, by the hand."

CORRESPONDENCE BETWEEN THE CONVENTION AND MR. LINCOLN.

The following letter was addressed to Mr. Lincoln by

the President of the Convention, and a committee appointed for that purpose :

"CHICAGO, *May* 18*th*, 1860.

"TO THE HON. ABRAHAM LINCOLN, OF ILLINOIS.

"SIR: The representatives of the Republican party of the United States, assembled in Convention at Chicago, have this day by a unanimous vote, selected you as the Republican candidate for the office of President of the United States to be supported at the next election; and the undersigned were appointed a Committee of the Convention to apprise you of this nomination, and respectfully to request that you will accept it. A declaration of the principles and sentiments adopted by the Convention accompanies this communication.

"In the performance of this agreeable duty we take leave to add our confident assurance that the nomination of the Chicago Convention will be ratified by the suffrages of the people.

"We have the honor to be, with great respect and regard, your friends and fellow-citizens."

On the 23d, Mr. Lincoln addressed the following letter to the President of the Convention :

"SPRINGFIELD, ILLINOIS, *May* 23*rd*, 1860.

"HON. GEORGE ASHMAN, *President of the Republican National "Convention.*

"SIR: I accept the nomination tendered me by the Convention over which you presided, and of which I am formally apprised in the letter of yourself and others, acting as a Committee of the Convention for that purpose.

"The declaration of principles and sentiments, which accompanies your letter, meets my approval ; and it shall be my care not to violate, or disregard it, in any part.

"Imploring the assistance of Divine Providence, and with due regard to the views and feelings of all who were represented in the Convention ; to the rights of all the States and Territories, and people of the nation ; to the inviolability of the Constitution, and the perpetual union, harmony and prosperity of all, I am most happy to co-operate for the practical success of the principles declared by the Convention,

"Your obliged friend and fellow-citizen,

"ABRAHAM LINCOLN."

On the sixth of November, 1860, the election for President took place, with the following result : Mr. Lincoln received 491,275 over Mr. Douglas ; 1,018,499 over Mr. Breckenridge, and 1,275,821 over Mr. Bell; and the vote was subsequently proclaimed by Congress to be as follows:

For Abraham Lincoln, of Illinois.................. 180
For John C. Breckenridge, of Kentucky........... 72
For John Bell, of Tennessee...................... 39
For Stephen A. Douglas, of Illinois.............. 12

To describe the various movements and projects which were devised and consummated in the South between the time that Mr. Lincoln was elected and the date of his inauguration, would require a much larger work than that which we now offer to the public, and we will therefore confine our account merely to those which it is unavoidably necessary to mention. The principal and most diabolical plot conceived and recommended by the traitors, was to prevent the inauguration by obtaining possession of the Federal Capital, or by assassinating Mr. Lincoln while on his way thither, or upon the day that the ceremonies were to take place. Whatever may have been the plan, or however large the reward offered to the villain who would accomplish the murderous deed, the object of their vindictiveness escaped their machinations, and still continues to administer the government wisely and faithfully.

LEAVES SPRINGFIELD FOR WASHINGTON — OVATIONS ON THE ROUTE.

The President Elect left his home in Springfield, Illinois, on the eleventh of February, 1861, for Washington, having before leaving the depot addressed the following words of farewell to the thousands of his fellow-citizens who had assembled at the place of departure:

" *My friends:* No one not in my position can appreciate the sadness I feel at this parting. To this people I owe all that I am. Here I have lived more than a quarter of a century. Here my children were born, and here one of them lies buried. I know not how soon I shall see you again. A duty devolves upon me which is perhaps greater than that which has devolved upon any other man since the days of Washington. He never would have succeeded except for the aid of Divine Providence, upon which he at all times relied. I feel that I cannot succeed without the same Divine aid which sustained him, and in the same Almighty Being 1 place my reliance for support; and I hope you, my friends, will all pray that I may receive that Divine assistance, without which I cannot succeed, but with which success is certain. Again, I bid you all an affectionate farewell."

Along the route, multitudes assembled at the railway stations to greet him. At Toledo, in response to repeated calls, Mr. Lincoln appeared on the platform and said:

"I am leaving you on an errand of national importance, attended, as you are aware, with considerable difficulties. Let us believe, as some poet has expressed it, 'Behind the cloud the sun is shining still.' I bid you an affectionate farewell."

He next proceeded to Indianapolis, where Mr. Lincoln was welcomed by the Governor of the State, and escorted by a procession composed of both Houses of the Legislature, the public officers, municipal authorities, military, and firemen. On reaching the Hotel he addressed the people as follows:

"*Fellow-citizens of the State of Indiana:* I am here to thank you much for this magnificent welcome, and still more for the very generous support given by your State to that political cause, which I think is the true and just cause of the whole country and the whole world. Solomon says 'there is a time to keep silence;' and when men wrangle by the mouth, with no certainty that they mean the same thing while using the same words, it perhaps were as well if they would keep silence. The words 'coercion' and 'invasion' are much used in these days, and often with some temper and hot blood. Let us make sure, if we can, that we do not misunderstand the meaning of those who use them. Let us get the exact definitions of these words, not from dictionaries, but from the men themselves, who certainly deprecate the things they would represent by the use of the words. What, then, is 'coercion?' What is 'invasion?' Would the marching of an army into South Carolina, without the consent of her people, and with hostile intent towards them, be invasion? I certainly think it would, and it would be 'coercion' also if the South Carolinians were forced to submit. But if the United States should merely hold and retake its own forts and other property, and collect the duties on foreign importations,

or even withhold the mails from places where they were habitually violated, would any or all of these things be 'invasion' or
'coercion?' Do our professed lovers of the Union, but who
spitefully resolve that they will resist coercion and invasion, understand that such things as these, on the part of the United
States, would be coercion or invasion of a State? If so, their
idea of means to preserve the object of their great affection
would seem to be exceedingly thin and airy. If sick, the little
pills of the homœopathist would be much too large for it to
swallow. In their view, the Union, as a family relation, would
seem to be no regular marriage, but rather a sort of 'free-love'
arrangement, to be maintained on passional attraction. By the
way, in what consists the special sacredness of a State? I
speak not of the position assigned to a State in the Union by
the Constitution, for that is the bond we all recognize. That
position, however, a State cannot carry out of the Union with
it. I speak of that assumed primary right of a State to rule
all which is less than itself, and to ruin all which is larger than
itself. If a State and a County, in a given case, should be
equal in extent of territory and equal in number of inhabitants,
in what, as a matter of principle, is the State better than the
County? Would an exchange of name be an exchange of
rights? Upon what principle, upon what rightful principle, may
a State, being no more than one-fiftieth part of the nation in
soil and population, break up the nation, and then coerce a pro-
portionably larger subdivision of itself in the most arbitrary
way? What mysterious right to play tyrant is conferred on a
district of country with its people, by merely calling it a State?
Fellow-citizens, I am not asserting any thing. I am merely
asking questions for you to consider. And now allow me to bid
you farewell."

Proceeding to Cincinnati, he received a most enthusiastic welcome. Having been addressed by the mayor of
the city, and escorted by a civic and military procession
to the Burnet House, he addressed the assemblage in
these words :

"*Fellow-citizens :* I have spoken but once before this in Cincinnati. That was a year previous to the late Presidential election. On that occasion, in a playful manner, but with sincere
words, I addressed much of what I said to the Kentuckians. / I
gave my opinion that we, as Republicans, would ultimately beat
them as Democrats, but that they could postpone the result
longer by nominating Senator Douglas for the Presidency than
they could in any other way. They did not, in any true sense
of the word, nominate Mr. Douglas, and the result has come
certainly as soon as ever I expected.

" I also told them how I expected they would be treated after they should have been beaten, and now wish to call their attention to what I then said :

" ' When we do, as we say we will, beat you, you perhaps want to know what we will do with you.   I will tell you—as far as I am authorized to speak for the opposition—what we mean to do with you.   We mean to treat you as near as we possibly can, as Washington, Jefferson, and Madison treated you.   We mean to leave you alone, and in no way to interfere with your institutions ; to abide by all and every compromise of the Constitution.   In a word, coming back to the original proposition, to treat you, as far as degenerate men—if we have degenerated —may, according to the example of those noble fathers, Washington, Jefferson, and Madison.   We mean to remember that you are as good as we ; that there is no difference between us other than the difference of circumstances.   We mean to recognize and bear in mind always that you have as good hearts in your bosoms as other people, or as we claim to have, and to treat you accordingly.'

" Fellow-citizens of Kentucky, friends, brethren : May I call you such ?   In my new position I see no occasion and feel no inclination to retract a word of this.   If it shall not be made good be assured that the fault shall not be mine.'

In the evening he had a reception, when large crowds called upon him.

On the next morning he left Cincinnati, and arrived at Columbus, where he was received with every demonstration of enthusiasm.   He visited the Governor in the Executive Chamber, and was subsequently introduced to the members of the Legislature in joint session, when he was formally welcomed by the Lieutenant-Governor, to whom Mr. Lincoln responded in these words :

" It is true, as has been said by the President of the Senate, that very great responsibility rests upon me in the position to which the votes of the American people have called me.   I am deeply sensible of that weighty responsibility.   I cannot but know, what you all know, that without a name—perhaps without a reason why I should have a name—there has fallen upon me a task such as did not rest upon the Father of his Country.   And so feeling, I cannot but turn and look for the support without which it will be impossible for me to perform that great task   I turn, then, and look to the American people, and to that God who has never forsaken them.

"Allusion has been made to the interest felt in relation to the policy of the new Administration.   In this, I have received from some a degree of credit for having kept silence, from others some depreciation. I still think I was right. In the varying and repeatedly shifting scenes of the present, without a precedent which could enable me to judge for the past, it has seemed fitting, that before speaking upon the difficulties of the country I should have gained a view of the whole field. To be sure, after all, I would be at liberty to modify and change the course of policy as future events might make a change necessary.

" I have not maintained silence from any want of real anxiety. It is a good thing that there is no more than anxiety, for there is nothing going wrong. It is a consoling circumstance that when we look out there is nothing that really hurts anybody. We entertain different views upon political questions, but nobody is suffering any thing. This is a most consoling circumstance, and from it I judge that all we want is time and patience, and a reliance on that God who has never forsaken this people."

On the 14th of February, Mr. Lincoln proceeded to Pittsburgh. At Steubenville, on the route, in reply to an address, he said :

" I fear the great confidence placed in my ability is unfounded. Indeed, I am sure it is. Encompassed by vast difficulties, as I am, nothing shall be wanted on my part, if sustained by the American people and God. I believe the devotion to the Constitution is equally great on both sides of the river. It is only the different understanding of that instrument that causes difficulties. The only dispute is ' What are their rights ?' If the majority should not rule who should be the judge ? Where is such a judge to be found ? We should all be bound by the majority of the American people—if not, then the minority must control. Would that be right ? Would it be just or generous ? Assuredly not." He reiterated, the majority should rule. If he adopted a wrong policy, then the opportunity to condemn him would occur in four years' time. " Then I can be turned out and a better man with better views put in my place."

The next morning he left for Cleveland, but before his departure he made an address to the people of Pittsburgh, in which he said :

" In every short address I have made to the people, and in every crowd through which I have passed of late, some allusion has been made to the present distracted condition of the country. It is naturally expected that I should say something upon this subject, but to touch upon it at all would involve an elaborate discussion of a great many questions and circumstances, would require more time than I can at present command, and would perhaps unnecessarily commit me upon matters which have not yet fully developed themselves.

" The condition of the country, fellow-citizens, is an extraordinary one, and fills the mind of every patriot with anxiety and solicitude. My intention is to give this subject all the consideration which I possibly can before I speak fully and definitely in regard to it, so that, when I do speak, I may be as nearly right as possible. And when I do speak, fellow-citizens, I hope to say nothing in opposition to the spirit of the Constitution, contrary to the integrity of the Union, or which will in any way prove inimical to the liberties of the people or to the peace of the whole country. And, furthermore, when the time arrives for me to speak on this great subject, I hope to say nothing which will disappoint the reasonable expectations of any man, or disappoint the people generally throughout the country, especially if their expectations have been based upon any thing which I may have heretofore said.

" Notwithstanding the troubles across the river, [the speaker, smiling, pointed southwardly to the Monongahela River,] there is really no crisis springing from any thing in the Government itself. In plain words, there is really no crisis except an artificial one. What is there now to warrant the condition of affairs presented by our friends ' over the river'? Take even their own view of the questions involved, and there is nothing to justify the course which they are pursuing. I repeat it, then, there is no crisis, except such a one as may be gotten up at any time by turbulent men, aided by designing politicians. My advice, then, under such circumstances, is to keep cool. If the great American people will only keep their temper on both sides of the line, the trouble will come to an end, and the question which now distracts the country will be settled just as surely as all other difficulties of like character which have originated in this Government have been adjusted. Let the people on both sides keep their self-possession, and just as other clouds have cleared away in due time, so will this, and this great nation shall continue to prosper as heretofore."

He then referred to the subject of the tariff, and said :

" According to my political education, I am inclined to believe that the people in the various portions of the country should have their own views carried out through their representatives in Congress. That consideration of the Tariff bill should not be postponed until the next session of the National Legislature. No subject should engage your representatives more closely than that of the tariff. If I have any recommendation to make, it will be that every man who is called upon to serve the people, in a representative capacity, should study the whole subject thoroughly, as I intend to do myself, looking to all the varied interests of the common country, so that, when the time for action arrives, adequate protection shall be extended to the coal and iron of Pennsylvania and the corn of Illinois. Permit me to express the hope that this important subject may receive such consideration at the hands of your representatives that the interests of no part of the country may be overlooked, but that all sections may share in the common benefits of a just and equitable tariff."

Mr. Lincoln, upon his arrival in Cleveland, adverted to the same subject in the following terms :

" It is with you, the people, to advance the great cause of the Union and the Constitution, and not with any one man. It rests with you alone. This fact is strongly impressed on my mind at present. In a community like this, whose appearance testifies to their intelligence, I am convinced that the cause of liberty and the Union can never be in danger. Frequent allusion is made to the excitement at present existing in national politics. I think there is no occasion for any excitement. The crisis, as it is called, is altogether an artificial crisis. In all parts of the nation, there are differences of opinion in politics. There are differences of opinion even here. You did not all vote for the person who now addresses you. And how is it with those who are not here? Have they not all their rights as they ever had? Do they not have their fugitive slaves returned now as ever? Have they not the same Constitution that they have lived under for seventy odd years? Have they not a position as citizens of this common country, and have we any power to change that position? What, then, is the matter with them? Why all this excitement? Why all these complaints? As I said before, this crisis is all artificial. It has no foundation in fact. It was 'argued up,' as the saying is, and cannot be argued down. Let it alone, and it will go down itself."

On Saturday he proceeded to Buffalo, where he arrived at evening, and was met by an immense concourse of citizens, headed by Ex-President Fillmore.

Arriving at the hotel, Mr. Lincoln was welcomed in a brief speech by the acting chief magistrate, to which he made a brief reply, as follows :

"*Mr. Mayor and Fellow-Citizens* :—I am here to thank you briefly for this grand reception given to me, not personally, but as the representative of our great and beloved country. Your worthy mayor has been pleased to mention in his address to me, the fortunate and agreeable journey which I have had from home—only it is rather a circuitous route to the Federal Capital. I am very happy that he was enabled, in truth, to congratulate myself and company on that fact. It is true, we have had nothing thus far to mar the pleasure of the trip. We have not been met alone by those who assisted in giving the election to me; I say not alone, but by the whole population of the country through which we have passed. This is as it should be. Had the election fallen to any other of the distinguished candidates instead of myself, under the peculiar circumstances, to say the least, it would have been proper for all citizens to have greeted him as you now greet me. It is an evidence of the devotion of the whole people to the Constitution, the Union, and the perpetuity of the liberties of this country. 1 am unwilling, on any occasion, that I should be so meanly thought of as to have it supposed for a moment that these demonstrations are tendered to me personally. They are tendered to the country, to the institutions of the country, and to the perpetuity of the liberties of the country for which these institutions were made and created. Your worthy mayor has thought fit to express the hope that I may be able to relieve the country from the present, or, I should say, the threatened difficulties. I am sure I bring a heart true to the work. For the ability to perform it, I trust in that Supreme Being who has never forsaken this favored land, through the instrumentality of this great and intelligent people. Without that assistance I should surely fail; with it I cannot fail. When we speak of the threatened difficulties to the country, it is natural that it should be expected that something should be said by myself with regard to particular measures. Upon more mature reflection, however—and others will agree with me—that, when it is considered that these difficulties are without precedent, and never have been acted upon by any individual situated as I am, it is most proper I should wait and see the developments, and get all the light possible, so that, when I do speak authoritatively, I may be as near right as possible. When I shall speak authoritatively, I hope to say nothing inconsistent with the Constitution, the Union, the rights of all the States, of each State, and of each section of the country, and not to disappoint the reasonable expectations of those who have confided to me their votes. In this connection, allow me to say that you, as a portion of the great American people, need only to maintain your composure, stand up to your sober convictions of right, to your obligations to the Constitution, and act in accordance with those sober convictions, and the clouds which now arise in the horizon will be dispelled, and we shall have a bright and glorious future; and, when this generation shall have passed away, tens of thousands shall inhabit this country where only thousands inhabit it now. I do not propose to address you at length. I have no voice for it. Allow me again to thank you for this magnificent reception, and bid you farewell."

Mr. Lincoln then proceeded from Buffalo to Albany. Here he was met by the Mayor, the City Councils, and the Legislative Committees, and was conducted to the Capitol, where he was welcomed by Governor Morgan, and responded briefly, as follows:

"*Governor Morgan:*—I was pleased to receive an invitation to visit the capital of the great Empire State of this nation, while on my way to the Federal capital. I now thank you, and you, the people of the capital of the State of New York, for this most hearty and magnificent welcome. If I am not at fault, the great Empire State at this time contains a larger population than did the whole of the United States of America at the time they achieved their national independence; and I was proud to be invited to visit its capital, to meet its citizens as I now have the honor to do. I am notified by your governor that this reception is tendered by citizens without distinction of party. Because of this, I accept it the more gladly. In this country, and in any country where freedom of thought is tolerated, citizens attach themselves to political parties. It is but an ordinary degree of charity to attribute this act to the supposition that, in thus attaching themselves to the various parties, each man, in his own judgment, supposes he thereby best advances the interests of the whole country. And when an election is passed, it is altogether befitting a free people that, until the next election, they should be one people. The reception you have extended me to-day is not given to me personally. It should not be so, but as the representative, for the time being, of the majority of the nation. If the election had fallen to any of the more distinguished citizens, who received the support of the people, this same honor should have greeted him that greets me this day, in testimony of the unanimous devotion of the whole people to the Constitution, the Union, and to the perpetual liberties of succeeding generations in this country. I have neither the voice nor the strength to address you at any greater length. I beg you will, therefore, accept my most grateful thanks for this manifest devotion—not to me but to the institutions of this great and glorious country."

He was then conducted to the Legislative halls, where, in reply to an address of welcome, he again adverted to the troubles of the country in the following terms:

"*Mr. President and Gentlemen of the Legislature of the*

State of New York :—It is with feelings of great diffidence, and, I may say, feelings even of awe, perhaps greater than I have recently experienced, that I meet you here in this place. The history of this great State, the renown of its great men, who have stood in this chamber, and have spoken their thoughts, all crowd around my fancy, and incline me to shrink from an attempt to address you. Yet I have some confidence given me by the generous manner in which you have invited me, and the still more generous manner in which you have received me. You have invited me and received me without distinction of party. I could not for a moment suppose that this has been done in any considerable degree with any reference to my personal self. It is very much more grateful to me that this reception and the invitation preceding it were given to me as the representative of a free people than it could possibly have been were they but the evidence of devotion to me or to any one man. It is true that, while I hold myself, without mock-modesty, the humblest of all the individuals who have ever been elected President of the United States, I yet have a more difficult task to perform than any one of them has ever encountered. You have here generously tendered me the support, the united support, of the great Empire State. For this, in behalf of the nation—in behalf of the President and of the future of the nation—in behalf of the cause of civil liberty in all time to come—I most gratefully thank you. I do not propose now to enter upon any expressions as to the particular line of policy to be adopted with reference to the difficulties that stand before us in the opening of the incoming Administration. I deem that it is just to the country, to myself, to you, that I should see every thing, hear every thing, and have every light that can possibly be brought within my reach to aid me before I shall speak officially, in order that, when I do speak, I may have the best possible means of taking correct and true grounds. For this reason, I do not now announce any thing in the way of policy for the new Administration. When the time comes, according to the custom of the government, I shall speak, and speak as well as I am able for the good of the present and of the future of this country—for the good of the North and of the South—for the good of one and of the other, and of all sections of it. In the meantime, if we have patience, if we maintain our equanimity, though some may allow themselves to run off in a burst of passion, I still have confidence that the Almighty Ruler of the Universe, through the instrumentality of this great and intelligent people, can and will bring us through this difficulty, as he has heretofore brought us through all preceding difficulties of the country. Relying upon this, and again thanking you, as I forever shall, in my heart, for this generous reception you have given me, I bid you farewell."

At Albany, he was met by a delegation from the city authorities of New York, and on the 19th started for that city. At Poughkeepsie, he was welcomed by the Mayor of the city. Mr. Lincoln, in reply, said :

"I am grateful for this cordial welcome, and I am gratified that this immense multitude has come together, not to meet the individual man, but the man who, for the time being, will humbly but earnestly represent the majesty of the nation. These receptions have been given me at other places, and, as here, by men of different parties, and not by one party alone. It shows an earnest effort on the part of all to save, not the country, for the country can save itself, but to save the institutions of the country—those institutions under which, for at least three-quarters of a century, we have become the greatest, the most intelligent, and the happiest people in the world. These manifestations show that we all make common cause for these objects ; that if some of us are successful in an election, and others are beaten, those who are beaten are not in favor of sinking the ship in consequence of defeat, but are earnest in their purpose to sail it safely through the voyage in hand, and, in so far as they may think there has been any mistake in the election, satisfying themselves to take their chance at setting the matter right the next time. That course is entirely right. I am not sure—I do not pretend to be sure—that in the selection of the individual who has been elected this term, the wisest choice has been made. I fear it has not. In the purposes and in the principles that have been sustained, I have been the instrument selected to carry forward the affairs of this Government. I can rely upon you, and upon the people of the country ; and with their sustaining hand, I think that even I shall not fail in carrying the Ship of State through the storm."

The reception of President Lincoln in New York City was a most imposing demonstration. Places of business were generally closed, and hundreds of thousands were in the streets. On the next day, he was welcomed to the city by Mayor Wood, and replied as follows :

"*Mr. Mayor :* It is with feelings of deep gratitude that I make my acknowledgments for the reception given me in the great commercial city of New York. I cannot but remember that this is done by a people who do not, by a majority, agree with me in political sentiment. It is the more grateful, because in this I see that, for the great principles of our Government, the people are almost unanimous. In regard to the difficulties that confront us at this time, and of which your Honor has thought fit to speak so becomingly and so justly, as I suppose, I can only say that I agree in the sentiments expressed. In my devotion to the Union, I hope I am behind no man in the nation. In the wisdom with which to conduct the affairs tending to the preservation of the Union, I fear that too great confidence may have been reposed in me; but I am sure I bring a heart devoted to the work. There is nothing that could ever bring me to willingly consent to the destruction of this Union, under which not only the great commercial city of New York, but the whole country, acquired its greatness, except it be the purpose for which the Union itself was formed. I understand the ship to be made for the carrying and the preservation of the cargo, and so long as the ship can be saved with the cargo, it should never be abandoned, unless it fails the possibility of its preservation, and shall cease to exist, except at the risk of throwing overboard both freight and passengers. So long, then, as it is possible that the prosperity and the liberties of the people be preserved in this Union, it shall be my purpose at all times to use all my powers to aid in its perpetuation. Again thanking you for the reception given me, allow me to come to a close."

On the next day, he left for Philadelphia. At Trenton, ne remained a few hours, and visited both Houses of the Legislature. On being received in the Senate, he thus addressed that body :

"*Mr. President and Gentlemen of the Senate of the State of New Jersey:* I am very grateful to you for the honorable reception of which I have been the object. I cannot but remember the place that New Jersey holds in our early history. In the early Revolutionary struggle, few of the States among the old Thirteen had more of the battle-fields of the country within its limits than old New Jersey. May I be pardoned, if, upon this occasion, I mention, that away back in my childhood, the earliest days of my being able to read, I got hold of a small book, such a one as few of the younger members have ever seen, ' Weems' Life of Washington.' I remember all the accounts there given of the battle-fields and struggles for the liberties of the country, and none fixed themselves upon my imagination so deeply as the struggle here at Trenton, New Jersey. The crossing of the river—the contest with the Hessians—the great hardships endured at that time—all fixed themselves on my memory more than any single revolutionary event; and you all know, for you have all been boys, how these early impressions last longer than any others. I recollect thinking then, boy even though I was, that there must have been something more than common that those men struggled for. I am exceedingly anxious that that thing which they struggled for—that something even more than National Independence—that something that held out a great promise to all the people of the world to all time to come—I am

5

exceedingly anxious that this Union, the Constitution, and the liberties of the people, shall be perpetuated in accordance with the original idea for which that struggle was made, and I shall be most happy indeed if I shall be an humble instrument in the hands of the Almighty, and of this, His almost chosen people, for perpetuating the object of that great struggle. You give me this reception, as I understand, without distinction of party. I learn that this body is composed of a majority of gentlemen who, in the exercise of their best judgment in the choice of a Chief Magistrate, did not think I was the man. I understand, nevertheless, that they came forward here to greet me as the constitutional President of the United States—as citizens of the United States, to meet the man who, for the time being, is the representative man of the nation, united by a purpose to perpetuate the Union and liberties of the people. As such, I accept this reception more gratefully than I could do did I believe it was tendered to me as an individual."

He then passed into the Chamber of the Assembly, and upon being introduced by the Speaker, addressed that body as follows:

"Mr. Speaker and Gentlemen: I have just enjoyed the honor of a reception by the other branch of this Legislature, and I return to you and them my thanks for the reception which the people of New Jersey have given, through their chosen representatives, to me, as the representative, for the time being, of the majesty of the people of the United States. I appropriate to myself very little of the demonstrations of respect with which I have been greeted. I think little should be given to any man, but that it should be a manifestation of adherence to the Union and the Constitution. I understand myself to be received here by the representatives of the people of New Jersey, a majority of whom differ in opinion from those with whom I have acted. This manifestation is therefore to be regarded by me as expressing their devotion to the Union, the Constitution, and the liberties of the people. You, Mr. Speaker, have well said, that this is the time when the bravest and wisest look with doubt and awe upon the aspect presented by our national affairs. Under these circumstances, you will readily see why I should not speak in detail of the course I shall deem it best to pursue. It is proper that I should avail myself of all the information and all the time at my command, in order that when the time arrives in which I must speak officially, I shall be able to take the ground which I deem the best and safest, and from which I may have no occasion to swerve. I shall endeavor to take the ground I deem most just to the North, the East, the West, the South, and the whole country. I take it, I hope, in good temper—certainly

with no malice towards any section. I shall do all that may be in my power to promote a peaceful settlement of all our difficulties. The man does not live who is more devoted to peace than I am—none who would do more to preserve it. But it may be necessary to put the foot down firmly. And if I do my duty, and do right, you will sustain me, will you not? Received, as I am, by the members of a Legislature, the majority of whom do not agree with me in political sentiments, I trust that I may have their assistance in piloting the Ship of State through this voyage, surrounded by perils as it is ; for if it should suffer shipwreck now, there will be no pilot ever needed for another voyage."

On his arrival in Philadelphia, he was received with great enthusiasm, and the Mayor greeted him with the following address :

" *Sir :* In behalf of the Councils of Philadelphia and of its citizens, who, with common respect for their chief Magistrate-elect, have greeted your arrival, I tender you the hospitality of this city. I do this as the official representative of ninety thousand hearths, around which dwell six hundred thousand people, firm and ardent in their devotion to the Union ; and yet it may not be withheld, that there are but few of these firesides whose cheer is not straitened and darkened by the calamitous condition of our country. The great mass of this people are heartily weary and sick of the selfish schemes and wily plots of mere politicians, who bear no more relation to true statesmanship than do the barnacles which incrust the ship to the master who stands by the helm. Your fellow-countrymen look to you in the earnest hope that true statesmanship and unalloyed patriotism may, with God's blessing, restore peace and prosperity to this distracted land. It is to be regretted that your short stay precludes that intercourse with the merchants, manufacturers, mechanics, and other citizens of Philadelphia, which might afford you a clear discernment of their great interests. And, sir, it could not be other than grateful to yourself to have the opportunity of communicating with the memories of the past, in those historic walls where were displayed the comprehensive intellects, and the liberal, disinterested virtues of our fathers, who framed the Constitution of the Federal States, over which you have been called upon to preside."

Mr. Lincoln replied :

" *Mr. Mayor and Fellow-citizens of Philadelphia :* I appear before you to make no lengthy speech but to thank you for this reception. The reception you have given me to-night is not to me, the man, the individual, but to the man who temporarily represents, or should represent, the majesty of the nation.   It is true, as your worthy Mayor has said, that there is anxiety among the citizens of the United States at this time.   I deem it a happy circumstance that this dissatisfied portion of our fellow-citizens do not point us to any thing in which they are being injured, or are about to be injured; for which reason I have felt all the while justified in concluding that the crisis, the panic, the anxiety of the country at this time, is artificial.   If there be those who differ with me upon this subject, they have not pointed out the substantial difficulty that exists.   I do not mean to say that an artificial panic may not do considerable harm; that it has done such I do not deny.   The hope that has been expressed by your Mayor, that I may be able to restore peace, harmony, and prosperity to the country, is most worthy of him; and happy indeed will I be if I shall be able to verify and fulfil that hope.   I promise you, in all sincerity, that I bring to the work a sincere heart.   Whether I will bring a head equal to that heart, will be for future times to determine.   It were useless for me to speak of details of plans now; I shall speak officially next Monday week, if ever.   If I should not speak then, it were useless for me to do so now.   If I do speak then, it is useless for me to do so now.   When I do speak, I shall take such ground as I deem best calculated to restore peace, harmony, and prosperity to the country, and tend to the perpetuity of the nation, and the liberty of these States and these people.   Your worthy Mayor has expressed the wish, in which I join with him, that it were convenient for me to remain with your city long enough to consult your merchants and manufacturers; or, as it were, to listen to those breathings rising within the consecrated walls wherein the Constitution of the United States, and, I will add, the Declaration of Independence, were originally framed and adopted.   I assure you and your Mayor, that I had hoped on this occasion, and upon all occasions during my life, that I shall do nothing inconsistent with the teachings of these holy and most sacred walls.   I never asked any thing that does not breathe from those walls.   All my political warfare has been in favor of the teachings that come forth from these sacred walls.   May my right hand forget its cunning, and my tongue cleave to the roof of my mouth, if ever I prove false to those teachings.   Fellow-citizens, now allow me to bid you good-night."

On the next morning, Mr. Lincoln visited the old "Independence Hall," for the purpose of raising the national flag over it.   Here he was received with a warm welcome, and made the following address:

"I am filled with deep emotion at finding myself standing here, in this place, where were collected the wisdom, the patriotism, the devotion to principle, from which sprang the institutions under which we live. You have kindly suggested to me that in my hands is the task of restoring peace to the present distracted condition of the country. I can say in return, sir, that all the political sentiments I entertain have been drawn, so far as I have been able to draw them, from the sentiments which originated and were given to the world from this hall. I have never had a feeling politically that did not spring from the sentiments embodied in the Declaration of Independence. I have often pondered over the dangers which were incurred by the men who assembled here, and framed and adopted that Declaration of Independence. I have pondered over the toils that were endured by the officers and soldiers of the army who achieved that independence. I have often inquired of myself what great principle or idea it was that kept this Confederacy so long together. It was not the mere matter of the separation of the colonies from the mother-land, but that sentiment in the Declaration of Independence which gave liberty, not alone to the people of this country, but, I hope, to the world for all future time. It was that which gave promise that in due time the weight would be lifted from the shoulders of all men. This is a sentiment embodied in the Declaration of Independence. Now, my friends, can this country be saved upon this basis? If it can, I will consider myself one of the happiest men in the world if I can help to save it. If it cannot be saved upon that principle, it will be truly awful. But if this country cannot be saved without giving up that principle, I was about to say I would rather be assassinated on this spot than surrender it. Now, in my view of the present aspect of affairs, there need be no bloodshed or war. There is no necessity for it. I am not in favor of such a course, and I may say, in advance, that there will be no bloodshed unless it be forced upon the government, and then it will be compelled to act in self-defence.

"My friends, this is wholly an unexpected speech, and I did not expect to be called upon to say a word when I came here. I supposed it was merely to do something towards raising the flag. I may, therefore, have said something indiscreet. I have said nothing but what I am willing to live by, and, if it be the pleasure of Almighty God, to die by."

The party then proceeded to a platform erected in front of the State House, and Mr. Benton, of the Select Council, invited the President-elect to raise the flag. Mr. Lincoln responded in a brief speech, stating his cheerful compliance with the request, and alluded to the original flag of thirteen stars, saying that the number had increased as time rolled on, and we became a happy and a powerful people, each star adding to its prosperity. "The future," he added, "is in the hands of the people. It is on such an occasion as this that we can reason together, reaffirm our devotion to the country and the principles of the Declaration of Independence. Let us make up our mind, that when we do put a new star upon our banner, it shall be a fixed one, never to be dimmed by the horrors of war, but brightened by the contentment and prosperity of peace. Let us go on to extend the area of our usefulness, add star upon star, until their light shall shine upon five hundred millions of a free and happy people."

The President-elect then raised the flag to the top of the staff.

At half-past 9 o'clock the party left for Harrisburg. Both Houses of the Legislature were visited by Mr. Lincoln, and to an address of welcome he thus replied :

"I appear before you only for a very few brief remarks, in response to what has been said to me. I thank you most sincerely for this reception, and the generous words in which support has been promised me upon this occasion. I thank your great commonwealth for the overwhelming support it recently gave, not to me personally, but the cause, which I think a just one, in the late election. Allusion has been made to the fact—the interesting fact, perhaps we should say—that I, for the first time, appear at the Capital of the great Commonwealth of Pennsylvania upon the birthday of the Father of his Country, in connection with that beloved anniversary connected with the history of this country. I have already gone through one exceedingly interesting scene this morning in the ceremonies at Philadelphia. Under the high conduct of gentlemen there, I was, for the first time, allowed the privilege of standing in Old Independence Hall, to have a few words addressed to me there, and opening up to me an opportunity of expressing, with much regret, that I had not more time to express something of my own feelings, excited by the occasion, somewhat to harmonize and give shape to the feelings that had been really the feelings of my whole life. Besides this, our friends there had provided a magnificent flag of the country. They had arranged it so that I was given the honor of raising it to the head of its staff. And when it went up I was pleased that it went to its place by the strength of my own feeble arm ; when, according to the arrangement, the cord was pulled, and it flaunted gloriously to the wind without an accident, in the bright glowing sunshine of the morning. I could not help hoping that there was in the entire success of that beautiful ceremony at least something of an omen of what is to come. Nor could I help feeling then, as I often have felt, in the whole of that proceeding, I was a very humble instrument. I had not provided the flag; I had not made the arrangements for elevating it to its place. I had applied but a very small portion of my feeble strength in raising it. In the whole transaction I was in the hands of the people who had arranged it, and if I can have the same generous coöperation of the people of the nation, I think the flag of our country may yet be kept flaunting gloriously. I recur for a moment but to repeat some words uttered at the hotel in regard to what has been said about the military support which the General Government may expect from the Commonwealth of Pennsylvania in a proper emergency. To guard against any possible mistake do I recur to this. It is not with any pleasure that I contemplate the possibility that a necessity may arise in this country for the use of the military arm. While I am exceedingly gratified to see the manifestation upon your streets of your military force here, and exceedingly gratified at your promise here to use that force upon a proper emergency—while I make these acknowledgments, I desire to repeat, in order to preclude any possible misconstruction, that I do most sincerely hope that we shall have no use for them; that it will never become their duty to shed blood, and most especially never to shed fraternal blood. I promise that, so far as I may have wisdom to direct, if so painful a result shall in any wise be brought about, it shall be through no fault of mine. Allusion has also been made by one of your honored speakers to some remark recently made by myself at Pittsburg, in regard to what is supposed to be the especial interests of this great Commonwealth of Pennsylvania. I now wish only to say, in regard to that matter, that the few remarks which I uttered on that occasion were rather carefully worded. I took pains that they should be so. I have seen no occasion since to add to them or subtract from them. I leave them precisely as they stand, adding only now, that I am pleased to have an expression from you, gentlemen of Pennsylvania, significant that they are satisfactory to you. And now, gentlemen of the General Assembly of the Commonwealth of Pennsylvania, allow me to return you again my most sincere thanks."

PLOT TO ASSASSINATE HIM—HOW IT WAS THWARTED.

Arrangements had been made for his departure from

Harrisburg on the following morning, but the discovery of a plot to assassinate him as he passed through Baltimore—a plot in which some of the principal residents of that city were interested, although their projects were to be accomplished by means of paid emissaries—caused a change in the schedule, and on the evening of the day that he had been received by the Legislature, he left in a special train for Philadelphia, and from thence proceeded in the sleeping-car attached to the regular midnight train to Washington, where he arrived at an early hour on the morning of the twenty-third.

The sudden departure of Mr. Lincoln from the Pennsylvania State Capital naturally astonished the people of the country; and while the loyal citizens exulted in the fact that he was safe in Washington, the traitors and their sympathizers were greatly exasperated at the failure of their nefarious designs, and pronouncing the movement an act of cowardice, solemnly declared that he should never be inaugurated.

IS WELCOMED TO WASHINGTON BY THE AUTHORITIES.

A few days after his arrival he was waited upon by the Mayor and other municipal authorities, who welcomed him to the city, and to whom he made the following reply:

"*Mr. Mayor:* I thank you, and through you the municipal authorities of this city who accompany you, for this welcome. And as it is the first time in my life since the present phase of politics has presented itself in this country, that I have said any thing publicly within a region of country where the institution of slavery exists, I will take this occasion to say that I think very much of the ill-feeling that has existed, and still exists, between the people in the sections from whence I came and the people here, is dependent upon a misunderstanding of one another. I therefore avail myself of this opportunity to assure you, Mr. Mayor, and all the gentlemen present, that I have not now, and never have had, any other than as kindly feelings towards you as the people of my own section. I have not now, and never have had, any disposition to treat you in any respect otherwise than as my own neighbors. I have not now any purpose to withhold from you any of the benefits of the Constitution, under any circumstances, that I would not feel myself constrained to withhold from my neighbors ; and I hope, in a word, that, when we shall become better acquainted, and I say it with great confidence, we shall like each other the more. I thank you for the kindness of this reception."

ADDRESSES THE REPUBLICAN ASSOCIATION.

On the following evening the Republican Association tendered him a delightful serenade, at the conclusion of which he made the following remarks to the assembled crowd :

"*My friends*: I suppose that I may take this as a compliment paid to me, and as such please accept my thanks for it. I have reached this city of Washington under circumstances considerably differing from those under which any other man has ever reached it. I am here for the purpose of taking an official position amongst the people, almost all of whom were politically opposed to me, and are yet opposed to me as I suppose. I propose no lengthy address to you. I only propose to say, as I did on yesterday, when your worthy Mayor and Board of Aldermen called upon me, that I thought much of the ill-feeling that has existed between you and the people of your surroundings and that people from amongst whom I came, has depended, and now depends, upon a misunderstanding.

"I hope that, if things shall go along as prosperously as I believe we all desire they may, I may have it in my power to remove something of this misunderstanding; that I may be enabled to convince you, and the people of your section of the country, that we regard you as in all things our equals, and in all things entitled to the same respect and the same treatment that we claim for ourselves ; that we are in nowise disposed, if it were in our power, to oppress you, to deprive you of any of your rights under the Constitution of the United States, or even narrowly to split hairs with you in regard to those rights, but are determined to give you, as far as lies in our hands, all your rights under the Constitution—not grudgingly, but fully and fairly. I hope that, by thus dealing with you, we will become better acquainted, and be better friends. And now, my friends, with these few remarks, and again returning my thanks for this compliment, and expressing my desire to hear a little more of your good music, I bid you good-night."

IS INAUGURATED PRESIDENT OF THE UNITED STATES.

On the fourth of March, 1861, Abraham Lincoln was inaugurated the Sixteenth President of the United States, the ceremonies incident to the event being of the most imposing description. A large number of troops participated in the procession, and every arrangement was made to frustrate any movement the Secessionists or their friends might make to prevent the choice of a majority of the voters of the nation from taking the oath of office. From a platform erected in the usual position on the east front of the capitol, and in the presence of not less than ten thousand persons, Mr. Lincoln delivered the following Inaugural Address :

INAUGURAL ADDRESS OF ABRAHAM LINCOLN.

"Fellow-citizens of the United States :

"In compliance with a custom as old as the Government itself, I appear before you to address you briefly, and to take, in your presence, the oath prescribed by the Constitution of the United States to be taken by the President, before he enters on the execution of his office.

"I do not consider it necessary, at present, for me to discuss those matters of administration about which there is no special anxiety or excitement. Apprehension seems to exist among the people of the Southern States, that, by the accession of a Republican Administration, their property and their peace and personal security are to be endangered. There has never been any reasonable cause for such apprehension. Indeed, the most ample evidence to the contrary has all the while existed, and been open to their inspection. It is found in nearly all the published speeches of him who now addresses you. I do but quote from one of those speeches, when I declare that ' I have no purpose, directly or indirectly, to interfere with the institution of slavery in the States where it exists.' I believe I have no lawful right to do so ; and I have no inclination to do so. Those who nominated and elected me, did so with the full knowledge that I had made this, and made many similar declarations, and had never recanted them. And more than this, they placed in the platform. for my acceptance, and as a law to themselves and to me, the clear and emphatic resolution which I now read :

" '*Resolved,* That the maintenance inviolate of the rights of the States, and especially the right of each State to order and control its own domestic institutions according to its own judgment exclusively, is essential to that balance of power on which the perfection and endurance of our political fabric depend ; and we denounce the lawless invasion by armed force of the soil of any State or Territory, no matter under what pretext, as among the gravest of crimes.'

" I now reiterate these sentiments ; and in doing so I only press upon the public attention the most conclusive evidence of which the case is susceptible, that the property, peace, and security of no section are to be in anywise endangered by the now incoming Administration.

" I add, too, that all the protection which, consistently with the Constitution and the laws, can be given, will be cheerfully given to all the States when lawfully demanded, for whatever cause, as cheerfully to one section as to another.

" There is much controversy about the delivering up of fugitives from service or labor. The clause 1 now read is as plainly written in the Constitution as any other of its provisions :

" 'No person held to service or labor in one State under the laws thereof, escaping into another, shall, in consequence of any law or regulation therein, be discharged from such service or labor, but shall be delivered up on claim of the party to whom such service or labor may be due.'

" It is scarcely questioned that this provision was intended by those who made it for the reclaiming of what we call fugitive slaves ; and the intention of the lawgiver is the law.

"All members of Congress swear their support to the whole Constitution—to this provision as well as any other. To the proposition, then, that slaves whose cases come within the terms of this clause ' shall be delivered up,' their oaths are unanimous. Now, if they would make the effort in good temper, could they not, with nearly equal unanimity, frame and pass a law by means of which to keep good that unanimous oath?

" 'There is some difference of opinion whether this clause should be enforced by national or by State authority; but surely that difference is not a very material one. If the slave is to be surrendered, it can be of but little consequence to him or to others by which authority it is done ; and should any one, in any case, be content that this oath shall go unkept on a merely unsubstantial controversy as to how it shall be kept ?

"Again, in any law upon this subject, ought not all the safeguards of liberty known in the civilized and humane jurisprudence to be introduced, so that a free man be not, in any case, surrendered as a slave? And might it not be well at the same time to provide by law for the enforcement of that clause in the Constitution, which guarantees that ' the citizens of each State shall be entitled to all the privileges and immunities of citizens in the several States ?'

"I take the official oath to-day with no mental reservations, and with no purpose to construe the Constitution or laws by any hypercritical rules; and while I do not choose now to specify particular acts of Congress as proper to be enforced, I do suggest that it will be much safer for all, both in official and private stations, to conform to and abide by all those acts which stand unrepealed, than to violate any of them, trusting to find impunity in having them held to be unconstitutional.

"It is seventy-two years since the first inauguration of a President under our national Constitution. During that period fifteen different and very distinguished citizens have in succession administered the executive branch of the government. They have conducted it through many perils, and generally with great success. Yet, with all this scope for precedent, I now enter upon the same task, for the brief constitutional term of four years, under great and peculiar difficulties.

"A disruption of the Federal Union, heretofore only menaced, is now formidably attempted. I hold that in the contemplation of universal law and of the Constitution, the Union of these States is perpetual. Perpetuity is implied, if not expressed, in the fundamental law of all national governments. It is safe to assert that no government proper ever had a provision in its organic law for its own termination. Continue to execute all the express provisions of our national Constitution, and the Union will endure forever, it being impossible to destroy it except by some action not provided for in the instrument itself.

"Again, if the United States be not a government proper, but an association of States in the nature of a contract merely, can it, as a contract, be peaceably unmade by less than all the parties who made it? One party to a contract may violate it—break it, so to speak; but does it not require all to lawfully rescind it? Descending from these general principles, we find the proposition that in legal contemplation the Union is perpetual, confirmed by the history of the Union itself.

"The Union is much older than the Constitution. It was formed, in fact, by the Articles of Association in 1774. It was matured and continued in the Declaration of Independence in 1776. It was further matured, and the faith of all the then thirteen States expressly plighted and engaged that it should be perpetual, by the Articles of Confederation, in 1778; and, finally, in 1787, one of the declared objects for ordaining and establishing the Constitution was to form a more perfect Union. But if the destruction of the Union by one or by a part only of the States be lawfully possible, the Union is less than before, the Constitution having lost the vital element of perpetuity.

"It follows from these views that no State, upon its own mere motion, can lawfully get out of the Union; that resolves and ordinances to that effect are legally void; and that acts of vio-

lence within any State or States against the authority of t1
United States are insurrectionary or revolutionary, according to
circumstances.

" I therefore consider that, in view of the Constitution and
the laws, the Union is unbroken, and, to the extent of my
ability, I shall take care, as the Constitution itself expressly
enjoins upon me, that the laws of the Union shall be faithfully
executed in all the States.   Doing this, which I deem to be only
a simple duty on my part, I shall perfectly perform it, so far as
is practicable, unless my rightful masters, the American people,
shall withhold the requisition, or, in some authoritative manner,
direct the contrary.

" I trust this will not be regarded as a menace, but only as the
declared purpose of the Union that it will constitutionally defend
and maintain itself.

" In doing this there need be no bloodshed or violence, and
there shall be none unless it is forced upon the national authority.

" The power confided to me *will be used to hold, occupy, and
possess the property and places belonging to the government,* and
collect the duties and imposts ; but beyond what may be necessary for these objects there will be no invasion, no using of force
against or among the people anywhere.

" Where hostility to the United States shall be so great and
so universal as to prevent competent resident citizens from holding
the Federal offices, there will be no attempt to force obnoxious
strangers among the people that object.   While strict legal right
may exist of the government to enforce the exercise of these
offices, the attempt to do so would be so irritating, and so
nearly impracticable withal, that I deem it better to forego for
the time the uses of such offices.

" The mails, unless repelled, will continue to be furnished to
all parts of the Union.

" So far as possible, the people everywhere shall have that
sense of perfect security which is most favorable to calm thought
and reflection.

" The course here indicated will be followed, unless current
events and experience shall show a modification or change to be
proper ; and in every case and exigency my best discretion will
be exercised according to the circumstances actually existing,
and with a view and hope of a peaceful solution of the national
troubles, and the restoration of fraternal sympathies and af-
fections.

" That there are persons, in one section or another, who seek
to destroy the Union at all events, and are glad of any pretext
to do it, I will neither affirm nor deny.   But if there be such, I
need address no word to them.

" To those, however, who really love the Union, may I not
speak, before entering upon so grave a matter as the destruc-

tion of our national fabric, with all its benefits, its memories, and its hopes? Would it not be well to ascertain why we do it? Will you hazard so desperate a step, while any portion of the ills you fly from have no real existence? Will you, while the certain ills you fly to, are greater than all the real ones you fly from? Will you risk the commission of so fearful a mistake? All profess to be content in the Union if all constitutional rights can be maintained. Is it true, then, that any right, plainly written in the Constitution, has been denied? I think not. Happily the human mind is so constituted, that no party can reach to the audacity of doing this.

"Think, if you can, of a single instance in which a plainly-written provision of the Constitution has ever been denied. If, by the mere force of numbers, a majority should deprive a minority of any clearly-written constitutional right, it might, in a moral point of view, justify revolution; it certainly would, if such right were a vital one. But such is not our case.

"All the vital rights of minorities and of individuals are so plainly assured to them by affirmations and negations, guarantees and prohibitions in the Constitution, that controversies never rise concerning them. But no organic law can ever be framed with a provision specifically applicable to every question which may occur in practical administration. No foresight can anticipate, nor any document of reasonable length contain, express provisions for all possible questions. Shall fugitives from labor be surrendered by national or by State authorities? The Constitution does not expressly say. Must Congress protect slavery in the territories? The Constitution does not expressly say. From questions of this class spring all our constitutional controversies, and we divide upon them into majorities and minorities.

"If the minority will not acquiesce, the majority must, or the government must cease. There is no alternative for continuing the government but acquiescence on the one side or the other. If a minority in such a case will secede rather than acquiesce, they make a precedent which in turn will ruin and divide them, for a minority of their own will secede from them whenever a majority refuses to be controlled by such a minority. For instance, why not any portion of a new confederacy, a year or two hence, arbitrarily secede again, precisely as portions of the present Union now claim to secede from it? All who cherish disunion sentiments are now being educated to the exact temper of doing this. Is there such perfect identity of interests among the States to compose a new Union as to produce harmony only, and prevent renewed secession? Plainly, the central idea of secession is the essence of anarchy.

"A majority held in restraint by constitutional check and limitations, and always changing easily with deliberate changes of popular opinions and sentiments, is the only true sovereign of a free people. Whoever reject it, does, of necessity, fly to anarchy or to despotism. Unanimity is impossible; the rule of a majority, as a permanent arrangement, is wholly inadmissible. So that, rejecting the majority principle, anarchy or despotism in some form is all that is left.

"I do not forget the position assumed by some that constitutional questions are to be decided by the Supreme Court, nor do I deny that such decisions must be binding in any case upon the parties to a suit, as to the object of that suit, while they are also entitled to very high respect and consideration in all parallel cases by all other departments of the government: and while it is obviously possible that such decision may be erroneous in any given case, still the evil effect following it, being limited to that particular case, with the chance that it may be overruled and never become a precedent for other cases, can better be borne than could the evils of a different practice.

"At the same time, the candid citizen must confess that, if the policy of the government upon the vital questions affecting the whole people is to be irrevocably fixed by the decisions of the Supreme Court, the instant they are made, as in ordinary litigation between parties in personal actions, the people will have ceased to be their own masters, unless having to that extent practically resigned their government into the hands of that eminent tribunal.

"Nor is there in this view any assault upon the court or the judges. It is a duty from which they may not shrink, to decide cases properly brought before them; and it is no fault of theirs if others seek to turn their decisions to political purposes. One section of our country believes slavery is right, and ought to be extended, while the other believes it is wrong, and ought not to be extended; and this is the only substantial dispute; and the fugitive slave clause of the Constitution, and the law for the suppression of the foreign slave-trade, are each as well enforced, perhaps, as any law can ever be in a community where the moral sense of the people imperfectly supports the law itself. The great body of the people abide by the dry legal obligation in both cases, and a few break over in each. This, I think, cannot be perfectly cured, and it would be worse, in both cases, after the separation of the sections, than before. The foreign slave-trade, now imperfectly suppressed, would be ultimately revived, without restriction, in one section; while fugitive slaves, now only partially surrendered, would not be surrendered at all by the other.

"Physically speaking, we cannot separate—we cannot remove our respective sections from each other, nor build an impassable wall between them. A husband and wife may be divorced, and go out of the presence and beyond the reach of the other, but the different parts of our country cannot do that. They cannot but remain face to face; and intercourse, either amicable or hostile, must continue between them. Is it possible, then, to make that intercourse more advantageous or more satisfactory after separation than before? Can aliens make treaties easier than friends can make laws? Can treaties be more faithfully enforced between aliens than laws can among friends? Suppose you go to war, you cannot fight always; and when, after much loss on both sides, and no gain on either, you cease fighting, the identical questions as to terms of intercourse are again upon you.

"This country, with its institutions, belongs to the people who inhabit it. Whenever they shall grow weary of the existing government, they can exercise their constitutional right of amending, or their revolutionary right to dismember or over-throw it. I cannot be ignorant of the fact that many worthy and patriotic citizens are desirous of having the national Con-stitution amended. While I make no recommendation of amend-ment, I fully recognize the full authority of the people over the whole subject, to be exercised in either of the modes pre-scribed in the instrument itself, and I should, under existing circumstances, favor, rather than oppose, a fair opportunity being afforded the people to act upon it.

"I will venture to add that to me the convention mode seems preferable, in that it allows amendments to originate with the people themselves, instead of only permitting them to take or reject propositions originated by others not especially chosen for the purpose, and which might not be precisely such as they would wish either to accept or refuse. I understand that a pro-posed amendment to the Constitution (which amendment, how-ever, I have not seen) has passed Congress, to the effect that the Federal Government shall never interfere with the domestic institutions of States, including that of persons held to service. To avoid misconstruction of what I have said, I depart from my purpose not to speak of particular amendments, so far as to say that, holding such a provision to now be implied constitutional law, I have no objections to its being made express and irrevo-cable.

"The chief magistrate derives all his authority from the peo-ple, and they have conferred none upon him to fix the terms for the separation of the States. The people themselves, also, can do this if they choose, but the Executive, as such, has nothing to do with it. His duty is to administer the present government as it came to his hands, and to transmit it, unimpaired by him, to his successor. Why should there not be a patient confidence in the ultimate justice of the people? Is there any better or equal hope in the world? In our present differences, is either party without faith of being in the right? If the Almighty Ruler of nations, with his eternal truth and justice, be on your side of the North, or on yours of the South, that truth and that justice will surely prevail by the judgment of this great tribunal, the American people. By the frame of the government under which we live, this same people have wisely given their public servants but little power for mischief, and have, with equal wisdom, provided for the return of that little to their own hands at very short intervals. While the people retain their virtue and vigilance, no administration, by any extreme wickedness or folly, can very seriously injure the government in the short space of four years.

"My countrymen, one and all, think calmly and well upon this whole subject. Nothing valuable can be lost by taking time.

"If there be an object to hurry any of you, in hot haste, to a step which you would never take deliberately, that object will be frustrated by taking time; but no good object can be frustrated by it.

"Such of you as are now dissatisfied still have the old Constitution unimpaired, and, on the sensitive point, the laws of your own framing under it; while the new administration will have no immediate power, if it would, to change either.

"If it were admitted that you who are dissatisfied hold the right side in the dispute, there is still no single reason for precipitate action. Intelligence, patriotism, Christianity, and a firm reliance on Him who has never yet forsaken this favored land, are still competent to adjust, in the best way, all our present difficulties.

"In your hands, my dissatisfied fellow-countrymen, and not in mine, is the momentous issue of civil war. The government will not assail you.

"You can have no conflict without being yourselves the aggressors. You have no oath registered in heaven to destroy the government: while I shall have the most solemn one to 'preserve, protect, and defend it.'

"I am loth to close. We are not enemies, but friends. We must not be enemies. Though passion may have strained, it must not break our bonds of affection.

"The mystic cords of memory, stretching from every battle-field and patriot grave to every living heart and hearthstone all over this broad land, will yet swell the chorus of the Union, when again touched, as surely they will be, by the better angels of our nature."

Chief Justice Taney then administered the oath of office, and President Lincoln left the Capitol for the White House, where he held a public reception.

PRESIDENT LINCOLN'S INTERVIEW WITH THE VIRGINIA COMMISSIONERS.

On the 13th of April, 1861, Messrs. Preston Stuart and

Randolph, a committee appointed by the Virginia Convention, were formally received by the President, and presented the resolutions under which they were appointed.
In response, Mr. Lincoln made the following address :

"GENTLEMEN : As a committee of the Virginia Convention,
now in session, you present me a preamble and resolution in
these words :

"'*Whereas*, in the opinion of this Convention, the uncertainty
which prevails in the public mind as to the policy which the
Federal Executive intends to pursue towards the seceded States
is extremely injurious to the industrial and commercial interests
of the country, tends to keep up an excitement which is un-
favorable to the adjustment of the pending difficulties, and
threatens a disturbance of the public peace ; therefore,

"'*Resolved*, That a committee of three delegates be appointed
to wait on the President of the United States, present to him
this preamble, and respectfully ask him to communicate to this
Convention the policy which the Federal Executive intends to
pursue in regard to the Confederate States.'

" In answer I have to say, that having, at the beginning of
my official term, expressed my intended policy as plainly as I
was able, it is with deep regret and mortification I now learn there
is great and injurious uncertainty in the public mind as to what
that policy is, and what course I intend to pursue. Not having
as yet seen occasion to change, it is now my purpose to pursue
the course marked out in the inaugural address. I commend a
careful consideration of the whole document as the best expression I can give to my purposes. As I then and therein said,
I now repeat, 'The power confided in me will be used to hold,
occupy, and possess property and places belonging to the Government, and to collect the duties and imports ; but beyond
what is necessary for these objects there will be no invasion, no
using of force against or among the people anywhere.' By the
words 'property and places belonging to the Government,' I
chiefly allude to the military posts and property which were in
possession of the government when it came into my hands.
But if, as now appears to be true, in pursuit of a purpose to
drive the United States authority from these places, an unpro-
voked assault has been made upon Fort Sumter, I shall hold
myself at liberty to repossess it, if I can, like places which had
been seized before the Government was devolved upon me, and
in any event I shall, to the best of my ability, repel force by
force. In case it proves true that Fort Sumter has been
assaulted, as is reported, I shall, perhaps, cause the United
States mails to be withdrawn from all the States which claim to
have seceded, believing that the commencement of actual war
against the Government justifies and possibly demands it. I

scarcely need to say that I consider the military posts and property situated within the States which claim to have seceded, as yet belonging to the Government of the United States as much as they did before the supposed secession. Whatever else I may do for the purpose, I shall not attempt to collect the duties and imposts by any armed invasion of any part of the country; not meaning by this, however, that I may not land a force deemed necessary to relieve a fort upon the border of the country. From the fact that I have quoted a part of the inaugural address, it must not be inferred that I repudiate any other part, the whole of which I reaffirm, except so far as what I now say of the mails may be regarded as a modification."

Two days later the following proclamation was issued:

THE FIRST CALL FOR TROOPS.---CONGRESS SUMMONED TO ASSEMBLE.

" *Whereas*, The laws of the United States have been for some time past, and now are opposed, and the execution thereof obstructed, in the States of South Carolina, Georgia, Alabama, Florida, Mississippi, Louisiana, and Texas, by combinations too powerful to be suppressed by the ordinary course of judicial proceedings, or by the powers vested in the marshals by law; now, therefore, I, ABRAHAM LINCOLN, President of the United States, in virtue of the power in me vested by the Constitution and the laws, have thought fit to call forth, and hereby do call forth, the militia of the several States of the Union to the aggregate number of 75,000, in order to suppress said combinations and to cause the laws to be duly executed.

" The details for this object will be immediately communicated to the State authorities through the War Department. I appeal to all loyal citizens to favor, facilitate, and aid this effort to maintain the honor, the integrity, and existence of our national Union, and the perpetuity of popular government, and to redress wrongs already long enough endured. I deem it proper to say that the first service assigned to the forces hereby called forth, will probably be to repossess the forts, places, and property which have been seized from the Union; and in every event the utmost care will be observed, consistently with the objects aforesaid, to avoid any devastation, any destruction of, or interference with property, or any disturbance of peaceful citizens of any part of the country; and I hereby command the persons composing the combinations aforesaid, to disperse and retire peaceably to their respective abodes, within twenty days from this date.

" Deeming that the present condition of public affairs presents an extraordinary occasion, I do hereby, in virtue of the power in me vested by the Constitution, convene both Houses of Congress. The Senators and Representatives are, therefore, summoned to assemble at their respective chambers at twelve o'clock, noon, on Thursday, the fourth day of July next, then and there to consider and determine such measures as, in their wisdom, the public safety and interest may seem to demand.

"In witness whereof, I have hereunto set my hand, and caused the seal of the United States to be affixed.

"Done at the City of Washington, this fifteenth day of April, in the year of our Lord, one thousand eight hundred and sixty-one, and of the independence of the United States the eighy-fifth.

"By the President: "ABRAHAM LINCOLN.

"WILLIAM H. SEWARD, *Secretary of State.*"

Within three days after the appeal had been made to the patriots of the North, six hundred of their number had arrived in Washington, prepared for active duty and ready to sacrifice their lives in defence of the capital. The avenues to the city of Washington were guarded night and day, and cannon were placed in position. The excitement was intense, but amid all the various apprehensions of the residents and the country, he, who really should have been more especially anxious and fearful, was always calm and collected. The murderous outbreak in Baltimore on the nineteenth only increased the excitement, but, as if indifferent to the scenes which were in progress immediately around him, the President issued the following Proclamation, ordering a blockade of the Southern ports:

A BLOCKADE OF SOUTHERN PORTS ORDERED.

"*Whereas*, An insurrection against the Government of the United States has broken out in the States of South Carolina, Georgia, Alabama, Florida, Mississippi, Louisiana, and Texas, and the laws of the United States for the collection of the revenue cannot be efficiently executed therein conformably to that provision of the Constitution which requires duties to be uniform throughout the United States.

"*And whereas*, A combination of persons, engaged in such insurrection, have threatened to grant pretended letters of marque to authorize the bearers thereof to commit assaults on the lives, vessels, and property of good citizens of the country lawfully engaged in commerce on the high seas, and in waters of the United States.

"*And whereas,* An Executive Proclamation has been already issued, requiring the persons engaged in these disorderly proceedings to desist therefrom, calling out a militia force for the purpose of repressing the same, and convening Congress in extraordinary session to deliberate and determine thereon.

"Now, therefore, I, ABRAHAM LINCOLN, President of the United States, with a view to the same purpose before mentioned, and to the protection of the public peace, and the lives and property of quiet and orderly citizens pursuing their lawful occupations, until Congress shall have assembled and deliberated on the said unlawful proceedings, or until the same shall have ceased, have further deemed it advisable to set on foot a blockade of the ports within the States aforesaid, in pursuance of the laws of the United States and of the laws of nations in such cases provided. For this purpose a competent force will be posted so as to prevent entrance and exit of vessels from the ports aforesaid. If, therefore, with a view to violate such blockade, a vessel shall approach, or shall attempt to leave any of the said ports, she will be duly warned by the commander of one of the blockading vessels, who will indorse on her register the fact and date of such warning; and if the same vessel shall again attempt to enter or leave the blockaded port, she will be captured and sent to the nearest convenient port, for such proceedings against her and her cargo as prize as may be deemed advisable.

"And I hereby proclaim and declare, that if any person, under the pretended authority of said States, or under any other pretence, shall molest a vessel of the United States, or the persons or cargo on board of her, such person will be held amenable to the laws of the United States for the prevention and punishment of piracy.

"By the President: "ABRAHAM LINCOLN.

" WILLIAM H. SEWARD, *Secretary of State.*

"*Washington, April* 19*th,* 1861."

THE PRESIDENT'S COMMUNICATION WITH THE MARYLAND AUTHORITIES.

On the twentieth of April, the President sent the following letter to the Governor of Maryland and also to the Mayor of Baltimore:

"WASHINGTON, *April* 20*th,* 1861.

" GOVERNOR HICKS AND MAYOR BROWN:

" GENTLEMEN :—Your letter by Messrs. Bond, Dobbin, and Brune, is received. I tender you both my sincere thanks for your efforts to keep the peace in the trying situation in which you are placed. For the future, troops *must* be brought here, but I make no point of bringing them *through* Baltimore.

"Without any military knowledge myself, of course I must leave details to General Scott. He hastily said this morning, in presence of those gentlemen, ' March them *around* Baltimore, and not through it.'

"I sincerely hope the general, on fuller reflection, will consider this practical and proper, and that you will not object to it. By this a collision of the people of Baltimore with the troops will be avoided, unless they go out of the way to seek it. I hope you will exert your influence to prevent this. Now and ever, I shall do all in my power for peace, consistently with the maintenance of government

" Your obedient servant,

"A. LINCOLN."

And on the twenty-first, he sent a despatch to Mayor Brown, requesting him to proceed immediately to Washington, a request that was obeyed, and upon arriving at the White House the invited guest was admitted to an interview with the Cabinet and General Scott. The President informed the Mayor, and three of the citizens of Baltimore who had accompanied him, that he recognized the good faith of the City and State authorities, but should insist upon a recognition of his own.

He admitted the excited state of feeling in Baltimore, and his desire and duty to avoid the fatal consequences of a collision with the people. He urged, on the other hand, the absolute, irresistible necessity of having a transit through the State for such troops as might be necessary for the protection of the Federal capital. The protection of Washington, he asseverated with great earnestness, was the sole object of concentrating troops there ; and he protested that none of the troops brought through Maryland were intended for any purposes hostile to the State, or aggressive as against the Southern States. Being now unable to bring them up the Potomac in security, the Government must either bring them through Maryland or abandon the capital.

He called on General Scott for his opinion, which the General gave at length, to the effect that troops might be brought through Maryland, without going through Balti-more, by either carrying them from Perryville to Annapo-lis, and thence by rail to Washington, or by bringing them to the Relay House on the Northern Central railroad, and marching them to the Relay House on the Washington railroad, and thence by rail to the capital. If the people would permit them to go by either of these routes uninter-ruptedly, the necessity of their passing through Baltimore would be avoided. If the people would not permit them a transit thus remote from the city, they must select their own best route, and, if need be, fight their way through Baltimore, a result which the General earnestly depre-cated.

The President expressed his hearty concurrence in the desire to avoid a collision, and said that no more troops should be ordered through Baltimore if they were per-mitted to go uninterrupted by either of the other routes suggested. In this disposition the Secretary of War ex-pressed his participation.

About this same date a deputation of sympathizers visited the President, and demanded a cessation of hostili-ties until the convening of Congress, accompanying the demand with the assertion that seventy-five thousand Marylanders would contest the passage of troops over their soil. Mr. Lincoln, in refusing to accede to the truce, quietly replied that he presumed there was room enough on her soil to bury seventy-five thousand men.

BLOCKADING OF VIRGINIA AND NORTH CAROLINA.

On the twenty-seventh of April, the following additional proclamation, extending the blockade, was issued :

"*Whereas*, For the reasons assigned in my proclamation of the 19th instant, a blockade of the ports of the States of South Carolina, Georgia, Florida, Alabama, Louisiana, Mississippi, and Texas, was ordered to be established ; *And whereas*, Since

that date public property of the United States has been seized,
the collection of the revenue obstructed, and duly commissioned
officers of the United States, while engaged in executing the
orders of their superiors, have been arrested and held in custody
as prisoners, or have been impeded in the discharge of their
official duties, without due legal process, by persons claiming to
act under authority of the States of Virginia and North Carolina, an efficient blockade of the ports of these States will therefore also be established.

"In witness whereof, I have hereunto set my hand, and caused
the seal of the United States to be affixed.

"Done at the City of Washington, this 27th day of April, in the
year of our Lord one thousand eight hundred and sixty-one,
and of the Independence of the United States the eighty-
fifth.

"By the President: "ABRAHAM LINCOLN.
"WILLIAM H. SEWARD, *Secretary of State.*"

Although the first call for troops had been responded to
in the most gratifying manner by the outraged citizens of
the free States, it was early ascertained that the number
asked was totally insufficient for the existing exigencies,
and on the third of May the following proclamation was
issued :

A CALL FOR ADDITIONAL TROOPS.

"WASHINGTON, FRIDAY, *May 3d,* 1861.

"*Whereas.* Existing exigencies demand immediate and adequate measures for the protection of the national Constitution
and the preservation of the national Union by the suppression
of the insurrectionary combinations now existing in several
States for opposing the laws of the Union and obstructing the
execution thereof, to which end a military force, in addition to
that called forth by my Proclamation of the fifteenth day of
April, in the present year, appears to be indispensably necessary, now, therefore, I, Abraham Lincoln, President of the
United States, and Commander-in-Chief of the Army and Navy
thereof, and of the militia of the several States, when called into
actual service, do hereby call into the service of the United
States forty-two thousand and thirty-four volunteers, to serve
for a period of three years, unless sooner discharged, and to be
mustered into service as infantry and cavalry. The proportions
of each arm and the details of enrolment and organization will
be made known through the Department of War; and I also
direct that the regular army of the United States be increased
by the addition of eight regiments of infantry, one regiment of

cavalry, and one regiment of artillery, making altogether a maximum aggregate increase of 22,714 officers and enlisted men, the details of which increase will also be made known through the Department of War; and I further direct the enlistment, for not less than one nor more than three years, of 18,000 seamen, in addition to the present force, for the naval service of the United States. The details of the enlistment and organization will be made known through the Department of the Navy. The call for volunteers, hereby made, and the direction of the increase of the regular army, and for the enlistment of seamen hereby given, together with the plan of organization adopted for the volunteers and for the regular forces hereby authorized, will be submitted to Congress as soon as assembled.

"In the meantime, I earnestly invoke the co-operation of all good citizens in the measures hereby adopted for the effectual suppression of unlawful violence, for the impartial enforcement of constitutional laws, and for the speediest possible restoration of peace and order, and with those of happiness and prosperity throughout our country.

"In testimony whereof, I have hereunto set my hand, and caused the seal of the United States to be affixed.

"Done at the City of Washington, this third day of May, in the year of our Lord one thousand eight hundred and sixty-one, and of the Independence of the United States the eighty-fifth.

"By the President: "ABRAHAM LINCOLN.
"WILLIAM H. SEWARD, *Secretary of State.*"

AN INTERVIEW WITH THE MARYLAND LEGISLATURE.

On the following day, the President had an interview with a Committee of the Maryland Legislature, who admitted the right of the Government to transport troops through Baltimore or Maryland, but expressed their belief that no immediate efforts would be made by the State authorities at secession or resistance, and asked that the State might be spared military occupation, or a mere revengeful chastisement for former transgressions. The President, in reply, promised to give their suggestions a respectful consideration, and stated that whatever measures might be adopted, would be actuated entirely by the public interests and not by any spirit of revenge.

A SPECIAL ORDER FOR FLORIDA.

On the tenth of May, 1861, the following proclamation was promulgated :

"*Whereas,* An insurrection exists in the State of Florida, by which the lives, liberty, and property of loyal citizens of the United States are endangered.

"*And whereas,* It is deemed proper that all needful measures should be taken for the protection of such citizens and all officers of the United States in the discharge of their public duties in the State aforesaid.

"Now, therefore, be it known that I, Abraham Lincoln, President of the United States, do hereby direct the Commander of the forces of the United States on the Florida coast to permit no person to exercise any office or authority upon the Islands of Key West, the Tortugas, and Santa Rosa, which may be inconsistent with the laws and Constitution of the United States, authorizing him at the same time, if he shall find it necessary, to suspend there the writ of *habeas corpus*, and to remove from the vicinity of the United States fortresses all dangerous or suspected persons.

" In witness whereof, I have hereunto set my hand, and caused the seal of the United States to be affixed.

" Done at the City of Washington, this tenth day of May, in the year of our Lord one thousand eight hundred and sixty-one, and of the Independence of the United States the eighty-fifth.

"By the President :　　　　"ABRAHAM LINCOLN.

" WILLIAM H. SEWARD, *Secretary of State.*"

PRESIDENT LINCOLN'S FIRST MESSAGE TO CONGRESS.

On the fourth of July, 1861, Congress assembled, in pursuance to the call of the President, and received from the Executive the following Message :

" FELLOW-CITIZENS OF THE SENATE AND HOUSE OF REPRESENTATIVES :—Having been convened on an extraordinary occasion, as authorized by the Constitution, your attention is not called to any ordinary subject of legislation.　At the beginning of the present Presidential term, four months ago, the functions of the Federal Government were found to be generally suspended within the several States of South Carolina, Georgia, Alabama, Mississippi, Louisiana, and Florida, excepting only those of the Post-Office Department.

"Within these States all the Forts, Arsenals, Dock-Yards, Custom-Houses, and the like, including the movable and stationary property in and about them, had been seized, and were held in open hostility to this Government, excepting only Forts Pickens, Taylor, and Jefferson, on and near the Florida coast, and Fort Sumter in Charleston harbor, South Carolina. The forts thus seized had been put in improved condition, new ones had been built, and armed forces had been organized, and were organizing, all avowedly for the same hostile purpose.

"The forts remaining in possession of the Federal Government in and near these States were either besieged or menaced by warlike preparations, and especially Fort Sumter was nearly surrounded by well-protected hostile batteries, with guns equal in quality to the best of its own, and outnumbering the latter as, perhaps, ten to one—a disproportionate share of the Federal muskets and rifles had somehow found their way into these States, and had been seized to be used against the Government.

"Accumulations of the public revenue lying within them had been seized for the same object. The navy was scattered in distant seas, leaving but a very small part of it within the immediate reach of the Government.

"Officers of the Federal army had resigned in great numbers, and of those resigning a large proportion had taken up arms against the Government.

"Simultaneously, and in connection with all this, the purpose to sever the Federal Union was openly avowed. In accordance with this purpose an ordinance had been adopted in each of these States, declaring the States respectively to be separated from the National Union. A formula for instituting a combined Government of these States had been promulgated, and this illegal organization, in the character of the 'Confederate States,' was already invoking recognition, aid, and intervention from foreign Powers.

"Finding this condition of things, and believing it to be an imperative duty upon the incoming Executive to prevent, if possible, the consummation of such attempt to destroy the Federal Union, a choice of means to that end became indispensable. This choice was made and was declared in the Inaugural Address.

"The policy chosen looked to the exhaustion of all peaceful measures before a resort to any stronger ones. It sought only to hold the public places and property not already wrested from the Government, and to collect the revenue, relying for the rest on time, discussion, and the ballot-box. It promised a continuance of the mails, at Government expense, to the very people who were resisting the Government, and it gave repeated pledges against any disturbances to any of the people, or any of their rights, of all that which a President might constitutionally and justifiably do in such a case; every thing was forborne, without which it was believed possible to keep the Government on foot.

"On the 5th of March, the present incumbent's first full day in office, a letter from Major Anderson, commanding at Fort Sumter, written on the 28th of February and received at the War Department on the 4th of March, was by that Department placed in his hands. This letter expressed the professional opinion of the writer, that reinforcements could not be thrown into that fort within the time for its relief rendered necessary by the limited supply of provisions, and with a view of holding possession of the same, with a force less than 20,000 good and well-disciplined men. This opinion was concurred in by all the officers of his command, and their memoranda on the subject were made inclosures of Major Anderson's letter. The whole was immediately laid before Lieutenant-General Scott, who at once concurred with Major Anderson in his opinion. On reflection, however, he took full time, consulting with other officers both of the army and navy, and at the end of four days came reluctantly but decidedly to the same conclusion as before. He also stated at the same time that no such sufficient force was then at the control of the Government, or could be raised and brought to the ground, within the time when the provisions in the fort would be exhausted. In a purely military point of view, this reduced the duty of the Administration in the case to the mere matter of getting the garrison safely out of the fort.

"It was believed, however, that to so abandon that position, under the circumstances, would be utterly ruinous; that the necessity under which it was to be done would not be fully understood; that by many it would be construed as a part of a voluntary policy; that at home it would discourage the friends of the Union, embolden its adversaries, and go far to insure to the latter a recognition abroad; that, in fact, it would be our national destruction consummated. This could not be allowed. Starvation was not yet upon the garrison, and ere it would be reached, Fort Pickens might be reinforced. This last would be a clear indication of policy, and would better enable the country to accept the evacuation of Fort Sumter as a military necessity. An order was at once directed to be sent for the landing of the troops from the steamship Brooklyn into Fort Pickens. This order could not go by land, but must take the longer and slower route by sea. The first return news from the order was received just one week before the fall of Sumter. The news itself was that the officer commanding the Sabine, to which vessel the troops had been transferred from the Brooklyn, acting upon some quasi armistice of the late Administration, and of the existence of which the present Administration, up to the time the order was despatched, had only too vague and uncertain rumors to fix attention, had refused to land the troops. To now reinforce Fort Pickens before a crisis would be reached at Fort Sumter was impossible, rendered so by the near exhaustion of provisions at the latter named fort. In precaution against such a conjuncture the Government had a few days before commenced preparing an expedition, as well adapted as might be to relieve Fort Sumter, which expedition was intended to be ultimately used or not, according to circumstances. The strongest anticipated case for using it was now presented, and it was resolved to send it forward as had been intended. In this contingency it was also resolved to notify the Governor of South Carolina that he might expect an attempt would be made to provision the fort, and that if the attempt should not be resisted, there would be no attempt to throw in men, arms, or ammunition, without further notice or in case of an attack upon the fort. This notice was accordingly given, whereupon the fort was attacked and bombarded to its fall, without even awaiting the arrival of the provisioning expedition.

" It is thus seen that the assault upon, and reduction of Fort Sumter, was, in no sense, a matter of self-defence on the part of the assailants. They well knew that the garrison in the fort could by no possibility commit aggression upon them ; they knew they were expressly notified that the giving of bread to the few brave and hungry men of the garrison was all which would on that occasion be attempted, unless themselves, by resisting so much, should provoke more. They knew that this Government desired to keep the garrison in the fort, not to assail them, but merely to maintain visible possession, and thus do preserve the Union from actual and immediate dissolution : trusting, as hereinbefore stated, to time, discussion, and the ballot-box for final adjustment, and they assailed and reduced the fort, for precisely the reverse object, to drive out the visible authority of the Federal Union, and thus force it to immediate dissolution ; that this was their object the Executive well understood, having said to them in the Inaugural Address, ' you can have no conflict without being yourselves the aggressors.' He took pains not only to keep this declaration good, but also to keep the case so far from ingenious sophistry as that the world should not misunderstand it. By the affair at Fort Sumter, with its surrounding circumstances, that point was reached. Then and thereby the assailants of the Government began the conflict of arms,—without a gun in sight or in expectancy to return their fire, save only the few in the fort sent to that harbor years before, for their own protection, and still ready to give that protection in whatever was lawful. In this act, discarding all else, they have forced upon the country the distinct issue, immediate dissolution or blood, and this issue embraces more than the fate of these United States. It presents to the whole family of man the question whether a Constitutional Republic or Democracy, a Government of the people, by the same people, can or cannot maintain its territorial integrity against its own domestic foes. It presents the question whether discontented individuals, too few in numbers to control the Administration according to the organic law in any case, can always, upon the pretences made in this case, or any other pretences or arbitrarily without any pretence, break up their Government, and thus practically put an end to free government upon the earth. It forces us to ask, 'Is there in all republics this inherent and fatal weakness?' Must a Government of necessity be too strong for the liberties of its own people, or too weak to maintain its own existence? So viewing the issue, no choice was left but to call out the war power of the Government, and so to resist the force employed for its destruction by force for its preservation. The call was made, and the response of the country was most gratifying, surpassing, in unanimity and spirit, the most sanguine expectation. Yet none of the States, commonly called slave States, except Delaware, gave a regiment through the regular State organization. A few regiments have been organized within some others of those States by individual enterprise, and received into the Government service. Of course the seceded States, so called, and to which Texas had been joined about the time of the inauguration, gave no troops to the cause of the Union. The Border States, so called, were not uniform in their action, some of them being almost for the Union, while in others as in Virginia, North Carolina, Tennessee, and Arkansas, the Union sentiment was nearly repressed and silenced. The course taken in Virginia was the most remarkable, perhaps the most important. A convention, elected by the people of that State to consider this very question of disrupting the Federal Union, was in session at the capital of Virginia when Fort Sumter fell.

"To this body the people had chosen a large majority of professed Union men. Almost immediately after the fall of Sumter many members of that majority went over to the original disunion minority, and with them adopted an ordinance for withdrawing the State from the Union. Whether this change was wrought by their great approval of the assault upon Sumter, or their great resentment at the Government's resistance to that assault, is not definitely known. Although they submitted the ordinance for ratification to a vote of the people, to be taken on a day then somewhat more than a month distant, the Convention and the Legislature, which was also in session at the same time and place, with leading men of the State, not members of either, immediately commenced acting as if the State was already out of the Union. They pushed military preparations vigorously forward all over the State. They seized the United States Armory at Harper's Ferry, and the Navy-Yard at Gosport, near Norfolk. They received, perhaps invited into their State large bodies of troops, with their warlike appointments, from the so-called seceded States.

"They formally entered into a treaty of temporary alliance with the so-called Confederate States, and sent members to their

Congress at Montgomery, and finally they permitted the insurrectionary Government to be transferred to their capitol at Richmond. The people of Virginia have thus allowed this giant insurrection to make its nest within her borders, and this Government has no choice left but to deal with it where it finds it, and it has the less to regret as the loyal citizens have in due form claimed its protection. Those loyal citizens this Government is bound to recognize and protect as being in Virginia. In the Border States, so called, in fact the middle States, there are those who favor a policy which they call armed neutrality, that is, an arming of those States to prevent the Union forces passing one way or the disunion forces the other over their soil. This would be disunion completed. Figuratively speaking, it would be the building of an impassable wall along the line of separation, and yet not quite an impassable one, for under the guise of neutrality it would tie the hands of the Union men, and freely pass supplies from among them to the insurrectionists, which it could not do as an open enemy. At a stroke it would take all the trouble off the hands of secession, except only what proceeds from the external blockade. It would do for the disunionists that which of all things they most desire, feed them well and give them disunion without a struggle of their own. It recognizes no fidelity to the Constitution, no obligation to maintain the Union, and while very many who have favored it are doubtless loyal citizens, it is nevertheless very injurious in effect.

"Recurring to the action of the Government it may be stated that at first a call was made for 75,000 militia, and rapidly following this a proclamation was issued for closing the ports of the insurrectionary districts by proceedings in the nature of a blockade. So far all was believed to be strictly legal.

"At this point the insurrectionists announced their purpose to enter upon the practice of privateering.

" Other calls were made for volunteers, to serve three years, unless sooner discharged, and also for large additions to the regular army and navy. These measures, whether strictly legal or not, were ventured upon under what appeared to be a popular demand and a public necessity, trusting then, as now, that Congress would ratify them.

" It is believed that nothing has been done beyond the constitutional competency of Congress. Soon after the first call for militia it was considered a duty to authorize the commanding general, in proper cases, according to his discretion, to suspend the privilege of the writ of habeas corpus; or, in other words, to arrest and detain, without resort to the ordinary processes and forms of law, such individuals as he might deem dangerous to the public safety. This authority has purposely been exercised but very sparingly. Nevertheless the legality and propriety of what has been done under it are questioned, and the attention of the country has been called to the proposition that one who is sworn to take care that the laws be faithfully executed, should not himself violate them. Of course some consideration was given to the questions of power and propriety before this matter was acted upon. The whole of the laws which were required to be faithfully executed were being resisted, and failing of execution in nearly one-third of the States. Must they be allowed to finally fail of execution, even had it been perfectly clear that by use of the means necessary to their execution, some single law, made in such extreme tenderness of the citizen's liberty that practically it relieves more of the guilty than the innocent, should to a very great extent be violated? To state the question more directly, are all the laws but one to go unexecuted, and the Government itself to go to pieces lest that one be violated? Even in such a case would not the official oath be broken if the Government should be overthrown when it was believed that disregarding the single law would tend to preserve it.

"But it was not believed that this question was presented. It was not believed that any law was violated. The provision of the Constitution, that the privilege of the writ of habeas corpus shall not be suspended, unless when, in cases of rebellion or invasion, the public safety may require it, is equivalent to a provision that such privilege may be suspended when, in cases of rebellion or invasion, the public safety does require it. It was decided that we have a case of rebellion, and that the public safety does require the qualified suspension of the privilege of the writ, which was authorized to be made. Now, it is insisted that Congress, and not the Executive, is vested with this power. But the Constitution itself is silent as to which or who is to exercise the power; and as the provision was plainly made for a dangerous emergency, it cannot be believed that the framers of the instrument intended that in every case the danger should run its course until Congress could be called together, the very assembling of which might be prevented, as was intended in this case by the rebellion. No more extended argument is now afforded, as an opinion at some length will probably be presented by the Attorney-General. Whether there shall be any legislation on the subject, and if so what, is submitted entirely to the better judgment of Congress. The forbearance of this Government had been so extraordinary, and so long continued, as to lead some foreign nations to shape their action as if they supposed the early destruction of our national Union was probable. While this, on discovery, gave the Executive some concern, he is now happy to say that the sovereignty and rights of the United States are now everywhere practically respected by foreign Powers, and a general sympathy with the country is manifested throughout the world.

"The reports of the Secretaries of the Treasury, War, and

the Navy, will give the information in detail deemed necessary and convenient for your deliberation and action, while the Executive and all the departments will stand ready to supply omissions or to communicate new facts considered important for you to know.

"It is now recommended that you give the legal means for making this contest a short and decisive one ; that you place at the control of the Government for the work at least 400,000 men and $400,000,000 ; that number of men is about one-tenth of those of proper ages within the regions where apparently all are willing to engage, and the sum is less than a twenty-third part of the money value owned by the men who seem ready to devote the whole. A debt of $600,000,000 now is a less sum per head than was the debt of our Revolution when we came out of that struggle, and the money value in the country bears even a greater proportion to what it was then than does the population. Surely each man has as strong a motive now to preserve our liberties as each had then to establish them.

"A right result at this time will be worth more to the world than ten times the men and ten times the money. The evidence reaching us from the country leaves no doubt that the material for the work is abundant, and that it needs only the hand of legislation to give it legal sanction, and the hand of the Executive to give it practical shape and efficiency. One of the greatest perplexities of the Government is to avoid receiving troops faster than it can provide for them ; in a word, the people will save their Government if the Government will do its part only indifferently well. It might seem at first thought to be of little difference whether the present movement at the South be called secession or rebellion. The movers, however, well understand the difference. At the beginning they knew that they could never raise their treason to any respectable magnitude by any name which implies violation of law ; they knew their people possessed as much of moral sense, as much of devotion to law and order, and as much pride in its reverence for the history and Government of their common country, as any other civilized and patriotic people. They knew they could make no advancement directly in the teeth of these strong and noble sentiments. Accordingly they commenced by an insidious debauching of the public mind ; they invented an ingenious sophism, which, if conceded, was followed by perfectly logical steps through all the incidents of the complete destruction of the Union. The sophism itself is that any State of the Union may, consistently with the nation's Constitution, and therefore lawfully and peacefully, withdraw from the Union without the consent of the Union or of any other State.

"The little disguise that the supposed right is to be exercised only for just cause, themselves to be the sole judge of its justice, is too thin to merit any notice with rebellion. Thus sugar-

7

coated, they have been drugging the public mind of their section for more than thirty years, and until at length they have brought many good men to a willingness to take up arms against the Government the day after some assemblage of men have enacted the farcical pretence of taking their State out of the Union, who could have been brought to no such thing the day before. This sophism derives much, perhaps the whole of its currency, from the assumption that there is some omnipotent and sacred supremacy pertaining to a State, to each State of our Federal Union. Our States have neither more nor less power than that reserved to them in the Union by the Constitution, no one of them ever having been a State out of the Union. The original ones passed into the Union before they cast off their British Colonial dependence, and the new ones came into the Union directly from a condition of dependence, excepting Texas, and even Texas, in its temporary independence, was never designated as a State. The new ones only took the designation of States on coming into the Union, while that name was first adopted for the old ones in and by the Declaration of Independence. Therein the United Colonies were declared to be *free* and *independent* States. But even then the object plainly was not to declare their independence of one another of the Union, but directly the contrary, as their mutual pledge and their mutual action before, at the time, and afterward, abundantly show. The express plight of faith by each and all of the original thirteen States in the Articles of Confederation two years later that the Union shall be perpetuated, is most conclusive. Having never been States either in substance or in name outside of the Union, whence this magical omnipotence of State rights, asserting a claim of power to lawfully destroy the Union itself. Much is said about the sovereignty of the States, but the word even is not in the National Constitution, nor, as is believed, in any of the State constitutions. What is sovereignty in the political sense of the word? Would it be far wrong to define it a political community without a political superior? Tested by this, no one of our States, except Texas, was a sovereignty, and even Texas gave up the character on coming into the Union, by which act she acknowledged the Constitution of the United States; and the laws and treaties of the United States, made in pursuance of States, have their status in the Union, made in pursuance of the Constitution, to be for her the supreme law. The States have their status in the Union, and they have no other legal status. If they break from this, they can only do so against law and by revolution. The Union, and not themselves separately, procured their independence and their liberty by conquest or purchase. The Union gave each of them whatever of independence and liberty it has. The Union is older than any of the States, and, in fact, it created them, as States. Originally, some dependent Colonies made the Union, and in turn the

Union threw off their old dependence for them and made them States, such as they are. Not one of them ever had a State constitution independent of the Union. Of course it is not forgotten that all the new States formed their constitutions before they entered the Union; nevertheless, dependent upon, and preparatory to coming into the Union. Unquestionably, the States have the powers and rights reserved to them in and by the National Constitution.

"But among these surely are not included all conceivable powers, however mischievous or destructive, but at most such only as were known in the world at the time as governmental powers, and certainly a power to destroy the Government itself had never been known as a governmental, as a merely administrative power. This relative matter of national power and State rights as a principle, is no other than the principle of generality and locality. Whatever concerns the whole should be conferred to the whole General Government, while whatever concerns only the State should be left exclusively to the State. This is all there is of original principle about it. Whether the National Constitution, in defining boundaries between the two, has applied the principle with exact accuracy, is not to be questioned. We are all bound by that defining without question. What is now combated, is the position that secession is consistent with the Constitution, is lawful and peaceful. It is not contended that there is any express law for it, and nothing should ever be implied as law which leads to unjust or absurd consequences. The nation purchased with money the countries out of which several of those States were formed. Is it just that they shall go off without leave and without refunding? The nation paid very large sums in the aggregate, I believe nearly a hundred millions, to relieve Florida of the aboriginal tribes. Is it just that she shall now be off without consent or without any return? The nation is now in debt for money applied to the benefit of these so-called seceding States, in common with the rest. Is it just, either that creditors shall go unpaid, or the remaining States pay the whole? A part of the present national debt was contracted to pay the old debt of Texas. Is it just that she shall leave and pay no part of this herself? Again, if one State may secede so may another, and when all shall have seceded none is left to pay the debts. Is this quite just to creditors? Did we notify them of this sage view of ours when we borrowed their money? If we now recognize this doctrine by allowing the seceders to go in peace, it is difficult to see what we can do if others choose to go, or to extort terms upon which they will promise to remain. The seceders insist that our Constitution admits of secession. They have assumed to make a National Constitution of their own, in which, of necessity, they have either discarded or retained the right of secession, as they insist exists in ours. If they have discarded it, they thereby admit that on principle it ought not to exist in ours; if they have retained it, by their own construction of ours that shows that to be consistent, they must secede from one another whenever they shall find it the easiest way of settling their debts, or effecting any other selfish or unjust object. The principle itself is one of disintegration, and upon which no Government can possibly endure. If all the States save one should assert the power to drive that one out of the Union, it is presumed the whole class of seceder politicians would at once deny the power, and denounce the act as the greatest outrage upon State rights. But suppose that precisely the same act, instead of being called driving the one out, should be called the seceding of the others from that one, it would be exactly what the seceders claim to do, unless, indeed, they made the point that the one, because it is a minority, may rightfully do what the others, because they are a majority, may not rightfully do. These politicians are subtle, and profound in the rights of minorities. They are not partial to that power which made the Constitution, and speaks from the preamble, calling itself, 'We, the people.' It may be well questioned whether there is to-day a majority of the legally-qualified voters of any State, except, perhaps, South Carolina, in favor of disunion. There is much reason to believe that the Union men are the majority in many, if not in every one of the so-called seceded States. The contrary has not been demonstrated in any one of them. It is ventured to affirm this, even of Virginia and Tennessee, for the result of an election held in military camps, where the bayonets are all on one side of the question voted upon, can scarcely be considered as demonstrating popular sentiment. At such an election all that large class who are at once for the Union and against coercion, would be coerced to vote against the Union. It may be affirmed, without extravagance, that the free institutions we enjoy have developed the powers and improved the condition of our whole people beyond any example in the world. Of this we now have a striking and impressive illustration. So large an army as the Government has now on foot was never before known, without a soldier in it but who has taken his place there of his own free choice. But more than this, there are many single regiments whose members, one and another, possess full practical knowledge of all the arts, sciences, professions, and whatever else, whether useful or elegant, is known in the whole world, and there is scarcely one from which there could not be selected a President, a Cabinet, a Congress, and perhaps a Court, abundantly competent to administer the Government itself. Nor do I say this is not true also in the army of our late friends, now adversaries, in this contest. But it is so much better the reason why the Government which has conferred such benefits on both them and us should not be broken up. Whoever in any section proposes to abandon such a Government, would do well to consider in deference to what principle it is that he does it. What better he is likely to get in its stead, whether the substitute will give, or be intended to give so much of good to the people. There are some foreshadowings on this subject. Our adversaries have adopted some declarations of independence in which, unlike the good old one penned by Jefferson, they omit the words, 'all men are created equal.' Why? They have adopted a temporary National Constitution, in the preamble of which, unlike our good old one signed by Washington, they omit 'We the people,' and substitute 'We, the deputies of the sovereign and independent States.' Why? Why this deliberate pressing out of view the rights of men and the authority of the people? This is essentially a people's contest. On the side of the Union it is a struggle for maintaining in the world that form and substance of Government whose leading object is to elevate the condition of men, to lift artificial weights from all shoulders, to clear the paths of laudable pursuit for all, to afford all an unfettered start and a fair chance in the race of life, yielding to partial and temporary departures from necessity. This is the leading object of the Government, for whose existence we contend.

"I am most happy to believe that the plain people understand and appreciate this. It is worthy of note that while in this, the Government's hour of trial, large numbers of those in the army and navy who have been favored with the offices, have resigned and proved false to the hand which pampered them, not one common soldier or common sailor is known to have deserted his flag. Great honor is due to those officers who remained true despite the example of their treacherous associates, but the greatest honor and the most important fact of all, is the unanimous firmness of the common soldiers and common sailors. To the last man, so far as known, they have successfully resisted the traitorous efforts of those whose commands but an hour before they obeyed as absolute law. This is the patriotic instinct of plain people. They understand without an argument that the destroying the Government which was made by Washington means no good to them. Our popular Government has often been called an experiment. Two points in it our people have settled : the successful establishing and the successful administering of it. One still remains. Its successful maintenance against a formidable internal attempt to overthrow it. It is now for them to demonstrate to the world that those who can fairly carry an election can also suppress a rebellion ; that ballots are the rightful and peaceful successors of bullets, and that when ballots have fairly and constitutionally decided, there can be no successful appeal back to bullets ; that there can be no successful appeal except to ballots themselves at succeeding elections. Such will be a great lesson of peace, teaching men that what they cannot take by an election, neither can they take by a war, teaching all the folly of being the beginners of a war.

"Lest there be some uneasiness in the minds of candid men

as to what is to be the course of the government toward the Southern States after the rebellion shall have been suppressed, the Executive deems it proper to say it will be his purpose, then, as ever, to be guided by the Constitution and the laws, and that he probably will have no different understanding of the powers and duties of the Federal Government relatively to the rights of the States and the people under the Constitution than that expressed in the inaugural address. He desires to preserve the government, that it may be administered for all, as it was administered by the men who made it. Loyal citizens everywhere have the right to claim this of their government, and the government has no right to withhold or neglect it. It is not perceived that, in giving it, there is any coercion, any conquest, or any subjugation in any sense of these terms.

" The Constitution provided, and all the States have accepted the provision, 'that the United States shall guarantee to every State in this Union a Republican form of government ;' but if a State may lawfully go out of the Union, having done so, it may also discard the Republican form of government. So that to prevent its going out is an indispensable means to the end of maintaining the guarantee mentioned ; and, when an end is lawful and obligatory, the indispensable means to it are also lawful and obligatory.

" It was with the deepest regret that the Executive found the duty of employing the war power forced upon him. In defence of the government he could but perform this duty or surrender the existence of the government. No compromise by public servants could, in this case, be a cure ; not that compromises are not often proper, but that no popular government can long survive a marked precedent, that those who carry an election can only save the government from immediate destruction by giving up the main point upon which the people gave the election. The people themselves and not their servants can safely reverse their own deliberate decisions.

"As a private citizen, the Executive could not have consented that these institutions shall perish, much less could he in betrayal of so vast and so sacred a trust as these free people had confided to him. He felt that he had no moral right to shrink, nor even to count the chances of his own life in what might follow.

" In full view of his great responsibility, he has so far done what he has deemed his duty. You will now, according to your own judgment, perform yours. He sincerely hopes that your views and your actions may so accord with his as to assure all faithful citizens who have been disturbed in their rights of a certain and speedy restoration to them under the Constitution and laws ; and, having thus chosen our cause without guile, and with pure purpose, let us renew our trust in God, and go forward without fear and with manly hearts.

" ABRAHAM LINCOLN."

A DAY OF FASTING AND PRAYER AP-POINTED.

On the twelfth of August, the following proclamation, appointing a day of fasting and prayer, was issued :

"*Whereas*, A joint committee of both Houses of Congress has waited on the President of the United States, and requested him to ' recommend a day of public humiliation, prayer, and fasting, to be observed by the people of the United States with religious solemnities, and the offering of fervent supplications to Almighty God for the safety and welfare of these States, His blessings on their arms, and a speedy restoration of peace.'

"*And whereas*, It is fit and becoming in all people, at all times, to acknowledge and revere the Supreme Government of God ; to bow in humble submission to his chastisements ; to confess and deplore their sins and transgressions, in the full conviction that the fear of the Lord is the beginning of wisdom, and to pray, with all fervency and contrition, for the pardon of their past offences, and for a blessing upon their present and prospective action.

"*And whereas*, When our own beloved country, once, by the blessing of God, united, prosperous, and happy, is now afflicted with faction and civil war, it is peculiarly fit for us to recognize the hand of God in this terrible visitation, and, in sorrowful remembrance of our own faults and crimes as a nation, and as individuals, to humble ourselves before Him, and to pray for His mercy—to pray that we may be spared further punishment, though most justly deserved ; that our arms may be blessed and made effectual for the re-establishment of law, order, and peace throughout the wide extent of our country ; and that the inestimable boon of civil and religious liberty, earned under His guidance and blessing by the labors and sufferings of our fathers, may be restored in all its original excellence ;

"Therefore I, Abraham Lincoln, President of the United States, do appoint the last Thursday in September next as a day of humiliation, prayer and fasting for all the people of the nation. And I do earnestly recommend to all the people, and especially to all ministers and teachers of religion, of all denominations, and to all heads of families, to observe and keep that day, according to their several creeds and modes of worship, in all humility, and with all religious solemnity, to the end that the united prayer of the nation may ascend to the Throne of Grace, and bring down plentiful blessings upon our country.

"In testimony whereof, I have hereunto set my hand, and caused the seal of the United States to be affixed, this [L. S.] 12th day of August, A. D. 1861, and of the Independence of the United States of America the eighty-sixth.

"By the President :   "ABRAHAM LINCOLN.

"WILLIAM H. SEWARD, *Secretary of State.*"

COMMERCIAL INTERCOURSE WITH THE RE-BELLIOUS STATES PROHIBITED.

Four days later he also promulgated the following:

"*Whereas*, On the 15th day of April, the President of the United States, in view of an insurrection against the laws, Constitution, and Government of the United States, which had broken out within the States of South Carolina, Georgia, Alabama, Florida, Mississippi, Louisiana, and Texas, and in pursuance of the provisions of the act entitled an act to provide for calling forth the militia to execute the laws of the Union, suppress insurrections, and repel invasions, and to repeal the act now in force for that purpose, approved February 28th, 1795, did call forth the militia to suppress said insurrection and cause the laws of the Union to be duly executed—and the insurgents have failed to disperse by the time directed by the President; *and whereas*, such insurrection has since broken out and yet exists within the States of Virginia, North Carolina, Tennessee, and Arkansas; *and whereas*, the insurgents in all the said States claim to act under authority thereof, and such claim is not disclaimed or repudiated by the persons exercising the functions of government in such State or States, or in the part or parts thereof, in which such combinations exist, nor has such insurrection been suppressed by said States.

"Now, therefore, I, Abraham Lincoln, President of the United States, in pursuance of the act of Congress approved July 13th, 1861, do hereby declare that the inhabitants of the said States of Georgia, South Carolina, Tennessee, Alabama, Louisiana, Texas, Arkansas, Mississippi, and Florida, except the inhabitants of that part of the State of Virginia lying west of the Alleghany Mountains, and of such other parts of that State and the other States hereinbefore named as may maintain a loyal adhesion to the Union and the Constitution, or may be, from time to time occupied and controlled by the forces of the United States engaged in the dispersion of said insurgents, as are in a state of insurrection against the United States, and that all commercial intercourse between the same and the inhabitants thereof, with the exception aforesaid, and the citizens of other States and other parts of the United States, is unlawful and will remain unlawful until such insurrection shall cease or has been suppressed; that all goods and chattels, wares and merchandize, coming from any of the said States, with the exceptions aforesaid, into other parts of the United States, without the special license and permission of the President, through the Secretary of the Treasury, or proceeding to any of the said States, with the exception aforesaid, by land or water, together with the vessel or vehicle conveying the same or conveying persons to and from the said States, with the said exceptions, will be forfeited to the United States; and that, from and after fifteen days from the issuing of this proclamation, all ships and vessels belonging, in whole or in part, to any citizen or inhabitant of any of the said States, with the said exceptions, found at sea in any part of the United States, will be forfeited to the United States; and I hereby enjoin upon all district attorneys, marshals, and officers of the revenue of the military and naval forces of the United States to be vigilant in the execution of the said act, and in the enforcement of the penalties and forfeitures imposed or declared by it, leaving any party who may think himself aggrieved thereby to his application to the Secretary of the Treasury for the remission of any penalty or forfeiture, which the said Secretary is authorized by law to grant if, in his judgment, the special circumstances of any case shall require such a remission.

" In witness whereof, I have hereunto set my hand, and caused the seal of the United States to be affixed.

" Done in the city of Washington, this, the 16th day of August, in the year of our Lord one thousand eight hundred and sixty-one, and of the Independence of the United States of America the eighty-sixth.

" By the President: "ABRAHAM LINCOLN.

" WILLIAM H. SEWARD."

HE MODIFIES AN ORDER OF GENERAL FREMONT.

In the latter part of August, General Fremont declared martial law throughout the State of Missouri, and at the same time ordered that the property of all persons within the limits of his Department who had been disloyal, should be confiscated, and their slaves declared free men, but the President promptly issued an order modifying that clause of the proclamation in relation to the confiscation of property and the liberation of slaves, so as to conform with, and not transcend the provisions on the same subject contained in the Act of Congress approved August 6th, 1861.

HIS SECOND MESSAGE TO CONGRESS.

On the 3d of December, 1861, Congress having convened on the preceding day, the President sent in his Message, a document which was eminently conservative and which was received with great satisfaction by the loyal men of the country. No general scheme of emancipation was urged, and in alluding to the policy to be adopted to en- sure the suppression of the rebellion, he stated that he had been anxious and careful that the inevitable conflict necessary for that purpose should not degenerate into a violent and remorseless revolutionary struggle. " I have, therefore," he continued, " in every case, thought it proper to keep the integrity of the Union prominent as the pri- mary object of the contest on our part, leaving all ques- tions which are not of vital military importance to the more deliberate action of the Legislature."

There can never be any difficulty in ascertaining Mr. Lincoln's views upon the exciting and absorbing topics of the day. His messages, proclamations, and correspond- ence all evince the same spirit of independence and deter- mination, while his language is so explicit that there can be no doubt of his meaning. In his letter to Governor Magoffin, of Kentucky, declining to remove the Union troops from that State, and rebuking that official for his indifference to the cause of his country—in the one to Gen- eral Fremont, in reference to the modification of his pro- clamation, and in fact in all his correspondence on matters connected with political movements, his views have been of such a force and exalted character that they could not fail to receive the hearty approbation of his fellow-country- men.

On the nineteenth of February, 1862, he issued a pro- clamation requesting the people of the United States to assemble on the twenty-second of the same month and celebrate the day by reading the Farewell Address of the " Father of his Country."

THE PRESIDENT'S MESSAGE RECOMMENDING GRADUAL EMANCIPATION.

On the sixth of March, 1862. the President sent into

Congress the following Message, recommending the adoption of measures looking to "gradual, and not sudden" emancipation :

"Fellow-Citizens of the Senate and House of Representatives :
" I recommend the adoption of a joint resolution by your honorable bodies which shall be substantially as follows :
" *'Resolved,* That the United States ought to coöperate with any State which may adopt a gradual abolishment of slavery, giving to such State pecuniary aid to be used by such State in its discretion, to compensate for the inconveniences, public and private, produced by such change of system.'
" If the proposition contained in the resolution does not meet the approval of Congress and the country, there is the end ; but if it does command such approval, I deem it of importance that the States and people immediately interested should be at once distinctly notified of the fact, so that they may begin to consider whether to accept or reject it. The Federal Government would find its highest interest in such a measure as one of the most efficient means of self-preservation. The leaders of the existing insurrection entertain the hope that the Government will ultimately be forced to acknowledge the independence of some part of the disaffected region, and that all the slave ·States north of such parts will then say : 'The Union for which we have struggled being already gone, we now choose to go with the southern section.' To deprive them of this hope, substantially ends the rebellion, and the initiation of emancipation completely deprives them of it as to all the States initiating it.
" The point is not that all the States tolerating slavery would very soon, if at all, initiate emancipation, but that while the offer is equally made to all, the more northern shall, by such initiation, make it certain to the more southern that in no event will the former ever join the latter in their proposed confederacy. I say 'initiation,' because, in my judgment, gradual and not sudden emancipation is better for all. In the mere financial or pecuniary view, any member of Congress, with the census tables and the treasury report before him, can readily see for himself how very soon the current expenditures of this war would purchase, at a fair valuation, all the slaves in any named State.
" Such a proposition on the part of the general Government sets up no claim of a right by Federal authority to interfere with slavery within State limits, referring as it does the absolute control of the subject in each case to the State and its people immediately interested. It is proposed as a matter of perfectly free choice with them.
" In the annual message last December I thought fit to say :

'The Union must be preserved, and hence all indispensable means must be employed.' I said this not hastily, but deliberately. War has been, and continues to be an indispensable means to this end. A practical re-acknowledgment of the national authority would render the war unnecessary, and it would at once cease. If, however, resistance continues, the war must also continue, and it is impossible to foresee all the incidents which may attend, and all the ruin which may follow it. Such as may seem indispensable, or may obviously promise great efficiency toward ending the struggle, must and will come. The proposition now made is an offer only, and I hope it may be esteemed no offence to ask whether the pecuniary consideration tendered would not be of more value to the States and private persons concerned than are the institution and property in it, in the present aspect of affairs. While it is true that the adoption of the proposed resolution would be merely initiatory, and not within itself a practical measure, it is recommended in the hope that it would soon lead to important results. In full view of my great responsibility to my God and to my country, I earnestly beg the attention of Congress and the people to the subject. "ABRAHAM LINCOLN."

This important recommendation was received with the most unbounded satisfaction in all sections of the great North and West, and the leading loyal journals vied with each other in the laudatory notices bestowed upon its illustrious author. The English press favorable to the preservation of the Union, were equally complimentary, and pronounced it a fair, moderate, and magnanimous policy, greatly in contrast with that adopted by the rebel authorities.

ASSUMES ACTIVE COMMAND OF THE ARMY AND NAVY.

On the eleventh of March, 1862, the President gave an additional evidence of his independence and fearlessness by promulgating, for the information of the service and the country, three important military orders, assuming the active duties of Commander-in-Chief of the Army and Navy of the United States; ordering a general and combined movement of the land and naval forces; requiring the Army of the Potomac to be organized into Corps; confining General McClellan to the command of the Department of the Potomac ; and organizing the Department of the Mississippi and the Mountain Department.

THANKSGIVING FOR SIGNAL VICTORIES.

The triumphant success of our arms in the South and West during the early spring months of that year of conflict and carnage, prompted Mr. Lincoln to call upon the patriots of the nation to offer up their thanks to the Almighty for his manifold kindnesses, and for the inestimable blessings he had showered upon them in their hour of need. The recommendation was scrupulously observed, and from almost every place of public worship arose upon the following Sabbath songs of thanksgiving, mingled with invocations for a continuance of the Divine guidance.

SLAVERY ABOLISHED IN THE DISTRICT OF COLUMBIA.

On the sixteenth of April, 1862, Mr. Lincoln consummated an act which had for many years been one of his most favorite projects, by sending into Congress the following Message :

"Fellow-Citizens of the Senate and House of Representatives:
" 'The act entitled 'An act for the release of certain persons held to service or labor in the District of Columbia,' has this day been approved and signed.

" I have never doubted the constitutional authority of Congress to abolish slavery in this District, and I have ever desired to see the national capital freed from the institution in some satisfactory way. Hence there has never been in my mind any question upon the subject except the one of expediency, arising in view of all the circumstances. If there be matters within and about this act, which might have taken a course or shape more satisfactory to my judgment, I do not attempt to specify them. I am gratified that the two principles of compensation and colonization are both recognized and practically applied in the act.

" In the matter of compensation, it is provided that claims may be presented within ninety days from the passage of the act, but not thereafter, and there is no saving for minors, *femmes coverts*, insane, or absent persons. I presume this is an omission by mere oversight, and I recommend that it be supplied by an amendatory or supplemental act. "ABRAHAM LINCOLN."

RE-OPENING OF SOUTHERN PORTS.

During the month of May, 1862, two important proclamations were published—one on the twelfth, declaring the ports of Beaufort, Port Royal, and New Orleans open for trade ; and the second, a week later, repudiating an emancipation order of Major-General Hunter. This last document is too important a part of the history of the rebellion to be omitted here, and we therefore give it in full. It is as follows :

" *Whereas*, There appears in the public prints what purports to be a proclamation of Major-General Hunter, in the words and figures following. to wit :

"'HEAD-QUARTERS, DEPARTMENT OF THE SOUTH,

"'HILTON HEAD, S. C., *May 9th*, 1862.

"'GENERAL ORDERS NO. 11.

"'The three States of Georgia, Florida, and South Carolina, comprising the Military Department of the South, having deliberately declared themselves no longer under the protection of the United States of America, and having taken up arms against the said United States, it becomes a military necessity to declare them under martial law. This was accordingly done on the twenty-fifth day of April, 1862. Slavery and martial law in a free country are altogether incompatible. The persons in these three States, Georgia, Florida, and South Carolina, heretofore held as slaves, are therefore declared forever free.

"'DAVID HUNTER, *Major-General Commanding.*

"'Official :

"'ED. W. SMITH, *Acting Assistant Adjutant-General.*'

"*And whereas*, The same is producing some excitement and misunderstanding,

"*Therefore*, I, Abraham Lincoln, President of the United States, proclaim and declare that the government of the United States had no knowledge or belief of an intention, on the part of General Hunter, to issue such a proclamation, nor has it yet any authentic information that the document is genuine ; and further, that neither General Hunter nor any other commander or person has been authorized by the government of the United States to make proclamation declaring the slaves of any State free, and that the supposed proclamation now in question, whether genuine or false, is altogether void, so far as respects such declaration.

"I further make known, that whether it be competent for me as commander-in-chief of the army and navy to declare the slaves of any State or States free, and whether at any time, or in any case, it shall have become a necessity indispensable to the maintenance of the government to exercise such supposed power, are questions which, under my responsibility, I reserve to myself, and which I cannot feel justified in leaving to the decision of commanders in the field. These are totally different questions from those of police regulations in armies and camps.

"On the sixth day of March last, by a special message, I recommended to Congress the adoption of a joint resolution, to be substantially as follows :

"'*Resolved*, That the United States ought to co-operate with any State which may adopt a gradual abolishment of slavery, giving to such State in its discretion to compensate for the inconveniences, public and private, produced by such change of system.'

"The resolution, in the language above quoted, was adopted by large majorities in both branches of Congress, and now stands an authentic, definite and solemn proposal of the nation to the States and people most immediately interested in the subject matter. To the people of these States I now earnestly appeal. I do not argue; I beseech you to make the arguments for yourselves. You cannot, if you would, be blind to the signs of the times. I beg of you a calm and enlarged consideration of them, ranging, if it may be, far above personal and partisan politics. This proposal makes common cause for a common object, casting no reproaches upon any. It acts not the Pharisee. The change it contemplates would come gently as the dews of Heaven, not rending or wrecking any thing. Will you not embrace it? So much good has not been done by one effort in all past time, as in the Providence of God it is now your high privilege to do. May the vast future not have to lament that you have neglected it.

"In witness whereof, I have hereunto set my hand, and caused the seal of the United States to be affixed.

"Done at the City of Washington, this nineteenth day of May, in the year of our Lord one thousand eight hundred and sixty-two, and of the Independence of the United States the eighty-sixth.

"By the President: "ABRAHAM LINCOLN.

"WM. H. SEWARD, *Secretary of State.*"

THE PRESIDENT'S CONFERENCE WITH THE LOYAL GOVERNORS—HIS INTERVIEW WITH THE BORDER CONGRESSMEN.

On the first of July, 1862, the President, in accordance with the Act for the collection of direct taxes in the insurrectionary districts, issued a proclamation declaring in what States and in what counties of Virginia insurrection existed ; and on the same day addressed a letter to the Governors of the loyal States, in reply to one received from them, asking that for the purpose of following up recent signal successes by measures which would ensure the speedy restoration of the Union, a sufficient number of men from each State to fill up existing regiments and to form new organizations, might be called for. Mr. Lincoln fully concurred in the views of the Executives, and expressed his intention to call for an additional force of three hundred thousand men.

On the twelfth of July, an interesting interview took place at the White House, the Senators and Representatives of the Border States having assembled there by invitation of the President, who wished to converse with them upon the important topic of gradual emancipation. During an extended conversation, he expressed his views clearly and explicitly, requesting their calm consideration of the subject, and charging them to commend his suggestions to their constituents, and to prevent all doubt of his meaning, read to them the following appeal :

"*Gentlemen :* After the adjournment of Congress, now near, I shall have no opportunity of seeing you for several months. Believing that you of the border States hold more power for good than any other equal number of members, I feel it a duty, which I cannot justifiably waive, to make this appeal to you.

" I intend no reproach or complaint when I assure you that, in my opinion, if you all had voted for the resolution in the gradual emancipation message of last March, the war would now be substantially ended. And the plan therein proposed is yet one of the most potent and swift means of ending it. Let the States which are in rebellion see definitely and certainly that, in no event, will the States you represent ever join their proposed confederacy, and they cannot much longer maintain the contest. But you cannot divest them of their hope to ultimately have you with them so long as you show a determination to perpetuate the institutions within your own States. Beat them at elections, as you have overwhelmingly done, and, nothing daunted, they still claim you as their own. You and I know what the lever of their power is. Break that lever before their faces, and they can shake you no more forever.

"Most of you have treated me with kindness and consideration, and I trust you will not now think I improperly touch what is exclusively your own, when, for the sake of the whole country, I ask, 'Can you, for your States, do better than to take the course I urge?' Discarding *punctilio* and maxims adapted to more manageable times, and looking only to the unprecedentedly stern facts of our case, can you do better in any possible event? You prefer that the constitutional relation of the States to the nation shall be practically restored without disturbance of the institution; and, if this were done, my whole duty, in this respect, under the Constitution and my oath of office, would be performed. But it is not done, and we are trying to accomplish it by war. The incidents of the war cannot be avoided. If the war continues long, as it must if the object be not sooner attained, the institution in your States will be extinguished by mere friction and abrasion—by the mere incidents of the war. It will be gone, and you will have nothing valuable in lieu of it. Much of its value is gone already. How much better for you and for your people to take the step which at once shortens the war, and secures substantial compensation for that which is sure to be wholly lost in any other event! How much better to thus save the money which else we sink forever in the war! How much better to do it while we can, lest the war, ere long, render us pecuniarily unable to do it! How much better for you, as seller, and the nation, as buyer, to sell out and buy out that without which the war could never have been, than to sink both the thing to be sold and the price of it in cutting one another's throats.

"I do not speak of emancipation *at once*, but of a *decision* at once to emancipate *gradually*. Room in South America for colonization can be obtained cheaply and in abundance; and, when numbers shall be large enough to be company and encouragement for one another, the freed people will not be so reluctant to go.

"I am pressed with a difficulty not yet mentioned—one which threatens division among those who, united, are none too strong. An instance of it is known to you. General Hunter is an honest man. He was, and I hope still is, my friend. I valued him none the less for his agreeing with me in the general wish that all men everywhere could be freed. He proclaimed all men free within certain States, and I repudiated the proclamation. He expected more good and less harm from the measure than I could believe would follow. Yet, in repudiating it, I gave dissatisfaction, if not offence, to many whose support the country cannot afford to lose. And this is not the end of it. The pressure in this direction is still upon me, and is increasing. By conceding what I now ask, you can relieve me, and, much more, can relieve the country in this important point.

8

" Upon these considerations I have again begged your attention to the message of March last. Before leaving the capital,
consider and discuss it among yourselves. You are patriots and
statesmen, and, as such, I pray you consider this proposition,
and, at the least, commend it to the consideration of your States
and people. As you would perpetuate popular government for
the best people in the world, I beseech you that you do in nowise
omit this. Our common country is in great peril, demanding
the loftiest views and boldest action to bring a speedy relief.
Once relieved, its form of government is saved to the world, its
beloved history and cherished memories are vindicated, and its
happy future fully assured and rendered inconceivably grand.
To you, more than to any others, the privilege is given to assure
that happiness and swell that grandeur, and to link your own
names therewith forever."

INSTRUCTIONS TO MILITARY AND NAVAL COMMANDERS.

On the twenty-second of July, he issued the following
order :

" WAR DEPARTMENT, WASHINGTON, *July* 22*d*, 1862.

" *First.* Ordered that military commanders within the States
of Virginia, North Carolina, Georgia, Florida, Alabama, Mississippi, Louisiana, Texas, and Arkansas, in an ordinary manner
seize and use any property, real or personal, which may be
necessary or convenient for their several commands, for supplies, or for other military purposes ; and that while property
may be destroyed for proper military objects, none shall be destroyed in wantonness or malice.

" *Second.* That military and naval commanders shall employ
as laborers, within and from said States, so many persons of
African descent as can be advantageously used for military or
naval purposes, giving them reasonable wages for their labor.

" *Third.* That, as to both property, and persons of African
descent, accounts shall be kept sufficiently accurate and in detail to show quantities and amounts, and from whom both property and such persons shall have come, as a basis upon which
compensation can be made in proper cases ; and the several departments of this government shall attend to and perform their
appropriate parts toward the execution of these orders.

" By order of the President.

" EDWIN M. STANTON,
"Secretary of War."

And on the twenty-fifth of July, by proclamation, he
warned all persons to cease participating in aiding, counte-
nancing, or abetting the rebellion, and to return to their

allegiance under penalty of the forfeitures and seizures provided by an Act "to suppress insurrection, to punish treason and rebellion, to seize and confiscate the property of rebels, and for other purposes," approved on the seventeenth of July, 1862.

A DRAFT FOR THREE HUNDRED THOUSAND MEN ORDERED.

On the fourth of August, 1862, the following order for a draft was issued :

" ORDERED : *First,* that a draft of three hundred thousand militia be immediately called into the service of the United States, *to serve for nine months, unless sooner discharged.* The Secretary of War will assign the quotas to the States and establish regulations for the draft.

" *Second,* that if any State shall not, by the fifteenth of August, furnish its quota of the additional three hundred thousand volunteers authorized by law, the deficiency of volunteers in that State will also be made up by a special draft from the militia. The Secretary of War will establish regulations for this purpose.

" *Third,* regulations will be prepared by the War Department, and presented to the President, with the object of securing the promotion of officers of the army and volunteers for meritorious and distinguished services, and of preventing the nomination and appointment in the military service of incompetent or unworthy officers.

" The regulations will also provide for ridding the service of such incompetent persons as now hold commissions.

" By order of the President.

" EDWIN M. STANTON,
"Secretary of War.'

THE PRESIDENT SPEAKS AT A WAR MEETING.

On the sixth of August, 1862, a large and enthusiastic Union meeting was held in Washington, at which a series of patriotic resolutions was adopted, and numerous eloquent speeches delivered, among others the following characteristic one by the Chief Magistrate of the nation :

"*Fellow-citizens:* I believe there is no precedent for my appearing before you on this occasion, [applause,] but it is also true that there is no precedent for your being here yourselves, [applause and laughter,] and I offer, in justification of myself and of you, that, upon examination, I have found nothing in the Constitution against it. [Renewed applause.] I, however, have an impression that there are younger gentlemen who will enter- tain you better, [voices—'No, no! none can do better than yourself. Go on!'] and better address your understanding than I will or could, and therefore I propose but to detain you a mo- ment longer. [Cries—'Go on! Tar and feather the rebels!']

"I am very little inclined on any occasion to say any thing unless I hope to produce some good by it. [A voice—'You do that; go on.'] The only thing I think of just now not likely to be better said by some one else is a matter in which we have heard some other persons blamed for what I did myself. [Voices—'What is it?'] There has been a very wide-spread at- tempt to have a quarrel between General McClellan and the Secretary of War. Now, I occupy a position that enables me to observe, at least these two gentlemen are not nearly so deep in the quarrel as some pretending to be their friends. [Cries of 'Good.'] General McClellan's attitude is such that, in the very selfishness of his nature, he cannot but wish to be successful, and I hope he will—and the Secretary of War is in precisely the same situation. If the military commanders in the field cannot be successful, not only the Secretary of War, but myself, for the time being the master of them both, cannot be but failures. [Laughter and applause.] I know General McClellan wishes to be successful, and I know he does not wish it any more than the Secretary of War for him, and both of them together no more than I wish it. [Applause and cries of 'Good.'] Sometimes we have a dispute about how many men General McClellan has had, and those who would disparage him say that he has had a very large number, and those who would disparage the Secretary of War insist that General McClellan has had a very small number. The basis for this is, there is always a wide difference, and on this occasion perhaps a wider one, between the grand total on McClellan's rolls and the men actually fit for duty; and those who would disparage him talk of the grand total on paper, and those who would disparage the Secretary of War talk of those at present fit for duty. General McClellan has sometimes asked for things that the Secretary of War did not give him. General McClellan is not to blame for asking what he wanted and needed, and the Secretary of War is not to blame for not giving when he had none to give. [Applause, laughter, and cries of 'Good, good.'] And I say here, as far as I know, the Secretary of War has withheld no one thing at any time in my power to give him. [Wild applause, and a voice—'Give him enough now!'] I have no accusation against him. I believe he is a brave and able man, [applause,] and I stand here, as justice re- quires me to do, to take upon myself what has been charged on the Secretary of War, as withholding from him.

"I have talked longer than I expected to, [cries of 'No, no—go on,'] and now I avail myself of my privilege of saying no more."

THE EMANCIPATION PROCLAMATIONS OF SEPTEMBER, 1862, AND JANUARY, 1863.

On the twenty-second of September, 1862, Mr. Lincoln issued one of the two most important proclamations ever penned by a President of the United States : that which announced to the negroes held as slaves in the rebellious States that on and after the first day of the new year, they should be forever released from bondage. This great document, which was read with joy by the loyal residents of the North, and which was a source of such infinite happiness to the unfortunate class of beings who were to be more particularly affected by its provisions, was as follows :

"I, Abraham Lincoln, President of the United States of America, and Commander-in-Chief of the Army and Navy thereof, do hereby proclaim and declare that hereafter as heretofore the war will be prosecuted for the object of practically restoring the constitutional relation between the United States and the people thereof in those States in which that relation is, or may be, suspended or disturbed ; that it is my purpose upon the next meeting of Congress to again recommend the adoption of a practical measure tendering pecuniary aid 'to the free acceptance or rejection of all the slave States, so-called, the people whereof may not then be in rebellion against the United States, and which States may then have voluntarily adopted, or thereafter may voluntarily adopt, the immediate or gradual abolishment of slavery within their respective limits, and that the effort to colonize persons of African descent, with their consent, upon the continent or elsewhere, with the previously obtained consent of the government existing there, will be continued ; that on the first day of January, in the year of our Lord one thousand eight hundred and sixty-three, all persons held as slaves within any State, or any designated part of a State, the people whereof shall then be in rebellion against the United States, shall be then, thenceforward and forever, free, and the executive government of the United States, including the military and naval authority thereof, will recognize and maintain the freedom of such persons, and will do no act or acts to repress such persons, or any of them, in any efforts they may make for their actual freedom ; that the Executive will, on the first day of January aforesaid, by proclamation, designate the States and parts of States, if any, in which the people thereof respectively shall then be in rebellion against the United States; and the fact that any State, or the people thereof, shall on that day be in good faith represented in the Congress of the United States by members chosen thereto, at elections wherein a majority of the qualified voters of such State shall have participated, shall, in the absence of strong countervailing testimony, be deemed conclusive evidence that such State and the people thereof have not been in rebellion against the United States.

"That attention is hereby called to an act of Congress entitled, 'An act to make an additional article of war,' approved March 13, 1862, and which act is in the words and figures following:

"'*Be it enacted by the Senate and House of Representatives of the United States of America, in Congress assembled,* That hereafter the following shall be promulgated as an additional article of war for the government of the army of the United States, and shall be observed and obeyed as such.

"'*Article* —. All officers or persons of the military or naval service of the United States are prohibited from employing any of the forces under their respective commands for the purpose of returning fugitives from service or labor who may have escaped from any persons to whom such service or labor is claimed to be due, and any officer who shall be found guilty by a court-martial of violating this article, shall be dismissed from the service.

"'*Sec.* 2. And be it further enacted, That this act shall take effect from and after its passage.'

" Also to the ninth and tenth sections of an act entitled, ' An act to suppress insurrection, to punish treason and rebellion, to seize and confiscate property of rebels, and for other purposes,' approved July 17, 1862, and which sections are in the words and figures following:

"'*Sec.* 9. And be it further enacted, That all slaves of persons who shall hereafter be engaged in rebellion against the government of the United States, or who shall in any way give aid or comfort thereto, escaping from such persons and taking refuge within the lines of the army; and all slaves captured from such persons or deserted by them, and coming under the control of the government of the United States, and all slaves of such persons found on (or being within) any place occupied by rebel forces and afterwards occupied by the forces of the United States, shall be deemed captives of war, and shall be forever free of their servitude and not again held as slaves.

"'*Sec.* 10. And be it further enacted, That no slave escaping into any State, Territory, or the District of Columbia, from any of the States, shall be delivered up, or in any way impeded or hindered of his liberty, except for crime, or some offence against the laws, unless the person claiming said fugitive shall first make oath that the person to whom the labor or service of such fugitive is alleged to be due, is his lawful owner, and has not been in arms against the United States in the present rebellion, nor in any way given aid and comfort thereto; and no person engaged in the military or naval service of the United States shall, under any pretence whatever, assume to decide on the validity of the claim of any person to the service or labor of any other person, or surrender up any such person to the claimant, on pain of being dismissed from the service.'

" And I do hereby enjoin upon, and order all persons engaged in the military and naval service of the United States to observe, obey and enforce within their respective spheres of service the act and sections above recited.

" And the executive will in due time recommend that all citizens of the United States who shall have remained loyal thereto throughout the rebellion, shall (upon the restoration of the constitutional relation between the United States and their respective States and people, if the relation shall have been suspended or disturbed) be compensated for all losses by acts of the United States, including the loss of slaves.

" In witness whereof, I have hereunto set my hand and caused the seal of the United States to be affixed.

" Done at the city of Washington, this twenty-second day of September, in the year of our Lord one thousand eight hundred and sixty-two, and of the Independence of the United States the eighty-seventh.

      " By the President: " ABRAHAM LINCOLN.
" WM. H. SEWARD, *Secretary of State.*"

Such a bold movement was necessarily distasteful to the traitors, and while the Southern journals pronounced it to be a bid for the slaves to rise in insurrection, a bid which none but a barbarian would devise, it was denounced in the Richmond Congress, and a resolution was there offered, exhorting the people to slay every Union soldier and raider found within their borders, and offering a reward to every negro, who would, after the first of January, 1863, kill a Unionist.

The other important proclamation was issued on the first of January, 1863, and was worded as follows :

" *Whereas*, on the twenty-second day of September, in the year of our Lord one thousand eight hundred and sixty-two, a proclamation was issued by the President of the United States containing among other things the following, to wit :

"That on the first day of January, in the year of our Lord one thousand eight hundred and sixty-three, all persons held as slaves within any State, or designated part of a State, the people whereof shall then be in rebellion against the United States, shall be then, thenceforth and forever free, and the Executive Government of the United States, including the military and naval authorities thereof, will recognize and maintain the freedom of such persons, and will do no act or acts to repress such persons, or any of them, in any efforts they may make for their actual freedom.

"That the Executive will, on the first day of January aforesaid, by proclamation, designate the States and parts of States, if any, in which the people therein respectively shall then be in rebellion against the United States, and the fact that any State, or the people thereof, shall on that day be in good faith represented in the Congress of the United States by members chosen thereto, at elections wherein a majority of the qualified voters of such States shall have participated, shall, in the absence of strong countervailing testimony, be deemed conclusive evidence that such State and the people thereof are not then in rebellion against the United States.

"Now, therefore, I, Abraham Lincoln, President of the United States, by virtue of the power in me vested as Commander-in-chief of the Army and Navy of the United States in time of actual armed rebellion against the authority and Government of the United States, and as a fit and necessary war measure for suppressing said rebellion, do, on this first day of January, in the year of our Lord one thousand eight hundred and sixty-three, and in accordance with my purpose so to do, publicly proclaimed for the full period of one hundred days from the day of the first above-mentioned order, and designate, as the States and parts of States wherein the people thereof respectively are this day in rebellion against the United States, the following to wit: Arkansas, Texas, Louisiana, except the parishes of St. Bernard, Plaquemines, Jefferson, St. John, St. Charles, St. James, Ascension, Assumption, Terre Bonne, Lafourche, St. Mary, St. Martin, and Orleans, including the City of New Orleans. Mississippi, Alabama, Florida, Georgia, South Carolina, North Carolina, and Virginia, except the forty-eight counties designated as West Virginia, and also the counties of Berkeley, Accomac, Northampton, Elizabeth City, York, Princess Ann, and Norfolk, including the cities of Norfolk and Portsmouth, and which excepted parts are, for the present, left precisely as if this proclamation were not issued.

"And by virtue of the power and for the purpose aforesaid, I do order and declare that all persons held as slaves within said designated States and parts of States are, and henceforward shall be free; and that the Executive Government of the United States, including the Military and Naval authorities thereof, will recognize and maintain the freedom of said persons.

"And I hereby enjoin upon the people so declared to be free, to abstain from all violence, unless in necessary self-defence, and I recommend to them, that in all cases, when allowed, they labor faithfully for reasonable wages.

"And I further declare and make known that such persons of suitable condition will be received into the armed service of the United States to garrison forts, positions, stations, and other places, and to man vessels of all sorts in said service.

"And upon this, sincerely believed to be an act of justice, warranted by the Constitution, upon military necessity, I invoke the considerate judgment of mankind and the gracious favor of Almighty God.

"In witness whereof, I have hereunto set my hand and caused the seal of the United States to be affixed.

"Done at the City of Washington, this first day of January, in the year of our Lord one thousand eight hundred and sixty-three, and of the Independence of the United States of America the eighty-seventh.

[L. s.]

"By the President :   "ABRAHAM LINCOLN.
"WILLIAM H. SEWARD, *Secretary of State.*"

SUSPENSION OF THE WRIT OF HABEAS CORPUS.

On the twenty-fourth of September, 1862, two days after the promulgation of the renowned Emancipation Proclamation, the following order was published :

" *Whereas*, It has become necessary to call into service, not only volunteers, but also portions of the militia of the State by draft, in order to suppress the insurrection existing in the United States, and disloyal persons are not adequately restrained by the ordinary processes of law from hindering this measure, and from giving aid and comfort in various ways to the insurrection :

" Now, therefore, be it ordered :

" *First.* That during the existing insurrection, and as a necessary measure for suppressing the same, all rebels and insurgents, their aiders and abettors, within the United States, and all persons discouraging volunteer enlistments, resisting militia drafts, or guilty of any disloyal practice affording aid and comfort to the rebels against the authority of the United States, shall be subject to martial law, and liable to trial and punishment by courts-martial or military commissions.

" *Third.* That the writ of *habeas corpus* is suspended in respect to all persons arrested, or who are now, or hereafter during the rebellion shall be imprisoned in any fort, camp, arsenal, military prison, or other place of confinement, by any military authority or by the sentence of any court-martial or military commission.

" In witness whereof, I have hereunto set my hand, and caused the seal of the United States to be affixed.

" Done at the City of Washington, this twenty-fourth day of September, in the year of our Lord one thousand eight hundred and sixty-two, and of the Independence of the United States the eighty-seventh.

" By the President.   " ABRAHAM LINCOLN.

" WM. H. SEWARD, *Secretary of State*."

The suspension of the Writ of Habeas Corpus was naturally obnoxious to Northern sympathizers with treason, and for some time their newspaper organs were daily filled with editorial and other articles, teeming with invidious criticism and abuse.   The act placed more power in the hands of the President than was acceptable to men who, by their voice and pen, if not by their pecuniary means, were aiding and abetting the enemies of the country, and as they were not aware what moment they might be arrested and imprisoned for their despicable crimes, in their regard for their personal safety, they forgot their prudence, and abused the Executive.   The beneficial effects of the order were not over-estimated by Mr. Lincoln, and with its promulgation almost entirely ceased the interference with enlistments, which had too often before that date delayed the organization of regiments in some of the loyal States.

THE SABBATH TO BE OBSERVED.

On the sixteenth of November, 1862, the following order was issued to the soldiers and sailors of the Union :

"The President, Commander-in-Chief of the Army and Navy, desires and enjoins the orderly observance of the Sabbath by the officers and men in the military and naval service.   The importance for man and beast of the prescribed weekly rest, the sacred rights of Christian soldiers and sailors, a becoming deference to the best sentiment of a Christian people, and a due regard for the Divine will, demand that Sunday labor in the Army and Navy be reduced to the measure of strict necessity.

· " The discipline and character of the National forces should not suffer, nor the cause they defend be imperilled, by the profanation of the day or name of the Most High. 'At this time of public distress' adopting the words of Washington in 1776, ' men may find enough to do in the service of God and their country without abandoning themselves to vice and immorality.' The first general order issued by the Father of his Country after the Declaration of Independence indicates the spirit in which our institutions were founded and should ever be defended : ' The General hopes and trusts that every officer and man will endeavor to live and act as becomes a Christian soldier defending the dearest rights and liberties of his country.'

"ABRAHAM LINCOLN."

HIS ANNUAL MESSAGE.—IMPORTANT RECOMMENDATIONS TO CONGRESS.

On the first of December, 1862, Mr. Lincoln sent in to Congress his annual message ; giving a satisfactory resumé of the events of the previous twelve months ; calling the attention of the Senators and Representatives to important matters which should receive their notice ; recommending the organization of national banking associations, under the hope and belief that they would be the means of promoting the early resumption of specie payments ; re-impressed upon them the importance of his plan of " compensated emancipation ;" repeated at length his views upon the slavery question, and recommended the adoption of the following resolutions and articles amendatory to the Constitution :

"*Resolved*, By the Senate and House of Representatives of the United States of America in Congress assembled, two-thirds of both houses concurring, that the following articles be proposed to the Legislatures or Conventions of the several States, as amendments to the Constitution of the United States, all or any of which articles, when ratified by three-fourths of the said Legislatures or Conventions, to be valid as part or parts of the said Constitution, namely :

"ARTICLE —. Every State wherein slavery now exists, which shall abolish the same therein at any time or times before the first day of January, in the year of our Lord one thousand nine hundred, shall receive compensation from the United States as follows, to wit :

"The President of the United States shall deliver to every such State, bonds of the United States, bearing interest at the rate of ——, for each slave shown to have been therein, by the eighth census of the United States; said bonds to be delivered to such State by instalments, or in one parcel at the completion of the abolishment, according as the same shall have been gradual or at one time within such State; and interest shall begin to run upon any such bond only from the proper time of its delivery as aforesaid, and afterward. Any State having received bonds as aforesaid, and afterward introducing or tolerating slavery therein, shall refund to the United States the bonds so received, or the value thereof, and all interest paid thereon.

"ARTICLE ——. All slaves who shall have enjoyed actual freedom, by the chances of the war at any time, before the end of the rebellion, shall be forever free; but all owners of such, who shall not have been disloyal, shall be compensated for them at the same rates as is provided for States adopting abolishment of slavery—but in such a way that no slave shall be twice accounted for.

"ARTICLE ——. Congress may appropriate money, and otherwise provide for colonizing free colored persons with their own consent, at any place or places without the United States."

The message and its recommendations were received with the same *eclat* which has attended all the official documents penned by the illustrious statesman. The proclamation of September had awakened the people of the Union to the vast advantages to be derived from the adoption of his views and suggestions on every thing relating to slavery, and as the day on which the unfortunate blacks were to be rescued from a life of degradation approached, thousands, who had hitherto protested against interference with the "peculiar institution," united with their old political opponents, and awaited anxiously the hour when the order of emancipation was to go into effect. Residents of foreign lands were no less eager for the time to arrive when the Federal Government should strike off the fetters of the slave, and among other complimentary addresses sent to the President, was one from Manchester, England, from which we make the following extracts:

"As citizens of Manchester, assembled at the Free-Trade Hall, we beg to express our fraternal sentiments toward you and your country. We rejoice in your greatness as an outgrowth of England, whose blood and language you share, whose orderly and legal freedom you have applied to new circumstances, over a region immeasurably greater than our own. We honor your Free States, as a singularly happy abode for the working millions where industry is honored. One thing alone has, in the past, lessened our sympathy with your country and our confidence in it—we mean the ascendency of politicians who not merely maintained negro slavery, but desired to extend and root it more firmly. We joyfully honor you, as the President, and the Congress with you, for many decisive steps toward practically exemplifying your belief in the words of your great founders : 'All men are created free and equal.' You have procured the liberation of the slaves in the district around Washington, and thereby made the centre of your Federation visibly free. You have enforced the laws against the slave-trade, and kept up your fleet against it, even while every ship was wanted for service in your terrible war. You have nobly decided to receive embassadors from the negro republics of Hayti and Liberia, thus forever renouncing that unworthy prejudice which refuses the rights of humanity to men and women on account of their color. In order more effectually to stop the slave-trade, you have made with our Queen a treaty, which your Senate has ratified, for the right of mutual search. Your Congress has decreed freedom as the law forever in the vast unoccupied or half unsettled Territories which are directly subject to its legislative power. It has offered pecuniary aid to all States which will enact emancipation locally, and has forbidden your generals to restore fugitive slaves who seek their protection. You have entreated the slave-masters to accept these moderate offers ; and after long and patient waiting, you, as Commander-in-chief of the Army, have appointed to-morrow, the first of January, 1863, as the day of unconditional freedom for the slaves of the rebel States. We implore you, for your own honor and welfare, not to faint in your providential mission. While your enthusiasm is aflame, and the tide of events runs high, let the work be finished effectually. Leave no root of bitterness to spring up and work fresh misery to your children. It is a mighty task, indeed, to reorganize the industry not only of four millions of the colored race, but of five millions of whites. Nevertheless, the vast progress you have made in the short space of twenty months, fill us with hope that every stain on your freedom will shortly be removed, and that the erasure of that foul blot upon civilization and Christianity— chattle slavery—during your Presidency, will cause the name of Abraham Lincoln to be honored and revered by posterity."

In answer to this flattering letter, Mr. Lincoln sent a happy response, in which he explained the motive which had prompted him to the undeviating course he has pursued since his inauguration. He had, he said, considered the duty of maintaining and preserving the Constitution and the integrity of the Federal Republic paramount to all others, and as a conscientious purpose to perform that duty was the key to all the measures of his administration, he could not, if he would, under his oath and our . frame of government, depart from that purpose.

THE PRESIDENT VISITS THE ARMY OF THE POTOMAC.

Early in April, 1863, the President left Washington on a visit to the Army of the Potomac. He had in the previous year, when the same noble troops were resting at Harrison's Landing, after their campaign before Richmond, gone thither to observe for himself their true condition, and upon other occasions has visited their camping-grounds, where he has been always received with great enthusiasm. Upon the visit to which we now refer, he was accompanied by Mrs. Lincoln and one of his sons, and an eye-witness thus describes the proceedings incident to the entertainment of such distinguished guests :

On the morning of April seventh, 1863, a reception was had in General Hooker's tent, the members of the staff passing in and being introduced to the President by the Chief of Staff. Mr. Lincoln was in unusual good humor, and completely banished the constraint felt by all by his sociability and shafts of wit. The interview lasted some time, much to the enjoyment of all, until finally the officers one by one dropped out, and the hour designated for the review arrived. Early in the morning the several cavalry brigades commenced moving towards the field selected for the review, and during the forenoon were engaged forming the lines and stationing guards to keep off the crowd. At noon the roar of artillery announced that the cortege had arrived. President Lincoln, mounted on a magnificent bay, adorned with heavy trappings, rode steadily and rapidly along the line, with Generals Hooker and Stoneman at his side, and followed by an imposing cavalcade of general officers, aides-de-camp and orderlies. Having returned to the right of the line, a position was selected for the President upon a slight eminence, while the cavalry at a walk passed in review before him, the bands playing and the bugles sounding merrily. Mrs. Lincoln occupied a carriage at the right of the President while the regiments passed in review, surrounded by major-generals and stars of lesser magnitude. After the cavalry had moved off the field, the lancers, in splendid order, wheeled around into line fronting the President, while the light artillery dashed at a gallop through the avenue thus formed, the guns and caissons bounding over the irregularities as though the wheels were of India rubber. The cannon were soon off the field, the lancers filed in behind the cavalcade of generals, spectators vanished, and the plateau, torn and trodden by the squadrons, was left to the scattering working parties engaged in preparing the ground for the grand review of infantry. The President also rode over to the head-quarters of several commanding officers, and during the day reviewed the reserve artillery.

Doubtless the lady readers are anxious to know in what dress the wife of the Chief Magistrate visited the army, how she appeared, what she said, and how she liked the contrast—the Executive mansion, with its costly furniture, and the bare floor, cot and camp stools of the field. Mrs. Lincoln's attire was exceedingly simple—of that peculiar style of simplicity which creates at the time no impression upon the mind, and prevents one from remembering any article of dress. In this case there was nothing to attract attention, and after she had entered the tent there was not one in twenty of those gathered about who could tell what she wore. A rich black silk dress, with narrow flounces; a black cape, with a broad trimming of velvet around the border, and a plain hat of the same hue, composed her costume. A shade of weariness, doubtless the result of her labors in behalf of the sick and wounded in Washington, rested upon her countenance; but the change seemed pleasant to her, and the scenes of camp were noted with evident interest. The President wore a dark sack overcoat and a fur muffler, while Master Lincoln sported a suit of gray, and rambled about among the tents, examining the quarters of the staff, and watched by the orderlies and sentries with a curiosity somewhat amusing.

THE ENROLMENT ACT AND THE RIGHTS OF ALIENS.

To enumerate all the proclamations which the President issued during the year 1863, would be impossible in this work, and we must therefore restrict ourselves to those which were of more than usual interest. The one in regard to the rights of aliens, under the act calling out the national forces, was one of these, and reads as follows:

"*Whereas*, The Congress of the United States at its last session enacted a law entitled, 'An act for enrolling and calling out the national forces and for other purposes,' which was approved on the third day of March last, and,

"*Whereas*, It is recited in the said act that there now exists in the United States an insurrection and rebellion against the authority thereof, and it is, under the Constitution of the United States, the duty of the Government to suppress insurrection and rebellion, to guarantee to each State a republican form of government, and to preserve the public tranquility, and

"*Whereas*, For these high purposes a military force is indispensable, to raise and support which all persons ought willingly to contribute; and

"*Whereas*, No service can be more praiseworthy and honorable than that which is rendered for the maintenance of the Constitution and the Union, and the consequent preservation of the Government; and

"*Whereas*, For the reasons thus recited, it was enacted by the said statute that all able-bodied male citizens of the United States and persons of foreign birth, who shall have declared on oath their intentions to become citizens, under and in pursuance of the laws thereof, between the ages of twenty and forty-five years, with certain exceptions not necessary to be here mentioned, are declared to constitute the national forces, and shall be liable to perform military duty in the service of the United States, when called out by the President for that purpose; and

"Whereas, It is claimed, and in behalf of persons of foreign birth within the ages specified in said act who have heretofore declared on oath their intentions to become citizens under and in pursuance of the laws of the United States, and who have not exercised the right of suffrage or any other political franchise under the laws of the United States, or any of the States thereof, are not absolutely precluded by their aforesaid declaration of intention from renouncing their purpose to become citizens, and that, on the contrary, such persons under treaties or the law of nations, retain a right to renounce that purpose and to forego the privilege of citizenship and residence within the United States under the obligations imposed by the aforesaid act of Congress.

"Now, therefore, to avoid all misapprehensions concerning the liability of persons concerned to perform the service required by such enactment, and to give it full effect, I do hereby order and proclaim that no plea of alienage will be received or allowed to exempt from the obligations imposed by the aforesaid act of Congress, any person of foreign birth who shall have declared, on oath, his intention to become a citizen of the United States under the laws thereof, and who shall be found within the United States at any time during the continuance of the present insurrection and rebellion, at or after the expiration of the sixty-five days from the date of this proclamation, nor shall any such plea of alienage be allowed in favor of any such person who has so as aforesaid declared his intention to become a citizen of the United States, and shall have exercised at any time the right of suffrage or any other political franchise within the United States, under the laws thereof, or under the laws of any of the several States.

"In witness whereof I have hereunto set my hand and caused the seal of the United States to be affixed.

"Done at the city of Washington, this eighth day of May, in the year of our Lord 1863, and of the independence of the United States the eighty-seventh.

"By the President,   "ABRAHAM LINCOLN.

"WILLIAM H SEWARD, *Secretary of State.*"

A NATIONAL THANKSGIVING ORDERED.

On the fifteenth day of July, 1863, the President ordered the sixth of the following month to be set apart as

9

a day of National Thanksgiving.   Victories had crowned
our arms on land and sea, and no greater cause for offering thanks to the Almighty ever prompted the Chief Magistrate of a country to call the people together, and few
proclamations were ever written more chaste and beautiful than the following :

"It has pleased Almighty God to hearken to the supplications
and prayers of an afflicted people, and to vouchsafe to the army
and the navy of the United States, on the land and on the sea,
victories so . signal and so effective as to furnish reasonable
grounds for augmented confidence that the union of these States
will be maintained, their constitutions preserved, and their peace
and prosperity permanently preserved.

"But these victories have been accorded not without sacrifice
of life, limb and liberty, incurred by the brave, patriotic and
loyal citizens.   Domestic affliction in every part of the country
follows in the train of these fearful bereavements.   It is meet
and right to recognize and confess the presence of the Almighty
Father, and the power of His hand equally in these triumphs
and these sorrows.

"Now, therefore, be it known, that I do set apart Thursday,
the sixth day of August next, to be observed as a day for national Thanksgiving, praise, and prayer, and I invite the people of
the United States to assemble on that occasion in their customary places of worship, and in the forms approved by their own
conscience, render the homage due to the Divine Majesty for
the wonderful things He has done in the nation's behalf, and
invoke the influence of His Holy Spirit to subdue the anger
which has produced and so long sustained a needless and cruel rebellion ; to change the hearts of the insurgents, to guide the
counsels of the government with wisdom adequate to so great a
national emergency, and to visit with tender care and consolation throughout the length and breadth of our land all those
who through the vicissitudes of marches, voyages, battles and
sieges, have been brought to suffer in mind, body or estate and
family, to lead the whole nation through paths of repentance
and submission to the Divine Will, back to the perfect enjoyment of Union and fraternal peace.

"In witness whereof, I have hereunto set my hand and caused
the seal of the United States to be affixed.

"Done at the city of Washington, this 15th day of July, in
the year of our Lord one thousand eight hundred and sixty-
three, and of the independence of the United States of America
the eighty-eighth.   "ABRAHAM LINCOLN.

"By the President :
   "WILLIAM H. SEWARD, Secretary of State."

LETTER FROM THE PRESIDENT ON THE EMANCIPATION PROCLAMATION.

The following letter, written in August, 1863, in answer to an invitation to attend a meeting of unconditional Union men held in Illinois, gives at length the President's views at that time on his Emancipation proclamation :

"EXECUTIVE MANSION, WASHINGTON, *August* 26*th*, 1863.

" My DEAR SIR :—Your letter inviting me to attend a mass meeting of unconditional Union men, to be held at the capitol of Illinois on the third day of September, has been received. It would be very agreeable to me thus to meet my old friends at my own home ; but I cannot just now be absent from this city so long as a visit there would require. The meeting is to be of all those who maintain unconditional devotion to the Union ; and I am sure that my old political friends will thank me for tendering, as I do, the nation's gratitude to those other noble men whom no partisan malice or partisan hope can make false to the nation's life. There are those who are dissatisfied with me. To such I would say :—You desire peace, and you blame me that we do not have it. But how can we attain it ? There are but three conceivable ways :—First, to suppress the rebellion by force of arms. This I am trying to do. Are you for it ? If you are, so far we are agreed. If, you are not for it, a second way is to give up the Union. I am against this. If you are, you should say so, plainly. If you are not for force, nor yet for dissolution, there only remains some imaginable compromise. 1 do not believe that any compromise embracing the maintenance of the Union is now possible. All that I learn leads to a directly opposite belief. The strength of the rebellion is its military—its army. That army dominates all the country and all the people within its range. Any offer of any terms made by any man or men within that range in opposition to that army is simply nothing for the present, because such man or men have no power whatever to enforce their side of a compromise, if one were made with them. To illustrate : Suppose refugees from the South and peace men of the North get together in convention, and frame and proclaim a compromise embracing the restoration of the Union. In what way can that compromise be used to keep General Lee's army out of Pennsylvania ? General Meade's army can keep Lee's army out of Pennsylvania, and I think can ultimately drive it out of existence. But no paper compromise to which the controllers of General Lee's army are not agreed, can at all affect that army. In an effort at such compromise we would waste time which the enemy would improve to our disadvantage, and that would be all. A compromise, to be effective, must be made either with those who control the rebel army, or with the people, first liberated from the domination of that army by the success of our army. Now, allow me to assure you that no word or intimation from the rebel army, or from any of the men controlling it, in relation to any peace compromise, has ever come to my knowledge or belief. All charges and intimations to the contrary are deceptive and groundless. And I promise you that if any such proposition shall hereafter come, it shall not be rejected and kept secret from you. I freely acknowledge myself to be the servant of the people, according to the bond of service, the United States constitution ; and that, as such, I am responsible to them. But, to be plain. You are dissatisfied with me about the negro. Quite likely there is a difference of opinion between you and myself upon that subject. I certainly wish that all men could be free, while you, I suppose, do not. Yet I have neither adopted nor proposed any measure which is not consistent with even your view, provided you are for the Union. I suggested compensated emancipation, to which you replied that you wished not to be taxed to buy negroes. But I have not asked you to be taxed to buy negroes, except in such way as to save you from greater taxation, to save the Union exclusively by other means.

"You dislike the emancipation proclamation, and perhaps would have it retracted. You say it is unconstitutional. I think differently. I think that the constitution invests its commander-in-chief with the law of war in time of war. The most that can be said, if so much, is, that the slaves are property. Is there, has there ever been, any question that by the law of war, property, both of enemies and friends, may be taken when needed ? And is it not needed whenever taking it helps us or hurts the enemy ? Armies, the world over, destroy enemies' property when they cannot use it; and even destroy their own to keep it from the enemy. Civilized belligerents do all in their power to help themselves or hurt the enemy, except a few things regarded as barbarous or cruel. Among the exceptions are the massacre of vanquished foes and non-combatants, male and female. But the proclamation, as law, is valid or is not valid. If it is not valid it needs no retraction. If it is valid it cannot be retracted, any more than the dead can be brought to life. Some of you profess to think that its retraction would operate favorably for the Union. Why better after the retraction than before the issue ? There was more than a year and a half of trial to suppress the rebellion before the proclamation was issued, the last one hundred days of which passed under an explicit notice, that it was coming unless averted by those in revolt returning to their allegiance. The war has certainly progressed as favorably for us since the issue of the proclamation as before. I know as fully as one can know the opinions of others, that some of the commanders of our armies in the field, who have given us our most important victories, believe the emancipation policy and the aid of colored troops constitute the heaviest blows yet dealt to the rebellion, and that at least one of those important successes could not have been achieved when it was but for the aid of black soldiers. Among the commanders holding these views are some who have never had any affinity with what is called abolitionism or with 'republican party politics.'—But who hold them purely as military opinions. I submit their opinions as being entitled to some weight against the objections often urged that emancipation and arming the blacks are unwise as military measures, and were not adopted as such in good faith. You say that you will not fight to free negroes. Some of them seem to be willing to fight for you— but no matter. Fight you, then, exclusively to save the Union. I issued the proclamation on purpose to aid you in saving the Union. Whenever you shall have conquered all resistance to the Union, if I shall urge you to continue fighting, it will be an apt time then for you to declare that you will not fight to free negroes. I thought that in your struggle for the Union, to whatever extent the negroes should cease helping the enemy, to that extent it weakened the enemy in his resistance to you. Do you think differently? I thought that whatever negroes can be got to do as soldiers, leaves just so much less for white soldiers to do in saving the Union. Does it appear otherwise to you? But negroes, like other people, act upon motives. Why should they do any thing for us if we will do nothing for them? If they stake their lives for us they must be prompted by the strongest motive, even the promise of freedom. And the promise, being made, must be kept. The signs look better. The Father of Waters again goes unvexed to the sea. Thanks to the great North-west for it. Not yet wholly to them. Three hundred miles up they met New England, Empire, Keystone and Jersey, hewing their way right and left. The Sunny South, too, in more colors than one, also lent a hand. On the spot their part of the history was jotted down in black and white. The job was a great national one, and let none be banned who bore an honorable part in it; and, while those who have cleared the great river may well be proud, even that is not all. It is hard to say that any thing has been more bravely and better done than at Antietam, Murfreesboro, Gettysburg, and on many fields of less note. Nor must Uncle Sam's webfleet be forgotten. At all the waters' margins they have been present:—not only on the deep sea, the broad bay and the rapid river, but also up the narrow, muddy bayou; and wherever the ground was a little damp they have been and made their tracks. Thanks to all. For the great republic—for the principles by which it lives and keeps alive—for man's vast future—thanks to all. Peace does not appear so far distant as it did. I hope it will come soon, and come to stay : and so come as to be worth the keeping in all future time. It will then have been proved that among freemen there can be no successful appeal from the ballot to the bullet, and that they who take such appeal are sure to lose their case and pay the cost. And then there will be some black men who can remember that, with silent tongue, and clenched teeth, and steady eye, and well poised bayonet, they have helped mankind on to this great consummation; while I fear that there will be some white men unable to forget that with malignant heart and deceitful speech they have striven to hinder it. Still let us not be over sanguine of a speedy final triumph. Let us be quite sober. Let us diligently apply the means, never doubting that a just God, in His own good time, will give us the rightful result. Yours very truly,   "A. LINCOLN."

During September and October, 1863, the following proclamations were published:

SUSPENSION OF THE WRIT OF HABEAS CORPUS IN CERTAIN CASES.

"WASHINGTON, *Sept.* 15*th*, 1863.

"*Whereas*, the Constitution of the United States has ordained that 'the privilege of the writ of habeas corpus shall not be suspended, unless when in cases of rebellion or invasion the public safety may require it;' and

"*Whereas*, a rebellion was existing on the third day of March, 1863, which rebellion is still existing; and

"*Whereas*, by a statute which was approved on that day, it was enacted by the Senate and House of Representatives of the United States in Congress assembled, that during the present insurrection the President of the United States, whenever in his judgment the public safety may require, is authorized to suspend the privilege of the writ of habeas corpus in any case throughout the United States, or any part thereof; and

"*Whereas*, in the judgment of the President the public safety does require that the privilege of the said writ shall now be suspended throughout the United States in cases where, by the authority of the President of the United States, military, naval and civil officers of the United States, or any of them, hold persons under their command or in their custody, either as prisoners of war, spies, or aiders or abettors of the enemy, or officers, soldiers, or seamen enrolled, drafted or mustered or enlisted in or belonging to the land or naval forces of the United States, or as deserters therefrom, or otherwise amenable to military law, or to the Rules and Articles of War, or to the rules and regulations prescribed for the military or naval service by the authority of the President of the United States, or for resisting a draft, or for any other offence against the military or naval service:

"Now, therefore, I, Abraham Lincoln, President of the United States, do hereby proclaim and make known to all whom it may concern, that the privilege of the writ of habeas corpus is suspended throughout the United States in the several cases before mentioned, and that the suspension will continue throughout the duration of the said rebellion; or until this proclamation shall by a subsequent one, to be issued by the President of the United States, be modified and revoked. And I do hereby require all magistrates, attorneys and other civil officers within the United States, and all officers and others in the military and naval services of the United States, to take distinct notice of this suspension, and give it full effect; and all citizens of the United States to conduct and govern themselves accordingly and in conformity with the Constitution of the United States and the laws of Congress in such cases made and provided.

"In testimony whereof I have hereunto set my hand and caused the seal of the United States to be affixed, this fifteenth day of September, in the year of our Lord one thousand eight hundred and sixty-three, and of the Independence of the United States of America the eighty-eighth.

"ABRAHAM LINCOLN.

"By the President:
"WILLIAM H. SEWARD, *Secretary of State*."

NATIONAL THANKSGIVING PROCLAMATION.

"The year that is drawing towards its close has been filled with the blessings of fruitful fields and healthful skies. To these bounties, which are so constantly enjoyed that we are prone to forget the source from which they come, others have been added, which are of so extraordinary a nature, that they cannot fail to penetrate and soften even the heart which is habitually insensible to the ever watchful providence of Almighty God.

"In the midst of a civil war of unequalled magnitude and severity, which has sometimes seemed to invite and provoke the aggression of foreign States, peace has been preserved with all nations, order has been maintained, the laws have been respected and obeyed, and harmony has prevailed everywhere, except in the theatre of military conflict; while that theatre has been greatly contracted by the advancing armies and navies of the Union.

"The needful diversions of wealth and strength from the fields of peaceful industry to the national defence have not arrested the plough, the shuttle or the ship. The axe has enlarged the borders of our settlements, and the mines, as well of iron and coal as of the precious metals, have yielded even more abundantly than heretofore. Population has steadily increased, notwithstanding the waste that has been made in the camp, the siege and the battle-field; and the country, rejoicing in the consequences of augmented strength and vigor, is permitted to expect continuance of years with large increase of freedom.

"No human counsel hath devised, nor hath any mortal hand worked out these great things. They are the gracious gifts of the Most High God, who, while dealing with us in anger for our sins, hath nevertheless remembered mercy.

"It has seemed to me fit and proper that they should be solemnly, reverently and gratefully acknowledged as with one heart and voice by the whole American people; I do, therefore, invite my fellow-citizens in every part of the United States, and also those who are at sea and those who are sojourning in foreign lands, to set apart and observe the last Thursday of November next as a Day of Thanksgiving and Prayer to our beneficent Father, who dwelleth in the heavens. And I recommend to them that, while offering up the ascriptions justly due to him for such singular deliverances and blessings; they do also, with humble penitence for our national perverseness and disobedience, commend to his tender care all those who have become widows, orphans, mourners or sufferers in the lamentable civil strife in which we are unavoidably engaged, and fervently implore the interposition of the Almighty hand to heal the wounds of the nation and to restore it, as soon as may be consistent with the Divine purposes, to the full enjoyment of peace, harmony, tranquillity, and union.

"In testimony whereof I have hereunto set my hand and caused the seal of the United States to be affixed.

"Done at the city of Washington this third day of October, in the year of our Lord one thousand eight hundred and sixty-three, and of the Independence of the United States the eighty-eighth.   "ABRAHAM LINCOLN.

"By the President:
  "WILLIAM H. SEWARD, *Secretary of State.*"

We have shown, in the first pages of this volume, that the early instruction of Abraham Lincoln was of that religious character which could not fail to have a proper effect upon his after life, and it is not therefore surprising that during his Presidential career he has embraced every opportunity to publicly acknowledge the source from whence have come all the blessings the people of the Union have received during the progress of the civil war; and the unanimity with which his numerous requests for a general Thanksgiving have been acquiesced in, can but be gratifying to their author.

THREE HUNDRED THOUSAND MORE MEN CALLED FOR.

" *Whereas*, The term of service of part of the volunteer forces of the United States will expire during the coming year; and *whereas*, in addition to the men raised by the present draft, it is deemed expedient to call out three hundred thousand volunteers, to serve for three years or the war—not, however, exceeding three years.

" Now, therefore, I, Abraham Lincoln, President of the United States and Commander-in-Chief of the Army and Navy thereof, and of the militia of the several States when called into actual service, do issue this my proclamation, calling upon the Governors of the different States to raise and have enlisted into the United States service, for the various companies and regiments in the field from their respective States, their quotas of three hundred thousand men.

" I further proclaim that all the volunteers thus called out and duly enlisted shall receive advance pay, premium and bounty, as heretofore communicated to the Governors of States by the War Department, through the Provost Marshal General's office, by special letters.

" I further proclaim that all volunteers received under this call, as well as all others not heretofore credited, shall be duly credited and deducted from the quotas established for the next draft.

" I further proclaim that, if any State shall fail to raise the quota assigned to it by the War Department under this call; then a draft for the deficiency in said quota shall be made in said State, or on the districts of said State, for their due proportion of said quota, and the said draft shall commence on the fifth day of January, 1864.

"And I further proclaim that nothing in this proclamation shall interfere with existing orders, or with those which may be issued for the present draft in the States where it is now in progress or where it has not yet been commenced.

" The quotas of the States and districts will be assigned by the War Department, through the Provost Marshal General's office, due regard being had for the men heretofore furnished, whether by volunteering or drafting, and the recruiting will be conducted in accordance with such instructions as have been or may be issued by that department.

" In issuing this proclamation I address myself not only to the Governors of the several States, but also to the good and loyal people thereof, invoking them to lend their cheerful, willing and effective aid to the measures thus adopted, with a view to reinforce our victorious armies now in the field and bring our needful military operations to a prosperous end, thus closing forever the fountains of sedition and civil war.

"In witness whereof I have hereunto set my hand and caused the seal of the United States to be affixed.

"Done at the city of Washington, this seventeenth day of October, in the year of our Lord one thousand eight hundred and sixty-three, and of the independence of the United States the eighty-eighth.   "ABRAHAM LINCOLN.

"By the President:
    "WM. H. SEWARD, *Secretary of State.*"

THE PRESIDENT'S DEDICATORY ADDRESS AT GETTYSBURG.

On the nineteenth of November, 1863, the President participated in the solemn and imposing ceremonies incident to the consecration of the National Cemetery at Gettysburg. Arriving in the town on the previous evening, he was the recipient of a delightful serenade, which he acknowledged in a brief speech. On the next day he delivered the following beautiful Dedicatory Address :

"Fourscore and seven years ago our fathers brought forth upon this continent a new nation, conceived in Liberty, and dedicated to the proposition that all men are created equal. Now we are engaged in a great civil war, testing whether that nation, or any nation so conceived and so dedicated, can long endure. We are met on a great battle-field of that war. We are met to dedicate a portion of it as the final resting-place of those who here gave their lives that nation might live. It is altogether fitting and proper that we should do this.

"But in a larger sense we cannot dedicate, we cannot consecrate, we cannot hallow this ground. The brave men, living and dead, who struggled here, have consecrated it far above our power to add or detract. The world will little note, nor long remember what we say here, but it can never forget what they did here. It is for us, the living, rather to be dedicated here to the unfinished work that they have thus far so nobly carried on. It is rather for us to be here dedicated to the great task remaining before us—that from these honored dead we take increased devotion to the cause for which they here gave the last full measure of devotion,—that we here highly resolve that the dead shall not have died in vain, that the nation shall, under God, have a new birth of freedom, and that the government of the people, by the people, and for the people, shall not perish from the earth."

THANKSGIVING PROCLAMATION.

On the seventh of December, 1863, the following recommendation was made to the people of the country :

" Executive Mansion, Washington, *Dec. 7th*, 1863.—Reliable information being received that the insurgent force is retreating from East Tennessee, under circumstances rendering it probable that the Union forces cannot hereafter be dislodged from that important position, and esteeming this to be of high National consequence, I recommend that all loyal people do, on the receipt of this, informally assemble at their places of worship, and render special homage and gratitude to Almighty God for this great advancement of the National cause.   "A. Lincoln."

THE ANNUAL MESSAGE OF 1863—FULL PARDON OFFERED TO THE REBELS.

On the ninth of December, 1863, President Lincoln sent into Congress his Annual Message, and never were his wisdom and moderation more satisfactorily exhibited than in this document. His review of our foreign relations and the operations of the various departments of the Government was comprehensive and clear, while on the subject of the rebellion he re-affirmed all that he had written in his previous messages, and in referring to the success which had attended the proclamation of emancipation, he said : " While I remain in my present position, I shall not attempt to retract or modify the emancipation proclamation ; nor shall I return to slavery any person who is free by the terms of that proclamation, or by any of the acts of Congress."

Accompanying the Message, was a proclamation offering for the acceptance of the traitors a fair and practicable mode, by which they might return to their allegiance, and once again become loyal citizens. It was worded as follows :

" *Whereas*, In and by the Constitution of the United States, it is provided that the President ' shall have power to grant reprieves and pardons for offences against the United States, except in cases of impeachment ;" and

" *Whereas*, A rebellion now exists whereby the loyal State governments of several States have for a long time been subverted, and many persons have committed and are now guilty of treason against the United States ; and

" *Whereas*, With reference to said rebellion and treason, laws have been enacted by Congress, declaring forfeitures and confiscations of property and liberation of slaves, all upon terms and conditions therein stated, and also declaring that the President was thereby authorized at any time thereafter, by proclamation, to extend to persons who may have participated in the existing rebellion in any State, or part thereof, pardon and amnesty, with such exceptions and at such times and on such conditions as he may deem expedient for the public welfare; and

"*Whereas*, The Congressional declaration for limited and conditional pardon accords with well-established judicial exposition of the pardoning power; and

"*Whereas*, With reference to said rebellion, the President of the United States has issued several proclamations, with provisions in regard to the liberation of slaves; and

"*Whereas*, It is now desired by some persons heretofore engaged in said rebellion to resume their allegiance to the United States, and to re-inaugurate loyal State governments within and for their respective States;

"Therefore, I, Abraham Lincoln, President of the United States, do proclaim, declare, and make known to all persons who have, directly or by implication, participated in the existing rebellion, except as hereinafter excepted, that a FULL PARDON is hereby granted to them and each of them, with restoration of all rights of property, except as to slaves, and in property cases where rights of third parties shall have intervened, and upon the condition that every such person shall take and subscribe an oath, and thenceforward keep and maintain said oath inviolate; and which oath shall be registered for permanent preservation, and shall be of the tenor and effect following, to wit:

"'I ——, do solemnly swear, in presence of Almighty God, that I will henceforth faithfully support, protect, and defend the Constitution of the United States, and the Union of the States thereunder; and that I will, in like manner, abide by and faithfully support all acts of Congress passed during the existing rebellion with reference to slaves, so long and so far as not repealed, modified, or held void by Congress, or by decision of the Supreme Court; and that I will, in like manner, abide by and faithfully support all proclamations of the President made during the existing rebellion having reference to slaves, so long and so far as not modified or declared void by decision of the Supreme Court. So help me God.'

"The persons excepted from the benefits of the foregoing provisions are all who are or shall have been civil or diplomatic officers or agents of the so-called Confederate Government; all who have left judicial stations under the United States to aid the rebellion; all who are or shall have been military or naval officers of said Confederate Government above the rank of Colonel in the army or of Lieutenant in the navy; all who left seats in the United States Congress to aid the rebellion; all who resigned their commissions in the army or navy of the United

States, and afterwards aided the rebellion, and all who have engaged in any way, in treating colored persons or white persons, in charge of such, otherwise than lawfully, as prisoners of war, and which persons may be found in the United States service, as soldiers, seamen, or in any other capacity.

"And I do further proclaim, declare, and make known, that whenever, in any of the States of Arkansas, Texas, Louisiana, Mississippi, Tennessee, Alabama, Georgia, Florida, South Carolina, and North Carolina, a number of persons, not less than one-tenth in number of the votes cast in such State at the Presidential election of the year of our Lord 1860, each having taken the oath aforesaid and not having since violated it, and being a qualified voter by the election law of the State existing immediately before the so-called act of secession, and excluding all others, shall re-establish a State government which shall be Republican, and in nowise contravening said oath, such shall be recognized as the true government of the State, and the State shall receive thereunder the benefits of the constitutional provision, which declares that ' the United States shall guarantee to every State in this Union a Republican form of government, and shall protect each of them against invasion ; and, on application of the Legislature, or the executive (when the Legislature cannot be convened), against domestic violence.'

"And I do further proclaim, declare, and make known, that any provision which may be adopted by such State Government in relation to the freed people of such State, which shall recognize and declare their permanent freedom, provide for their education, and which may yet be consistent, as a temporary arrangement, with their present condition as a laboring, landless, and homeless class, will not be objected to by the National Executive. And it is suggested as not improper, that, in constructing a loyal State government in any State, the name of the State, the boundary, the subdivisions, the Constitution, and the general code of laws, as before the rebellion, be maintained, subject only to the modifications made necessary by the conditions hereinbefore stated, and such ·others, if any, not contravening said conditions, and which may be deemed expedient by those framing the new State Government.

" 'To avoid misunderstanding, it may be proper to say that this proclamation, so far as it relates to State Governments, has no reference to States wherein loyal State Governments have all the while been maintained. And for the same reason, it may be proper to further say, that whether members sent to Congress from any State shall be admitted to seats constitutionally, rests exclusively with the respective Houses, and not to any extent with the Executive. And still further, that this proclamation is intended to present the people of the States wherein the National authority has been suspended, and loyal State Governments have been subverted, a mode in and by which the National authority and loyal State Governments may be re-established within said States, or in any of them; and, while the mode presented is the best the Executive can suggest, with his present impressions, it must not be understood that no other possible mode would be acceptable.

"Given under my hand at the City of Washington, the eighth day of December, A. D. one thousand eight hundred and sixty-three, and of the Independence of the United States of America the eighty-eighth.

"By the President: "ABRAHAM LINCOLN.
"WM. H. SEWARD, *Secretary of State.*"

CALLS MADE FOR SEVEN HUNDRED THOUSAND MEN.

Since the beginning of the present year, 1864, two orders have been issued by the President, with a view of augmenting the armies of the Union to correspond with the requirements of the service. The first, dated February first, is as follows:

"EXECUTIVE MANSION, WASHINGTON, *February 1st*, 1864.— Ordered, that a draft for five hundred thousand men, to serve three years or during the war, be made on the tenth of March next, for the military service of the United States, crediting and deducting therefrom so many as have been enlisted or drafted into the service prior to the first day of March, and not heretofore credited.

"(Signed)   . "ABRAHAM LINCOLN."

The other, dated March fourteenth, was worded as follows:

"EXECUTIVE MANSION, WASHINGTON, *March 14th*, 1864.—In order to supply the force required to be drafted for the navy, and to provide an adequate reserve force for all contingencies, in addition to the five hundred thousand men called for February 1st, 1864, the call is hereby made, and a draft ordered for two hundred thousand men, for the military service of the army, navy, and marine corps of the United States. The proportionate quotas for the different wards, towns, townships, precincts, election districts, or counties will be made known through the Provost Marshal General's bureau, and account will be taken of the credits and deficiencies on former quotas. The 15th day of April, 1864, is designated as the time up to which the numbers required in each ward of a city, town, etc., may be raised by voluntary enlistment; and drafts will be made in each ward of a city, town, etc., which shall not have filled the quota assigned to it within the time designated for the number required to fill the said quotas. The draft will be commenced as soon after the 15th of April as practicable. The Government bounties, as now paid, will be continued until April 15th, 1864, at which time the additional bounties cease. On and after that date, one hundred dollars only will be paid, as provided by the act approved July 22nd, 1861. "ABRAHAM LINCOLN.

" Official.   " E. D. TOWNSEND, *A. A. G.* "

EXPLANATORY PROCLAMATION.

On the twenty-sixth of March, 1864, the following proclamation, explanatory of the one issued on the eighth of December, 1863, was published :

" *Whereas*, It has become necessary to define the cases in which insurgent enemies are entitled to the benefits of the Proclamation of the President of the United States, which was made on the 8th day of December, 1863, and the manner in which they shall proceed to avail themselves of these benefits ;

"*And whereas*, The object of that proclamation were to suppress the insurrection and to restore the authority of the United States ;

"*And whereas*, The amnesty therein proposed by the President was offered with reference to these objects alone ;

" Now, therefore, I, Abraham Lincoln, President of the United States, do hereby proclaim and declare that the said proclamation does not apply to the cases of persons who, at the time when they seek to obtain the benefits thereof, by taking the oath thereby prescribed, are in military, naval or civil confinement or custody, or under bonds or on parole of the civil, military or naval authorities or agents of the United States, as prisoners of war, or persons detained for offences of any kind, either before or after conviction ; and that on the contrary, it does apply only to those persons who, being at large and free from any arrest, confinement or duress, shall voluntarily come forward and take the said oath, with the purpose of restoring peace and establishing the national authority.

" Prisoners excluded from the amnesty offered in the said proclamation may apply to the President for clemency, like all other offenders, and their application will receive due consideration.

" I do further declare and proclaim that the oath prescribed in the aforesaid proclamation of the 8th of December, 1863, may be taken and subscribed to before any commanding officer, civil, military or naval, in the service of the United States, or any civil or military officer of a State or territory not in insurrection, who, by the laws thereof, may be qualified for administering oaths.

"All officers who receive such oaths are hereby authorized to give certificates thereon to the persons respectively by whom they are made, and such officers are hereby required to transmit the original records of such oaths at as early a day as may be convenient to the Department of State, where they will be deposited and remain in the archives of the government.

"The Secretary of State will keep a register thereof, and will, on application, in proper cases, issue certificates of such records in the customary form of official certificates.

"In testimony whereof, I have hereunto set my hand, and caused the seal of the United States to be affixed.

"Done at the City of Washington, the twenty-sixth day of March, in the year of our Lord one thousand eight hundred and sixty-four, and of the Independence of the United States the eighty-eighth.

"By the President: "ABRAHAM LINCOLN.
" WM. H. SEWARD, *Secretary of State.*"

REVIEW OF THE PRESIDENT'S POLICY.

In the number of the *North American Review* for January, 1864, a most able article was published, reviewing the policy of President Lincoln, and from it we make the following extracts:

"'Bare is back,' says the Norse proverb, 'without brother behind it;' and this is, by analogy, true of an elective magistracy. The hereditary ruler in any critical emergency may reckon on the inexhaustible resources of *prestige*, of sentiment, of superstition, of dependent interest, while the new man must slowly and painfully create all these out of the unwilling material around him, by superiority of character, by patient singleness of purpose, by sagacious presentiment of popular tendencies and instinctive sympathy with the national character. Mr. Lincoln's task was one of peculiar and exceptional difficulty. Long habit had accustomed the American people to the notion of a party in power, and of a President as its creature and organ, while the more vital fact, that the executive for the time being represents the abstract idea of government as a permanent principle superior to all party and all private interest, had gradually become unfamiliar. They had so long seen the public policy more or less

directed by views of party, and often even of personal advantage, as to be ready to suspect the motives of a chief
magistrate compelled, for the first time in our history, to
feel himself the head and hand of a great nation, and to act
upon the fundamental maxim, laid down by all publicists,
that the first duty of a government is to defend and maintain its own existence.   Accordingly, a powerful weapon
seemed to be put into the hands of the opposition by the
necessity under which the administration found itself of
applying this old truth to new relations.   They were not
slow in turning it to use, but the patriotism and common-
sense of the people were more than a match for any
sophistry of mere party.   The radical mistake of the leaders of the opposition was in forgetting that they had a
country, and expecting a similar obliviousness on the part
of the people.   In the undisturbed possession of office for
so many years, they had come to consider the government
as a kind of public Gift Enterprise conducted by themselves, and whose profits were nominally to be shared
among the holders of their tickets, though all the prizes
had a trick of falling to the lot of the managers.   Amid
the tumult of war, when the life of the nation was at stake,
when the principles of despotism and freedom were grap- .
pling in deadly conflict, they had no higher conception of
the crisis than such as would serve the purpose of a con-
tested election; no thought but of advertising the tickets
for the next drawing of that private speculation which
they miscalled the Democratic party.   But they were too
little in sympathy with the American people to understand them, or the motives by which they were governed.
It became more and more clear that, in embarrassing the
administration, their design was to cripple the country;
that, by a strict construction of the Constitution, they
meant nothing more than the locking up of the only
arsenal whence effective arms could be drawn to defend the
nation.   Fortunately, insincerity by its very nature, by
10

its necessary want of conviction, must ere long betray itself by its inconsistencies.   It was hard to believe that men had any real horror of sectional war, who were busy in fomenting jealousies between East and West; that they could be in favor of a war for the Union as it was, who were for accepting the violent amendments of Rebellion; that they could be heartily opposed to insurrection in the South, who threatened government with forcible resistance in the North; or that they were humanely anxious to stay the effusion of blood, who did not scruple to stir up the mob of our chief city to murder and arson, and to compliment the patriotism of assassins with arms in their hands. Believers, if they believed any thing, in the divine right of Sham, they brought the petty engineering of the caucus to cope with the resistless march of events, and hoped to stay the steady drift of the nation's purpose, always setting deeper and stronger in one direction, with the scoopnets that had served their turn so well in dipping fish from the turbid eddies of politics.   They have given an example of the shortest and easiest way of reducing a great party to an inconsiderable faction.

"The change which three years have brought about, is too remarkable to be passed over without comment—too weighty in its lesson not to be laid to heart.   Never did a President enter upon office with less means at his command, outside his own strength of heart and steadiness of understanding, for inspiring confidence in the people, and so winning it for himself, than Mr. Lincoln.   All that was known of him was that he was a good stump-speaker, nominated for his *availability*—that is, because he had no history—and chosen by a party with whose more extreme opinions he was not in sympathy.   It might well be feared that a man past fifty, against whom the ingenuity of hostile partisans could rake up no accusation, must be lacking in manliness of character, in decision of principle, in strength of will,—that a man who was at best only the representative of a party, and who yet did not fairly represent even that—would fail of political, much more of popular support. And certainly no one ever entered upon office with so few resources of power in the past, and so many materials of weakness in the present, as Mr. Lincoln. Even in that half of the Union which acknowledged him as President, there was a large, and at that time dangerous minority, that hardly admitted his claim to the office, and even in the party that elected him there was also a large minority that suspected him of being secretly a communicant with the church of Laodicea. All that he did was sure to be virulently attacked as ultra by one side; all that he left undone, to be stigmatized as proof of lukewarmness and backsliding by the other. Meanwhile he was to carry on a truly colossal war by means of both ; he was to disengage the country from diplomatic entanglements of unprecedented peril undisturbed by the help or the hinderance of either, and to win from the crowning dangers of his administration, in the confidence of the people, the means of his safety and their own. He has contrived to do it, and perhaps none of our Presidents since Washington has stood so firm in the confidence of the people as he does after three years of stormy administration.

"Mr. Lincoln's policy was a tentative one, and rightly so. He laid down no programme which must compel him to be either inconsistent or unwise—no cast-iron theorem to which circumstances must be fitted as they rose, or else be useless to his ends. He seemed to have chosen Mazarin's motto, *Le temps et moi*. The *moi*, to be sure, was not very prominent at first; but it has grown more and more so, till the world is beginning to be persuaded that it stands for a character of marked individuality and capacity for affairs. Time was his prime-minister, and, we began to think at one period, his general-in-chief also. At first he was so slow that he tired out all those who see no evidence of progress but in blowing up the engine; then he was so fast, that he took the breath away from those who think there is no getting on safely while there is a spark of fire under the boilers. God is the only being who has time enough; but a prudent man, who knows how to seize occasion, can commonly make a shift to find as much as he needs. Mr. Lincoln, as it seems to us in reviewing his career, though we have sometimes in our impatience thought otherwise, has always waited, as a wise man should, till the right moment brought up all his reserves. *Semper nocuit differre paratis* is a sound axiom, but the really efficacious man will also be sure to know when he is *not* ready, and be firm against all persuasion and reproach till he is.

"One would be apt to think, from some of the criticisms made on Mr. Lincoln's course by those who mainly agree with him in principle, that the chief object of a statesman should be rather to proclaim his adhesion to certain doctrines than to achieve their triumph by quietly accomplishing his ends. In our opinion, there is no more unsafe politician than a conscientiously rigid *doctrinaire*, nothing more sure to end in disaster than a theoretic scheme of policy that admits of no pliability for contingencies. True, there is a popular image of an impossible He, in whose plastic hands the submissive destinies of mankind become as wax, and to whose commanding necessity the toughest facts yield with the graceful pliancy of fiction; but in real life we commonly find that the men who control circumstances, as it is called, are those who have learned to allow for the influence of their eddies, and have the nerve to turn them to account at the happy instant. Mr. Lincoln's perilous task has been to carry a rather shackly raft through the rapids, making fast the unrulier logs as he could snatch opportunity; and the country is to be congratulated that he did not think it his duty to run straight at all hazards, but cautiously to assure himself with his setting-pole where the main current was, and keep steadily to that. He is still in wild water, but we have faith that his skill and sureness of eye will bring him out right at last.

" A curious, and, as we think, not inapt parallel might be drawn between Mr. Lincoln and one of the most striking figures in modern history—Henry IV. of France. The career of the latter may be more picturesque, as that of a daring captain always is ; but, in all its vicissitudes, there is nothing more romantic than that sudden change, as by a rub of Aladdin's lamp, from the attorney's office in a country town of Illinois to the helm of a great nation in times like these. The analogy between the characters and circumstances of the two men is, in many respects, singularly close. Succeeding to a rebellion rather than a crown, Henry's chief material dependence was the Huguenot party, whose doctrines sat upon him with a looseness distasteful certainly, if not suspicious, to the more fanatical among them. King only in name over the greater part of France, and with his capital barred against him, it yet gradually became clear to the more far-seeing even of the Catholic party, that he was the only centre of order and legitimate authority round which France could reorganize itself. While preachers who held the divine right of kings made the churches of Paris ring with declamations in favor of democracy rather than submit to the heretic dog of a Béarnois—much as our *soi-disant* Democrats have lately been preaching the divine right of slavery, and denouncing the heresies of the Declaration of Independence—Henry bore both parties in hand till he was convinced that only one course of action could possibly combine his own interests and those of France

Meanwhile the Protestants believed somewhat doubtfully that he was theirs, the Catholics hoped somewhat doubtfully that he would be theirs, and Henry himself turned aside remonstrance, advice, and curiosity alike with a jest or a proverb, (if a little *high*, he liked them none the worse,) joking continually, as his manner was. We have seen Mr. Lincoln contemptuously compared to Sancho Panza by persons incapable of appreciating one of the deepest pieces of wisdom in the profoundest romance ever written—namely, that, while Don Quixote was incomparable in theoretic and ideal statesmanship, Sancho, with his stock of proverbs, the ready-money of human experience, made the best possible practical governor. Henry IV. was as full of wise saws and modern instances as Mr. Lincoln, but beneath all this was the thoughtful, practical, humane, and thoroughly earnest man, around whom the fragments of France were to gather themselves till she took her place again as a planet of the first magnitude in the European system. In one respect Mr. Lincoln was more fortunate than Henry. However some may think him wanting in zeal, the most fanatical can find no taint of apostasy in any measure of his, nor can the most bitter charge him with being influenced by motives of personal interest. The leading distinction between the policies of the two is one of circumstances. Henry went over to the nation; Mr. Lincoln has steadily drawn the nation over to him. One left a united France; the other, we hope and believe, will leave a re-united America. We leave our readers to trace the further points of difference and resemblance for themselves, merely suggesting a general similarity which has often occurred to us. One only point of melancholy interest we will allow ourselves to touch upon. That Mr. Lincoln is not handsome nor elegant, we learn from certain English tourists who would consider similar revelations in regard to Queen Victoria as thoroughly American in their want of *bienséance*.   It is no concern of ours, nor does it affect his fitness for the high place he so worthily occupies; but he is certainly as fortunate as Henry in the matter of good looks, if we may trust contemporary evidence.   Mr. Lincoln has also been reproached with Americanism by some not unfriendly British critics; but, with all deference, we cannot say that we like him any the worse for it, or see in it any reason why he should govern Americans the less wisely.

"The most perplexing complications that Mr. Lincoln's government has had to deal with have been the danger of rupture with the two leading commercial countries of Europe, and the treatment of the slavery question.   In regard to the former, the peril may be considered as nearly past, and the latter has been withdrawing steadily, ever since the war began, from the noisy debating-ground of faction to the quieter region of practical solution by convincingness of facts and consequent advance of opinion which we are content to call Fate.

"Even so long ago as when Mr. Lincoln, not yet convinced of the danger and magnitude of the crisis, was endeavoring to persuade himself of Union majorities at the South, and to carry on a war that was half peace in the hope of a peace that would have been all war,—while he was still enforcing the Fugitive Slave Law, under some theory that Secession, however it might absolve States from their obligations, could not escheat them of their claims under the Constitution, and that slaveholders in rebellion had alone among mortals the privilege of having their cake and eating it at the same time,—the enemies of free government were striving to persuade the people that the war was an Abolition crusade.   To rebel without reason was proclaimed as one of the rights of man, while it was carefully kept out of sight that to suppress rebellion is the first duty of government.   All the evils

that have come upon the country have been attributed to
the Abolitionists, though it is hard to see how any party
can become permanently powerful except in one of two
ways,—either by the greater truth of its principles, or the
extravagance of the party opposed to it. To fancy the
ship of state, riding safe at her constitutional moorings,
suddenly engulfed by a huge kraken of Abolitionism,
rising from unknown depths and grasping it with slimy
tentacles, is to look at the natural history of the matter
with the eyes of Pontoppidan. To believe that the
leaders in the Southern treason feared any danger from
Abolitionism, would be to deny them ordinary intelligence, though there can be little doubt that they made
use of it to stir the passions and excite the fears of their
deluded accomplices. They rebelled, not because they
thought slavery weak, but because they believed it strong
enough, not to overthrow the government, but to get possession of it; for it becomes daily clearer that they used
rebellion only as a means of revolution, and if they got
revolution, though not in the shape they looked for, is the
American people to save them from its consequences at
the cost of its own existence? The election of Mr. Lincoln, which it was clearly in their power to prevent had
they wished, was the occasion merely, and not the cause,
of their revolt. Abolitionism, till within a year or two,
was the despised heresy of a few earnest persons, without
political weight enough to carry the election of a parish
constable; and their cardinal principle was disunion, because they were convinced that within the Union the
position of slavery was impregnable. In spite of the
proverb, great effects do not follow from small causes,—
that is, disproportionately small,—but from adequate
causes acting under certain required conditions. To contrast the size of the oak with that of the parent acorn, as
if the poor seed had paid all costs from its slender strong

box, may serve for a child's wonder ; but the real miracle
lies in that divine league which bound all the forces of
nature to the service of the tiny germ in fulfilling its
destiny. Every thing has been at work for the past ten
years in the cause of antislavery, but Garrison and
Phillips have been far less successful propagandists than
the slaveholders themselves, with the constantly-growing
arrogance of their pretensions and encroachments. They
have forced the question upon the attention of every voter
in the Free States, by defiantly putting freedom and democracy on the defensive. But, even after the Kansas
outrages, there was no wide-spread desire on the part of
the North to commit aggressions, though there was a
growing determination to resist them. The popular
unanimity in favor of the war three years ago was but in
small measure the result of antislavery sentiment, far less
of any zeal for abolition. But every month of the war,
every movement of the allies of slavery in the Free
States, has been making Abolitionists by the thousands.
The masses of any people, however intelligent, are very
little moved by abstract principles of humanity and justice, until those principles are interpreted for them by the
stinging commentary of some infringement upon their own
rights, and then their instincts and passions, once aroused,
do indeed derive an incalculable reinforcement of impulse
and intensity from those higher ideas, those sublime tra-
ditions, which have no motive political force till they are
allied with a sense of immediate personal wrong or im-
minent peril. Then at last the stars in their courses begin to fight against Sisera. Had any one doubted before
that the rights of human nature are unitary, that oppression is of one hue the world over, no matter what the
color of the oppressed,—had any one failed to see what
the real essence of the contest was,—the efforts of the advocates of slavery among ourselves to throw discredit upon

the fundamental axioms of the Declaration of Independence and the radical doctrines of Christianity, could not fail to sharpen his eyes. This quarrel, it is plain, is not between Northern fanaticism and Southern institutions, but between downright slavery and upright freedom, between despotism and democracy, between the Old World and the New.

"The progress of three years has outstripped the expectation of the most sanguine, and that of our arms, great as it undoubtedly is, is trifling in comparison with the advance of opinion. The great strength of slavery was a superstition, which is fast losing its hold on the public mind. When it was first proposed to raise negro regiments, there were many even patriotic men who felt as the West Saxons did at seeing their high priest hurl his lance against the temple of their idol. They were sure something terrible, they knew not what, would follow. But the earth stood firm, the heavens gave no sign, and presently they joined in making a bonfire of their bugbear. That we should employ the material of the rebellion for its own destruction, seems now the merest truism. In the same way men's minds are growing wonted to the thought of emancipation; and great as are the difficulties which must necessarily accompany and follow so vast a measure, we have no doubt that they will be successfully overcome. The point of interest and importance is, that the feeling of our country in regard to slavery is no whim of sentiment, but a settled conviction, and that the tendency of opinion is unmistakably and irrevocably in one direction, no less in the Border Slave States than in the Free. The chances of the war, which at one time seemed against us, are now greatly in our favor. The nation is more thoroughly united against any shameful or illusory peace than it ever was on any other question, and the very extent of the territory to be subdued, which was the most serious cause of

misgiving, is no longer an element of strength, but of disintegration, to the conspiracy. The Rebel leaders can
make no concessions ; the country is unanimously resolved
that the war shall be prosecuted, at whatever cost ; and if
the war go on, will it leave slavery with any formidable
strength in the South ? and without that, need there be any
fear of effective opposition in the North ?

" While every day was bringing the people nearer to the
conclusion which all thinking men saw to be inevitable
from the beginning, it was wise in Mr. Lincoln to leave
the shaping of his policy to events. In this country,
where the rough and ready understanding of the people
is sure at last to be the controlling power, a profound
common-sense is the best genius for statesmanship.
Hitherto the wisdom of the President's measures has
been justified by the fact that they have always resulted
in more firmly uniting public opinion. It is a curious
comment on the sincerity of political professions, that the
party calling itself Democratic should have been the last
to recognize the real movement and tendency of the
popular mind. The same gentlemen who two years ago
were introducing resolutions in Congress against coercion,
are introducing them now in favor of the war, but against
subjugation. Next year they may be in favor of emancipation, but against abolition. It does not seem to have
occurred to them that the one point of difference between
a civil and a foreign war is, that in the former, one of the
parties must by the very nature of the case be put down,
and the other left in possession of the government. Unless the country is to be divided, no compromise is possible,
and, if one side must yield, shall it be the nation or the
conspirators ? A government may make, and any wise
government would make, concessions to men who have
risen against real grievances ; but to make them in favor
of a rebellion that had no juster cause than the personal

ambition of a few bad men, would be to abdicate. Southern politicians, however, have always been so dexterous in drawing nice distinctions, that they may find some consolation inappreciable by obtuser minds in being coerced instead of subjugated.

"If Mr. Lincoln continue to act with the firmness and prudence which have hitherto distinguished him, we think he has little to fear from the efforts of the opposition. Men without sincere convictions are hardly likely to have a well-defined and settled policy, and the blunders they have hitherto committed must make them cautious. If their personal hostility to the President be unabated, we may safely count on their leniency to the opinion of majorities, and the drift of public sentiment is too strong to be mistaken. They have at last discovered that there is such a thing as Country, which has a meaning for men's minds and a hold upon their hearts; they may make the further discovery, that this is a revolution that has been forced on us, and not merely a civil war. In any event, an opposition is a wholesome thing; and we are only sorry that this is not a more wholesome opposition.

"We believe it is the general judgment of the country on the acts of the present administration, that they have been, in the main, judicious and well-timed. The only doubt about some of them seems to be as to their constitutionality. It has been sometimes objected to our form of government, that it was faulty in having a written constitution which could not adapt itself to the needs of the time as they arose. But we think it rather a theoretic than a practical objection; for in point of fact there has been hardly a leading measure of any administration that has not been attacked as unconstitutional, and which was not carried nevertheless. Purchase of Louisiana, Embargo, Removal of the Deposits, Annexation of Texas, not to speak of others less important,—on the unconstitutionality of all these, powerful parties have appealed to the country, and invariably the decision has been against them. The will of the people for the time being has always carried it. In the present instance, we purposely refrain from any allusion to the moral aspects of the question. We prefer to leave the issue to experience and common-sense. Has any sane man ever doubted on which side the chances were in this contest? Can any sane man who has watched the steady advances of opinion, forced onward slowly by the immitigable logic of facts, doubt what the decision of the people will be in this matter? The Southern conspirators have played a desperate stake, and, if they had won, would have bent the whole policy of the country to the interests of slavery. Filibustering would have been nationalized, and the slave-trade re-established as the most beneficent form of missionary enterprise. But if they lose? They have, of their own choice, put the chance into our hands of making this continent the empire of a great homogeneous population, substantially one in race, language, and religion,—the most prosperous and powerful of nations. Is there a doubt what the decision of a victorious people will be? If we were base enough to decline the great commission which Destiny lays on us, should we not deserve to be ranked with those dastards whom the stern Florentine condemns as hateful alike to God and God's enemies?

"We would not be understood as speaking lightly of the respect due to constitutional forms, all the more essential under a government like ours and in times like these. But where undue respect for the form will lose us the substance, and where the substance, as in this case, is nothing less than the country itself, to be over-scrupulous would be unwise. Who are most tender in their solicitude that we keep sacred the letter of the law, in order that its spirit may not keep us alive? Mr. Jefferson Davis and those who, in the Free States, would have been his associates, but must content themselves with being his political *guerilleros*. If Davis had succeeded, would he have had any scruples of constitutional delicacy? And if he has not succeeded, is it not mainly owing to measures which his disappointed partisans denounce as unconstitutional?

"We cannot bring ourselves to think that Mr. Lincoln has done any thing that would furnish a precedent dangerous to our liberties, or in any way overstepped the just limits of his constitutional discretion. If his course has been unusual, it was because the danger was equally so. It cannot be so truly said that he has strained his prerogative, as that the imperious necessity has exercised its own. Surely the framers of the Constitution never dreamed that they were making a strait waistcoat, in which the nation was to lie helpless while traitors were left free to do their will. In times like these, men seldom settle precisely the principles on which they *shall* act, but rather adjust those on which they *have* acted to the lines of precedent as well as they can after the event. This is what the English Parliament did in the Act of Settlement. Congress, after all, will only be called on for the official draft of an enactment, the terms of which have been already decided by agencies beyond their control. Even while they are debating, the current is sweeping them onward toward new relations of policy. At worst, a new precedent is pretty sure of pardon, if it successfully meet a new occasion. It is a harmless pleasantry to call Mr. Lincoln 'Abraham the First,'—we remember when a similar title was applied to President Jackson; and it will not be easy, we suspect, to persuade a people who have more liberty than they know what to do with, that they are the victims of despotic tyranny.

"Mr. Lincoln probably thought it more convenient, to say the least, to have a country left without a constitution, than a constitution without a country. We have no doubt we shall save both; for if we take care of the one, the other will take care of itself. Sensible men, and it is the sensible men in any country who at last shape its policy, will be apt to doubt whether it is true conservatism, after the fire is got under, to insist on keeping up the flaw in the chimney by which it made its way into the house. Radicalism may be a very dangerous thing, and so is calomel, but not when it is the only means of saving the life of the patient. Names are of great influence in ordinary times, when they are backed by the *vis inertiæ* of life-long prejudice, but they have little power in comparison with a sense of interest; and though, in peaceful times, it may be highly respectable to be conservative merely for the sake of being so, though without very clear notions of any thing in particular to be conserved, what we want now is the prompt decision that will not hesitate between the bale of silk and the ship when a leak is to be stopped. If we succeed in saving the great landmarks of freedom, there will be no difficulty in settling our constitutional boundaries again. We have no sympathy to spare for the pretended anxieties of men who, only two years gone, were willing that Jefferson Davis should break all the ten commandments together, and would now impeach Mr. Lincoln for a scratch on the surface of the tables where they are engraved."

As soon as the publication was received and read by the President, he sent to the publishers the following letter:

"EXECUTIVE MANSION, WASHINGTON, *January 16th*, 1864. "*Messrs. Crosby & Nichols:*

"GENTLEMEN: The number for this month and year of the *North American Review* was duly received and for which please accept my thanks. Of course I am not the most impartial

judge ; yet, with due allowance for this, I venture to hope that
the article entitled 'The President's Policy' will be of value
to the country. I fear I am not quite worthy of all which is
therein kindly said of me personally.

" The sentence of twelve lines, commencing at the top of page
252, (which in this book is on page 165,) I could wish to be not
exactly as it is. In what is there expressed the writer has not
correctly understood me. I have never had a theory that secession could absolve States or people from their obligations. Precisely the contrary is asserted in the inaugural address ; and it
was because of my belief in the continuation of those *obligations*
that I was puzzled, for a time, as to denying the legal *rights* of
those citizens who remained individually innocent of treason or
rebellion. But I mean no more now than to merely call attention to this point.

" Yours respectfully,

"A. LINCOLN."

The sentence referred to by Mr. Lincoln, is as follows :

" Even so long ago as when Mr. Lincoln, not yet convinced of the danger and magnitude of the crisis, was
endeavoring to persuade himself of Union majorities at
the South, and to carry on a war that was half peace, in
the hope of a peace that would have been all war, while
he was still enforcing the Fugitive Slave law, under
some theory that secession, however it might absolve
States from their obligations, could not escheat them of
their claims under the constitution, and that slaveholders
in rebellion had alone among mortals, the privilege of
having their cake and eating it at the same time,—the
enemies of free government were striving to persuade the
people that the war was an abolition crusade. To rebel
without reason was proclaimed as one of the rights of man,
while it was carefully kept out of sight that to suppress
rebellion is the first duty of government."

RECENT ADDRESSES OF MR. LINCOLN.

On the night of the eighteenth of March, 1864, at the
close of the successful fair held in the Patent Office at
Washington, Mr. Lincoln spoke as follows :

"*Ladies and Gentlemen :*—I appear, to say but a word. This

extraordinary war in which we are engaged falls heavily upon all classes of people, but the most heavily upon the soldier. For it has been said, all that a man hath will he give for his life ; and, while all contribute of their substance, the soldier puts his life at stake, and often yields it up in his country's cause. The highest merit, then, is due to the soldier.

" In this extraordinary war, extraordinary developments have manifested themselves, such as have not been seen in former wars ; and among these manifestations nothing has been more remarkable than these fairs for the relief of suffering soldiers and their families. And the chief agents in these fairs are the women of America. I am not accustomed to the use of the language of eulogy ; I have never studied the art of paying compliments to women ; but I must say that, if all that has been said by orators and poets, since the creation of the world, in praise of women were applied to the women of America, it would not do them justice for their conduct during this war. I will close by saying, God bless the women of America !" (Great applause.)

Three days later, a committee appointed by the Workingmen's Democratic Republican Association of New York waited on the President, and presented him with an address informing him that he had been elected a member of that organization. After the chairman had stated the object of the visit, Mr. Lincoln made the following reply :

"*Gentlemen of the Committee :*—The honorary membership in your Association so generously tendered is gratefully accepted. You comprehend, as your address shows, that the existing rebellion means more and tends to more than the perpetuation of African slavery—that it is, in fact, a war upon the rights of all working people. Partly to show that the view has not escaped my attention, and partly that I cannot better express myself, I read a passage from the message to Congress in December, 1861 :

" ' It continues to develop that the insurrection is largely, if not exclusively, a war upon the first principle of popular Government—the rights of the people. Conclusive evidence of this is found in the most grave and maturely-considered public documents, as well as in the general tone of the insurgents. In those documents we find the abridgement of the existing right of suffrage, and the denial to the people of all right to participate in the selection of public officers, except the legislative body, boldly advocated with labored arguments, to prove that large control of the people in government is the source of all political evil. Monarchy is sometimes hinted at as a possible refuge from the power of the people. In my present position, I could scarcely

11

be justified were I to omit raising my voice against this approach
of returning despotism.

" 'It is not needed or fitting here that a general argument
should be made in favor of popular institutions; but there is one
point, with its connections, not so hackneyed as most others, to
which I ask a brief attention. It is the effort to place *capital*
on an equal footing with, if not above, *labor* in the structure of
the Government. It is assumed that labor is available only in
connection with capital; that nobody labors unless somebody
else owning capital somehow, by use of it, induces him to labor.

" 'This assumed, it is next considered whether it is best that
capital shall *hire* laborers, and thus induce them to work by their
own consent, or *buy them* and drive them to it without their
consent. Having proceeded so far, it is naturally concluded
that all laborers are either hired laborers or what we call slaves.
And, further, it is assumed that whoever is once a hired laborer
is fixed in that condition for life. Now there is no such relation
between capital and labor as assumed, nor is there any such
thing as a free man being fixed for life in the condition of a
hired laborer. Both of these assumptions are false, and all inferences from them are groundless.

" 'Labor is prior to and independent of capital. Capital is
only the fruit of labor, and never could have existed if labor had
not first existed. Labor is the support of capital, and deserves
much the higher consideration. Capital has its rights, which
are as worthy of protection as any other rights. Nor is it denied
that there is, and probably always will be, a relation between
labor and capital producing mutual benefits. The error is in
assuming that the whole labor of a community exists within that
relation. A few men own capital, and that few avoid labor
themselves, and with that capital hire or buy another few to
labor for them.

" 'A large majority belong to neither class—neither work
for others nor have others working for them. In most of the
Southern States a majority of the whole people, of all colors,
are neither slaves nor masters, while, in the Northern States, a
large majority are neither hirers nor hired. Men with their
families—wives, sons, and daughters—work for themselves on
their farms, in their houses, and in their shops, taking the whole
product to themselves, and asking no *favors* of capital on the
one hand nor of hired laborers or slaves on the other. It is
not forgotten that a considerable number of persons mingle their
own labor with capital—that is, they labor with their own hands
and also buy or hire others to labor for them; but this is only a
mixed and not a distinct class. No principle stated is disturbed
by the existence of this mixed class.

" 'Again. As has already been said, there is not of necessity
any such thing as the free hired laborer being fixed to that condition for life. Many independent men everywhere in these

States, a few years back in their lives, were hired laborers. The prudent, penniless beginner in the world labors for wages a while, saves a surplus with which to buy tools or lands for himself, then labors on his own account another while, and at length hires another new beginner to help him. This is the just, and generous, and prosperous system which opens the way to all—gives hope to all, and consequent energy, and progress, and improvement to all. No men living are more worthy to be trusted than those who toil up from poverty—none less inclined to take or touch aught with which they have not honestly earned. Let them beware of surrendering a political power which they already possess, and which, if surrendered, will surely be used to close the door of advancement against such as they, and to fix new disabilities and burdens upon them till all of liberty shall be lost.'

"The views then expressed remain unchanged—nor have I much to add. None are so deeply interested to resist the present rebellion as the working people. Let them beware of prejudices working disunion and hostility among themselves. The most notable feature of a disturbance in your city last summer was the hanging of some working people by other working people. It should never be so. The strongest bond of human sympathy, outside of the family relation, should be one uniting all working people, of all nations, tongues, and kindreds. Nor should this lead to a war upon property or the owners of property. Property is the fruit of labor; property is desirable; is a positive good in the world. That some should be rich, shows that others may become rich, and hence is just encouragement to industry and enterprise. Let not him who is houseless pull down the house of another, but let him labor diligently and build one for himself; thus, by example, assuring that his own shall be safe from violence when built."

ABRAHAM LINCOLN THE CHOICE OF THE PEOPLE FOR ANOTHER TERM.

Within the past few months, a movement has been in progress throughout the North and West, which can but be as gratifying to Abraham Lincoln as it is pleasing to the great mass of the loyal voters of the country.

No President ever encountered the same difficulties which have met the present incumbent of the "White House" at every step he has taken since the day of his inauguration. The traitors in the South have naturally opposed every important order he has issued; have ridi-

culed every proclamation he has promulgated; have criti-
cised and sneered at every message he has written; and
have vilified and maligned the character of their author.
This was to be expected; but there have been traitors at
the North who have been no less bitter, no less strenuous
in their opposition; but, under the guidance of Divine
Providence, he has been able to repel the assaults of both
of these classes of unprincipled advocates of treason; and,
strong in his holy purpose to rescue the country from the
machinations of its enemies, he has continued steadfast in
the path of official duty. He may have made some mis-
takes, but they have been few, and it must be remembered
that even those which have been more particularly referred to by his opponents were caused, not by ignorance,
but by the exigencies of the occasion, which compelled
him to give an important answer, or issue an important
order, without being allowed the time for reflection which
the magnitude of the subject demanded.

The importance, indeed the absolute necessity, of re-
taining Mr. Lincoln in his present exalted position, is now
the popular belief, and from every loyal Commonwealth
come tidings, pronouncing in language which cannot be
mistaken, that he alone is deemed the proper person to
rescue the country from its present danger. The Legislatures of fifteen States have declared that he is their
choice and the choice of their constituents. Union
Leagues, Conventions, and public assemblies of different
political characters, have indorsed the decision of their
legislative bodies; and the loyal people almost unanimously approve of the action which has again brought
Mr. Lincoln prominently forward as the best and only
man to nominate and elect to the Presidency. He has
been tried, and not found wanting, and no better return
for the perils encountered, the labors accomplished, and
the benefits derived to the country, could be offered, than

his re-nomination and re-election, both of which are now almost as certain as that the Union Convention will assemble at Baltimore in June next, and that the election will be held in November. Maine, New Hampshire, Connecticut, Rhode Island, Pennsylvania, New Jersey, Maryland, Ohio, Indiana, Michigan, Wisconsin, Iowa, Minnesota, Kansas, and California, have spoken, and, at the advent of the summer solstice, the other States will re-echo the popular sentiments, as so emphatically expressed by their sister Commonwealths. He is no longer the representative of any particular political party, but comes before the loyal voters of the country as an indefatigable, incorruptible, public servant, whose multiform and perplexing duties have been faithfully performed, and who has no other ambition than to so administer the affairs of the nation as will be most conducive to its welfare. Throughout his Presidential career he has never failed to prove himself equal to any emergency that might occur. To use the words of a patriotic Philadelphian, even in the darkest hour of our struggle, when every thing seemed lost, and the feeling of despondency with regard to the future was so great that those who had been confident before lost all hope, he who was at the helm of Government still maintained his self-command and a firm reliance in an overruling Providence, which, in due time, would order all things aright. Coolness, confidence, and courage, are only valuable when they are needed; and he who has passed through ordeals in which the possession of such qualities have been manifested, in no ordinary degree, obtains a hold on the confidence of the world which but few are fortunate enough to secure; men of extraordinary abilities, lacking these qualities, have, on great and trying occasions, too often demonstrated their incapacity for supreme command, like that which belongs to the head of a great government. Considerations such as these will make the people loth to part with one who, in the hour of trial, has proved himself equal to *the emergency.*

As an evidence of the sentiment to which we have referred, we publish the following resolutions, unanimously adopted by the Union League of Philadelphia, on the eleventh of January, 1864:

"*Whereas,* The skill, courage, fidelity and integrity with which, in a period of unparalleled trial, Abraham Lincoln has conducted the administration of the National Government, have won for him the highest esteem and the most affectionate regard of his grateful countrymen;

"*And whereas,* The confidence which all loyal men repose in his honesty, his wisdom and his patriotism, should be proclaimed on every suitable occasion, in order that his hands may be strengthened for the important work he has yet to perform;

"*And whereas,* The Union League of Philadelphia, composed as it is, of those who, having formerly belonged to various parties, in this juncture recognize no party but their country; and representing, as it does, all the industrial, mechanical, manufacturing, commercial, financial, and professional interests of the city, is especially qualified to give, in this behalf, an unbiased and authentic utterance to the public sentiment; therefore,

"*Resolved,* That to the prudence, sagacity, comprehension and perseverance of Mr. Lincoln, under the guidance of a benign Providence, the nation is more indebted for the grand results of the war, which southern rebels have wickedly waged against liberty and the Union, than to any other single instrumentality; and that he is justly entitled to whatever reward it is in the power of the nation to bestow.

"*Resolved,* That we cordially approve of the policy which Mr. Lincoln has adopted and pursued, as well the principles he has announced as the acts he has performed, and that we shall continue to give an earnest and energetic support to the doctrines and measures by which his administration has thus far been directed and illustrated.

"*Resolved,* That as Mr. Lincoln has had to endure the largest share of the labor required to suppress the rebellion, now rapidly verging to its close, he should also enjoy the largest share of the honors which await those who have contended for the right; and as, in all respects, he has shown pre-eminent ability in fulfilling the requirements of his great office, we recognize with pleasure the unmistakable indications of the popular will in all the loyal States, and heartily join with our fellow-citizens, without any distinction of party, here and elsewhere, in presenting him as the People's candidate for the Presidency at the approaching election.

"*Resolved*, That a Committee of Seventy-Six be appointed, whose duty it shall be to promote the object now proposed, by correspondence with other loyal organizations, by stimulating the expression of public opinion, and by whatever additional modes shall, in their judgment, seem best adapted to the end; and that this Committee have power to supply vacancies in their own body and to increase their numbers at their own discretion.

"*Resolved*, That a copy of these proceedings, properly engrossed and attested, be forwarded to President Lincoln; and that they also be published in the loyal newspapers."

The loyal papers have also, almost without exception, raised the name of Abraham Lincoln at the head of their columns, and are preparing to do battle with his opponents. To insert in this work extracts from all the editorials which have recently appeared in the leading journals of the North and West, recommending the renomination and re-election of Mr. Lincoln is impossible, but from the large number we cull a few of the most ably written and forcible.

The Philadelphia *Daily Evening Bulletin* says: " The re-election of President Lincoln appears to be a foregone conclusion. That he will be nominated for a second term by the Republican party is as manifest as any thing that is yet to come to pass can be, and in the event of his re-nomination, there is nothing to prevent his election. Unless the States that seceded from the Union in 1860 and 1861 vote, the election in November, 1864, will be a matter of form, a mere recording of the will of the people already plainly expressed; and no statesman, unless he belongs to the ten-pin school of politicians, who are willing to be set up to be knocked down again, will consent to accept the nomination of a Democratic Convention. At the State elections which took place in 1863, when the great issue was the question of supporting the policy of President Lincoln, every free State, except New Jersey, went for the Union cause. When Mr. Lincoln himself, as well as his policy, will be before the country for judgment in November next, what reasonable man can doubt the result?

"As regards the voting of the South, that possible contingency involves the disbanding of the Union army, and the return to their homes of nearly half a million of voters, the greater portion of whom did not cast their suffrages in 1863, and very many of whom, from General Butler down to the privates in the ranks, went into the war pro-slavery Democrats, to come out of it earnest, slavery-hating Republicans. The recent return home of so many veteran soldiers has convinced even the most skeptical that President Lincoln is the most popular man in the country with the army, and it is not difficult to understand what the effect will be of the permanent infusion among the voting people of the North of five hundred thousand patriotic soldiers who have had practical experience of the curse of slavery, and of the terrific social and political evils growing out of it, and who understand perfectly well that the present Democratic party have no platform to stand upon except that based upon sympathy with slavery and the slaveholders' rebellion, and persistent and wicked opposition to the war that has been conducted by the administration for the preservation of the Union and in defence of our nationality.

"Mr. Lincoln cannot fail to carry every State in 1864 that he carried in 1860, and by increased majorities too; while the probabilities are that he will carry other States. Mr. Lincoln received one hundred and eighty out of three hundred and three electoral votes, twenty-eight votes more than a majority of the whole. How this result can be changed, except to increase the majority of Mr. Lincoln at the next election, is, we confess, entirely beyond our comprehension."

The same paper in commenting upon the patriotic resolutions adopted by the New Hampshire Republican Union Convention, says: "This resolution, carried as it was amid every demonstration of the wildest enthusiasm, will find an echo in the hearts of millions of loyal citizens, from the White Mountains to the Pacific. No President could have more ably managed the affairs of this mighty Republic, during so terrible a period, than has Abraham Lincoln. His mingled wisdom, moderation and firmness, his justice and yet kindness show him a statesman of the noblest character, and the admiration accorded him by his country-men proves how thoroughly they appreciate such gifts in such a man. With Abraham Lincoln as the Union candi-date in 1864, we can sweep the loyal States with even more triumphant success than in 1860."

The Chicago *Tribune* thus dilates upon the affection of the armies of the Union for the President, and the truth of its assertions can be substantiated in every military de-partment :

"It is notorious that the army almost *en masse* desire the re-election of President Lincoln. Officers and men prefer him to any other candidate. They have faith in him ; they believe him to be their warm friend, and that he does all for them in his power. They know him to be as true to the cause of liberty as Jefferson, and to national unity as Jackson. He has done well so far, and, like wine, grows better as he grows older.

"Soldiers like to be commanded by experienced officers. Lincoln has had three years experience ; he begins to un-derstand the details of his manifold duties. He has pretty well learned his trade, and has now become a skilful workman. The boys in blue don't want him thrown over-board right in the middle of the voyage when he is bring-ing the ship of state safely into port after having success-fully piloted her through shoals, breakers, rocks, and hurri-canes. They want him to remain where he is until he finishes his big job, and sees the last rebel lay down his arms and submit to the national authority. The feeling of the army is pretty well expressed by the remarks of a returned veteran the other day in answer to the question of a citizen, whether the soldiers wanted Lincoln re-elected: 'Why, of course they do,' replied the blue-coat. 'We have all re-enlisted to see this thing through, and Old Abe must *re-enlist* too. He mustered us in, and must stay where he is until he has mustered us out. We'll never give it up till every rebel acknowledges that he is the Constitutional President. When they got beat at the election they kicked out of the traces, and swore they would not submit to a black Republican President; but they've got to. We will show them that elections in this country *have got to stand.* Old Abe must stay in the White House until every rebel climbs down, and agrees to behave himself, and obey the laws of his country. There mustn't be any fooling in this thing, for I wouldn't give a cuss for this country if the beaten side has a right to *bolt* after an election ; it wouldn't be fit to live in.'

"This is the sentiment that pervades the whole army. It is the talk that passes round the camp fires of fifteen hundred regiments of citizen soldiers. The rebellion must be put down, and the insurgents who *bolted* the election shall be compelled to submit to the rule of the man who was constitutionally elected President; there must be no more appeals from the ballot-box to the cartridge-box ; the minority must let the majority rule ; and, if there is any disturbing element in our country that stands in the way, it must be hewn down and cast into the fire. Free Governments can only endure and prosper by the steadfast adherence to the fundamental principle that the will of the majority shall govern."

The New York *Times*, in referring to the anxiety which the rebels evince for the retirement of Mr. Lincoln, says :

" In a speech delivered in Portland, General Neal Dow, who for nine months has been a prisoner at Richmond and other points, detailing his personal observations, made the statement that 'at present the rebels are looking anxiously at movements at the North in relation to the next Presidential election, and their hope is that some other man than Mr. Lincoln may be nominated and elected.' He testified that they would regard the election of any other person as a sure indication that the loyal North tires of the war and means to change its policy. This special spite of the rebel press against President Lincoln, has long indicated the same thing. His 'tyranny,' as it is termed, is uniformly treated as the special motive power of the war. Their fixed idea is, that if an end could somehow be made of that, the war itself would speedily come to an end.

"This idea, doubtless, springs quite as much from blind feeling as from sober thought. When a man is hard pressed, he is apt to fancy that a change of any sort would bring relief. So long as a change is in prospect, even though there may be nothing promising in it, he yet is very sure to keep up his hope by imagining that somehow it may turn to his advantage. This is as true of a whole people as of an individual   It is human nature. There has never been a people so unimaginative and unimpassioned that it did not have some influence over them. It always operates, more or less, even though reason is dead against it.

"But in this case reason is not dead against it. Just the contrary. If Abraham Lincoln shall be superseded by the nominee of the Democratic party, there would almost surely be an abatement of the war, and a resort to negotiation. The rebels would understand that this negotiation, once begun, would result, sooner or later, in securing their independence. It might take a long while to clear the way for this consummation, but it would in all probability be reached before the Copperhead Presidency ended. The war once suspended, would never be resumed. The path of peace once entered upon, there would be no steps backward. The rebels know this, and therefore attach not the slightest consequence to the protestations of our Copperheads that no peace is possible without the Union.

"But if Mr. Lincoln's successor were to be not a Copperhead, but a genuine Union man, the rebels yet would find in the fact some' hope of relief, from the uncertainty what the policy of the new President would be; whether that policy, when developed, would be acceptable to the Northern people, and whether it might not breed a disaffection and discord that would rend and ruin the Union party. Indeed, no Northern man can say that this is impossible. There certainly are policies, which have zealous advocates in some quarter, that never could be practically applied, without the most determined opposition of the great body of the Northern people—policies which bear against some of the most rooted popular convictions of political right and expediency. For instance, many Anti-Slavery leaders maintain, with great vehemence, that no rebel State ought to be restored without a guarantee that the liberated slaves shall have the right of suffrage and every privilege of highest citizenship. Does any sane man believe that the next President of the United States could devote himself persistently to that object without convulsing the Union party with internal strife? One of the chief official virtues of President Lincoln has been his consummate discretion in pushing no policy that the great loyal body of the people would not heartily accept, and aid in furthering. He has known how to keep Union sentiment, in a wonderful degree, united and compact. We do not believe that any other public man has the combination of qualities that could have so happily secured this. There can be no assurance that it would be realized at all under any man, however loyal, not yet tried. This is a matter of exceeding consequence, and the rebels recognize it. The great danger to the Union cause, from the beginning, has been the danger of dividing into two hostile camps upon some of the tremendous questions which the progress of the war is constantly evolving. Such a division, once established, would very soon so weaken the Government as to make the further effective prosecution of the war impossible, and would assure the success of the rebellion. We say, then, that the placing any other man in our Presidential chair, at this stage of the war, however zealous he might be for the war, would raise this strong hope in the rebel heart, and would be a new stimulus to keep the rebel flag flying.

"The re-election of President Lincoln by the unanimous vote of all the vast loyal majority of the North, would do more than any thing else to shut off the last hope of the rebels. His war policy, developed through three years, and thoroughly tested, needs only the complete ratification of the people to stand as an adamantine barrier against all possibility of 'Confederate' independence. It would confront the rebels like doom itself. Though yet only foreshadowed, the rebels even now shrink from it. The political event which, of all others, they most deprecate, is the election of Abraham Lincoln to a second term of office. As it is with them, so is it with their Northern sympathizers."

THE END.

T. B. PETERSON & BROTHERS' PUBLICATIONS.

THIS CATALOGUE CONTAINS AND

Describes the Most Popular and Best Selling Books in the World.

The Books will also be found to be the Best and Latest Publications by the most Popular and Celebrated Writers in the World. They are also the most Readable and Entertaining Books published.

Suitable for the Parlor, Library, Sitting-Room, Railroad Camp, Steamboat, Army, or Soldiers' Reading.

PUBLISHED AND FOR SALE BY

T. B. PETERSON & BROTHERS, Philadelphia.

Booksellers and all others will be Supplied at very Low Rates.

Copies of any of Petersons' Publications, or any other work or works Advertised, Published, or Noticed by any one at all, in any place, will be sent by us, Free of Postage, on receipt of Price.

TERMS: To those with whom we have no monthly account, Cash with Order.

MRS. SOUTHWORTH'S WORKS.

The Fatal Marriage. Complete in one or two volumes, paper cover. Price $1.00; or in one vol., cloth, $1.50.

Love's Labor Won. Two vols., paper cover. Price One Dollar; or in one vol., cloth, $1.50.

The Gipsy's Prophecy. Complete in two vols., paper cover. Price $1 00; or in one vol., cloth, $1.50.

Mother-in-Law. Complete in two volumes, paper cover. Price $1.00; or in one vol., cloth, $1.50.

The Lady of the Isle. Complete in two vols., paper cover. Price $1.00; or in one vol., cloth, $1.50.

The Two Sisters. Complete in two volumes, paper cover. Price $1.00; or in one vol., cloth, $1.50.

The Three Beauties. Complete in two vols., paper cover. Price $1.00; or in one vol., cloth, $1.50.

Vivia. The Secret of Power. Two vols., paper cover. Price $1.00; or in one vol., cloth, $1.50.

India. The Pearl of Pearl River. Two volumes, paper cover. Price $1.00; or in cloth, for $1.50.

The Wife's Victory. Two vols., paper cover. Price One Dollar; or in one volume, cloth, for $1.50.

The Lost Heiress. Two volumes, paper cover. Price One Dollar; or in one volume, cloth, for $1.50.

Hickory Hall. By Mrs. Southworth. Price 50 cents.

The Missing Bride. Two volumes, paper cover. Price One Dollar; or in one volume, cloth, for $1.50.

Retribution: A Tale of Passion. Two vols., paper cover. Price $1.00; or in one vol., cloth, $1.50.

The Haunted Homestead. Two vols., paper cover. Price One Dollar; or in one vol., cloth, $1.50.

The Curse of Clifton. Two vols., paper cover. Price One Dollar; or in one volume, cloth, for $1.50.

The Discarded Daughter. Two vols., paper cover. Price One Dollar; or in one vol., cloth, $1.50.

The Deserted Wife. Two volumes, paper cover. Price One Dollar; or in one volume, cloth, for $1.50.

The Jealous Husband. Two volumes, paper cover. Price $1.00; or in one vol., cloth, for $1.50.

The Belle of Washington. Two vols., paper cover. Price One Dollar; or in one vol., cloth, $1.50.

The Initials. A Love Story. Two vols., paper cover. Price One Dollar; or in one vol., cloth, $1.50.

Kate Aylesford. Two vols., paper cover. Price One Dollar; or bound in one vol., cloth, for $1.50.

The Dead Secret. Two volumes, paper cover. Price One Dollar; or bound in one vol., cloth, $1.50.

The Broken Engagement. By Mrs. Southworth. Price 25 cents.

MRS. ANN S. STEPHENS' WORKS.

The Rejected Wife. One volume, paper cover. Price One Dollar; or in one volume, cloth, for 1.50.

Fashion and Famine. One volume, paper cover. Price $1.00; or in one vol., cloth, $1.50.

Mary Derwent. One volume, paper cover. Price One Dollar; or in one volume, cloth, for $1.50.

The Heiress. One volume, paper cover. Price One Dollar; or in one volume, cloth, for $1.50.

The Old Homestead. One volume, paper cover. Price One Dollar; or in one vol., cloth, $1.50.

The edition of these books in one volume, paper cover, is the "Railway Edition."

CAROLINE LEE HENTZ'S WORKS.

Planter's Northern Bride. Two volumes, paper cover. Price One Dollar; or in cloth, $1.50.

Linda. The Young Pilot of the Belle Creole. Price $1.00 in paper; or $1.50 in cloth.

Robert Graham. The Sequel to, and Continuation of Linda. Price $1.00 in paper; or $1.50 in cloth.

The Lost Daughter. Two vols., paper cover. Price One Dollar; or bound in one vol., cloth, $1.50.

Courtship and Marriage. Two vols., paper cover. Price One Dollar; or in one vol., cloth, $1.50.

Rena; or, The Snow Bird. Two vols., paper cover. Price One Dollar; or one vol., cloth, $1.50.

Marcus Warland. Two volumes, paper cover. Price One Dollar; or bound in one vol., cloth, $1.50.

Love after Marriage. Two vols., paper cover. Price One Dollar; or in one volume, cloth, for $1.50.

The Planter's Daughter. Two vols., paper cover. Price One Dollar; or in one vol., cloth, $1.50.

Eoline; or, Magnolia Vale. Two vols., paper cover. Price One Dollar; or in one vol., cloth, $1.50.

The Banished Son. Two vols., paper cover. Price One Dollar; or in one volume, cloth, for $1.50.

Helen and Arthur. Two volumes, paper cover. Price One Dollar; or in one volume, cloth, for $1.50.

Ernest Linwood. Two volumes, paper cover. Price One Dollar; or in one volume, cloth, for $1.50.

Courtship and Matrimony. Two vols., paper cover. Price One Dollar; or in one vol., cloth, $1.50.

MRS. HENRY WOOD'S BOOKS.

The Shadow of Ashlydyat. Two vols., paper cover. Price One Dollar; or in one vol., cloth, for $1.25.

Squire Trevlyn's Heir. Two vols., paper cover. Price One Dollar; or in one vol., cloth, for $1.25.

The Castle's Heir. Two volumes, octavo, paper cover. Price One Dollar; or in one vol., cloth, for $1.25.

Verner's Pride. Two vols., octavo, paper cover. Price $1.00; or in one vol., cloth, for $1.25.

We also publish a "Railway Edition" of all the above, each one in one volume, paper cover. Price One Dollar each.

The Earl's Heirs. Price Fifty cents; or one vol., cloth, 75 cents.

The Mystery. One vol., octavo, paper cover. Price Fifty cents; or bound in one vol., cloth, 75 cents.

A Life's Secret. One vol., octavo, paper cover. Price Fifty cents; or in one vol., cloth, 75 cents.

The Channings. One vol., octavo, paper cover. Price 75 cents; or in one vol., cloth, $1.00.

Aurora Floyd. Price 50 cents; or a finer edition, in cloth, for $1.00.

Better For Worse. One vol., octavo, paper cover. Price 50 cents.

Martyn Ware's Temptation. One vol., paper cover. Price 25 cents

The Foggy Night at Offord. Price 25 cents.

THE GREAT NOVEL OF THE WAR.

Shoulder Straps. A novel of New York and the Army in 1862. By Henry Morford, editor of the "New York Atlas." It is the book for Ladies! Gentlemen! Soldiers! Wives and Widows, Fast Young Ladies, Slow Young Ladies, Married Men and Bachelors, Young Ladies about to be Married, and those who have no Matrimonial Prospects whatever! Stay-at-Home Guards, Government officials, Army Contractors, Aldermen, Doctors, Judges, Lawyers, etc. Complete in two large volumes, illustrated, and neatly done up in paper covers, price One Dollar a copy; or bound in one volume, cloth, for $1.50. We also publish a "Railway Edition" of it, complete in one vol., paper cover, price One Dollar

CHARLES DICKENS' WORKS.

ILLUSTRATED OCTAVO EDITION.

Pickwick Papers,.....Cloth, $2.00	David Copperfield,......Cloth, 2.00
Nicholas Nickleby,.....Cloth, 2 00	Barnaby Rudge,.........Cloth, 2.00
Great Expectations,...Cloth, 2.00	Martin Chuzzlewit,...Cloth, 2.00
Lamplighter's Story,..Cloth, 2.00	Old Curiosity Shop,....Cloth, 2.00
Oliver Twist,.............Cloth, 2.00	Christmas Stories,.....Cloth, 2.00
Bleak House,.............Cloth, 2.00	Dickens' New Stories,......2.00
Little Dorrit,.............Cloth, 2.00	A Tale of Two Cities,......2.00
Dombey and Son,......Cloth, 2.00	American Notes and
Sketches by "Boz,"....Cloth, 2.00	Pic-Nic Papers,........Cloth, 2.00

Price of a set, in Black cloth, in 17 volumes...$32.00
    "   " ·   Full Law Library style.. 42 00
    "   "   Half calf, sprinkled edges 48.00
    "   "   Half calf, marbled edges. 50.00
    "   "   Half calf, antique 60.00
    "   "   Half calf, full gilt backs, etc.. 60.00

PEOPLE'S DUODECIMO EDITION.

Pickwick Papers, ...Cloth, $1.75	Little Dorrit,.............Cloth 1.75
Nicholas Nickleby,...Cloth, 1.75	Dombey and Son,.......Cloth, 1.75
Great Expectations,...Cloth, 1.75	Christmas Stories......Cloth, 1.75
Lamplighter's Story,..Cloth, 1.75	Sketches by "Boz,"....Cloth, 1.75
David Copperfield, ...Cloth, 1.75	Barnaby Rudge, ...Cloth, 1.75
Oliver Twist,.............Cloth, 1.75	Martin Chuzzlewit,...Cloth, 1.75
Bleak House,.............Cloth, 1.75	Old Curiosity Shop,....Cloth, 1.75
A Tale of Two Cities,......1.75	Dickens' Short Stories,......1.50
Dickens' New Stories,........1.50	Message from the Sea,.......1.50

Price of a set, in Black cloth, in 17 volumes..$29.00
    "   "   Full Law Library style.. 35.60
    "   "   Half calf, sprinkled edges..................................... 42.00
    "   "   Half calf, marbled edges. 44 00
    "   "   · Half calf, antique.. 50.00
    "   "   Half calf, full gilt backs, etc................................ 50.00
    "   "   Full calf, antique... 60.00
    "   "   Full calf, gilt edges, backs, etc.............................. 60.00

ILLUSTRATED DUODECIMO EDITION.

Pickwick Papers,......Cloth, $3.00	Sketches by "Boz,"...Cloth, 3.00
Tale of Two Cities,....Cloth, 3.00	Barnaby Rudge,.........Cloth, 3.00
Nicholas Nickleby,....Cloth, 3.00	Martin Chuzzlewit,...Cloth, 3.00
David Copperfield,......Cloth, 3.00	Old Curiosity Shop,...Cloth, 3.00
Oliver Twist,.............Cloth, 3.00	Little Dorrit,.............Cloth, 3.00
Christmas Stories,......Cloth, 3.00	Dombey and Son........Cloth, 3 00
Bleak House,.............Cloth, 3.00	

Each of the above are complete in two volumes, illustrated.

Great Expectations,...Cloth, 1.75	Dickens' New Stories,.........1.75
Lamplighter's Story,...........1.75	Message from the Sea,..... ..1.75

Price of a set, in Thirty volumes, bound in Black cloth, gilt backs................$45.00
    "   "   Full Law Library style... 55.00
    "   "   Half calf, antique 90.00
    "   "   Half calf, full gilt back.. 90.00
    "   "   Full calf, antique......................................~.......... 100.00
    "   "   Full calf, gilt edges, backs, etc................... ....100.00

CHARLES DICKENS' WORKS.

CHEAP EDITION, PAPER COVER.

This edition is published complete in Twenty-two large octavo volumes, in paper cover, as follows. Price Fifty cents a volume.

Pickwick Papers.	Oliver Twist.
Great Expectations.	Lamplighter's Story.
A Tale of Two Cities.	Dombey and Son.
New Years' Stories.	Nicholas Nickleby.
Barnaby Rudge.	Holiday Stories.
Old Curiosity Shop.	Martin Chuzzlewit.
Little Dorrit.	Bleak House.
David Copperfield.	Dickens' Short Stories.
Sketches by "Boz."	Message from the Sea.
Dickens' New Stories.	Christmas Stories.
American Notes.	Pic-Nic Papers.

LIBRARY OCTAVO EDITION. IN SEVEN VOLUMES.

This edition is in SEVEN very large octavo volumes, with a Portrait on steel of Charles Dickens, and bound in the following various styles.

Price of a set, in Black Cloth, in seven volumes,......................................$14.00
"   "   Scarlet cloth, extra,... 15.00
"   "   Law Library style,.. 17.50
"   "   Half calf, sprinkled edges, ... 20.00
"   ";   Half calf, marbled edges,.................................. 21.00
"   "   Half calf, antique,.. 25.00
"   "   Half calf, full gilt backs, etc.,.......................... 25.00

CHARLES LEVER'S WORKS.

Fine Edition, bound separately.

Charles O'Malley, cloth,......$1.50	Arthur O'Leary, cloth,......... 1.50
Harry Lorrequer, cloth,...... 1.50	Con Cregan, cloth,.................. 1.50
Jack Hinton, cloth,............. 1.50	Knight of Gwynne, cloth,.. 1.50
Davenport Dunn, cloth,....... 1.50	Valentine Vox, cloth,........... 1.50
Tom Burke of Ours, cloth,. 1.50	Ten Thousand a Year,.... 1.50

CHARLES LEVER'S NOVELS.

All neatly done up in paper covers.

Charles O'Malley,....Price 50 cts.	Arthur O'Leary,..............50 cts.
Harry Lorrequer,..........50 "	The Knight of Gwynne, 50 "
Horace Templeton,.........50 "	Kate O'Donoghue,..........50 "
Tom Burke of Ours,.....50 "	Con Cregan, the Irish
Jack Hinton, the Guards-	Gil Blas,...........................50 "
man,.....................................50 "	Davenport Dunn,.............50 "

LIBRARY EDITION.

THIS EDITION is complete in FIVE large octavo volumes, containing Charles O'Malley, Harry Lorrequer, Horace Templeton, Tom Burke of Ours, Arthur O'Leary, Jack Hinton the Guardsman, The Knight of Gwynne, Kate O'Donoghue, etc., handsomely printed, and bound in various styles, as follows:

Price of a set in Black cloth,.. $7.50
"   "   Scarlet cloth,... 8.00
"   "   Law Library sheep,.. 8.75
"   "   Half Calf, sprinkled edges,..... .... 12.00
"   "   Half Calf, marbled edges,.................................. 12.50
"   "   Half Calf, antique,.. 15.00

WILKIE COLLINS' GREAT WORKS.

The Dead Secret. One volume, octavo, paper cover. Price fifty cents; or bound in one vol., cloth, for 75 cts.; or a fine 12mo. edition, in two vols., paper cover, in large type, for One Dollar, or in one vol., cloth, for $1.50.

The Crossed Path; or, Basil. Complete in two volumes, paper cover. Price One Dollar; or bound in one volume, cloth, for $1.50.

The Stolen Mask. Price 25 cents.

Hide and Seek. One vol., octavo, paper cover. Price fifty cents; or bound in one vol., cloth, for 75 cents.

After Dark. One vol., octavo, paper cover. Price fifty cents; or bound in one vol., cloth, for 75 cents.

Sights A-foot; or Travels Beyond Railways. One volume, octavo, paper cover. Price 50 cents.

The Yellow Mask. Price 25 cts.

Sister Rose. Price 25 cents.

COOK BOOKS.

Petersons' New Cook Book; or Useful Receipts for the Housewife and the Uninitiated. Full of valuable receipts, all original and never before published, all of which will be found to be very valuable and of daily use. One vol., bound. Price $1.50.

Miss Leslie's New Cookery Book. Being her last new book. One volume, bound. Price $1.50.

Widdifield's New Cook Book; or, Practical Receipts for the Housewife. Cloth. Price $1.25.

Mrs. Hale's New Cook Book. By Mrs. Sarah J. Hale. One volume, bound. Price $1.25.

Miss Leslie's New Receipts for Cooking. Complete in one volume, bound. Price $1.25.

MRS. HALE'S RECEIPTS.

Mrs. Hale's Receipts for the Million. Containing 4545 Receipts. By Mrs. Sarah J. Hale. One vol., 800 pages, strongly bound. Price, $1.50.

MISS LESLIE'S BEHAVIOUR BOOK.

Miss Leslie's Behaviour Book. A complete Guide and Manual for Ladies. Price $1.50.

FRANCATELLI'S FRENCH COOK.

Francatelli's Celebrated French Cook Book. The Modern Cook. A Practical Guide to the Culinary Art, in all its branches; comprising, in addition to English Cookery, the most approved and recherché systems of French, Italian, and German Cookery; adapted as well for the largest establishments, as for the use of private families. By CHARLES ELME FRANCATELLI, pupil to the celebrated CAREME, and late Maitre-d'Hôtel and Chief Cook to her Majesty, the Queen of England. With Sixty-Two Illustrations of various dishes. Reprinted from the last London Edition, carefully revised and considerably enlarged. Complete in one large octavo volume of Six Hundred pages, strongly bound, and printed on the finest double super-calendered paper. Price Three Dollars a copy.

J. A. MAITLAND'S GREAT WORKS.

The Three Cousins. By J. A. Maitland. Two vols., paper. Price $1.00; or in one vol., cloth, $1.50.

The Watchman. Complete in two large vols., paper cover. Price $1.00; or in one vol., cloth, $1.50.

The Wanderer. Complete in two volumes, paper cover. Price $1.00; or in one vol., cloth, for $1.50.

The Diary of an Old Doctor. Two vols., paper cover. Price $1.00; or bound in cloth for $1.50.

The Lawyer's Story. Two volumes, paper cover. Price $1.00; or bound in cloth for $1.50.

Sartaroe. A Tale of Norway. Two vols., paper cover. Price $1.00; or in cloth for $1.50.

MRS. DANIELS' GREAT WORKS.

Marrying for Money. One vol., octavo, paper cover. Price fifty cents; or one vol., cloth, 75 cents.

The Poor Cousin. Price 50 cents

Kate Walsingham. Price 50 cents.

ALEXANDER DUMAS' WORKS.

Count of Monte-Cristo. By Alexander Dumas. Beautifully illustrated. One volume, cloth, $1.50 ; or in two volumes, paper cover, for $1.00.

The Conscript. Two vols., paper cover. Twice One Dollar ; or in one volume, cloth, for $1.50.

amille; or the Fate of a Coquette. Only correct Translation from the Original French. Two volumes, paper, price $1.00 ; cloth, $1.50.

The Three Guardsmen. Price 75 cents, in paper cover, or a finer edition in cloth, for $1.50.

Twenty Years After. A Sequel to the "Three Guardsmen." Price 75 cents, in paper cover, or a finer edition, in one volume, cloth, for $1.50.

Bragelonne; the Son of Athos: being the continuation of "Twenty Years After." Price 75 cents, in paper, or a finer edition, in cloth, for $1.50.

The Iron Mask. Being the continuation of the "Three Guardsmen." Two vols., paper cover. Price One Dollar ; or in one vol., cloth, $1.50.

Louise La Valliere; or, The Second Series and end of the "Iron Mask." Two volumes, paper cover. Price $1.00, or in one vol., cloth, $1.50.

The Memoirs of a Physician. Beautifully Illustrated. Two vols., paper cover. Price One Dollar ; or bound in one volume, cloth, for $1.50.

The Queen's Necklace. A Sequel to the "Memoirs of a Physician." Two vols., paper cover. Price $1.00 ; or in one vol., cloth, for $1.50.

Six Years Later; or, Taking of the Bastile. A Continuation of "The Queen's Necklace." Two vols., paper cover. Price One Dollar ; or in one vol., cloth, for $1.50.

Countess of Charny; or, The Fall of the French Monarchy. Sequel to Six Years Later. Two vols., paper cover. Price One Dollar ; or in one volume, cloth, for $1.50.

Andree de Taverney. A Sequel to and continuation of the Countess of Charny. Two volumes, paper. Price $1.00 ; or in one vol., cloth, for $1.50.

The Chevalier. A Sequel to, and final end of "Andree De Taverney." One vol. Price 75 cents.

The Adventures of a Marquis. Two vols., paper cover. Price 1.00 ; or in one vol., cloth, for $1.50.

The Forty-Five Guardsmen. Price 75 cents, or a finer edition in one volume, cloth. Price $1.50.

The Iron Hand. Price 75 cents, in paper cover, or a finer edition in one volume, cloth, for $1.50.

Diana of Meridor. Two volumes, paper cover. Price One Dollar ; or in one vol., cloth, for $1.50.

Edmond Dantes. Being a Sequel to Dumas' celebrated novel of the "Count of Monte-Cristo." Price 50 cts.

Annette; or, The Lady of the Pearls. A Companion to "Camille." Price 50 cents.

The Fallen Angel. A Story of Love and Life in Paris. One volume. Price 50 cents.

The Man with Five Wives. Complete in one volume. Price 50 cts.

George; or, The Planter of the Isle of France. One volume. Price Fifty cents.

Genevieve; or, The Chevalier of Maison Rouge. One volume. Illustrated. Price 50 cents.

The Mohicans of Paris. 50 cts.

Sketches in France. 50 cents.

Isabel of Bavaria. Price 50 cts.

Felina de Chambure; or, The Female Fiend. Price 50 cents.

The Horrors of Paris. 50 cents.

The Twin Lieutenants. One vol. Price 50 cts.

The Corsican Brothers. 25 cts

FRANK E. SMEDLEY'S WORKS.

Harry Coverdale's Courtship and Marriage. Two vols., paper. Price $1.00 ; or cloth, $1.50.

Lorrimer Littlegood. By author of "Frank Fairleigh." Two vols., paper. Price $1.00 ; or cloth, $1.50.

Frank Fairleigh. One volume, cloth, $1.50 ; or cheap edition in paper cover, for 75 cents

Lewis Arundel. One vol., cloth. Price $1.50 ; or cheap edition in paper cover, for 75 cents.

Fortunes and Misfortunes of Harry Racket Scapegrace. Cloth. Price $1.50 ; or cheap edition in paper cover, for 50 cents.

Tom Racquet; and His Three Maiden Aunts. Illustrated. 50 cents.

MISS BREMER'S NEW WORKS.

The Father and Daughter. By Fredrika Bremer. Two vols. paper. Price $1.00; or cloth, $1.50.

The Four Sisters. Two vols., paper cover. Price One Dollar; or in one volume, cloth, for $1.50.

The Neighbors. Two vols., paper cover. Price One Dollar; or in one volume, cloth, for $1.50.

The Home. Two volumes, paper cover. Price One Dollar; or in one volume, cloth, for $1.50.

Life in the Old World; or, Two Years in Switzerland and Italy. Complete in two large duodecimo volumes, of near 1000 pages. Price $3.00.

GREEN'S WORKS ON GAMBLING.

Gambling Exposed. By J. H. Green, the Reformed Gambler. Two vols., paper cover. Price $1.00; or in one volume, cloth, gilt, for $1.50.

The Gambler's Life. Two vols., paper cover. Price One Dollar; or in one vol., cloth, gilt, for $1.50.

The Secret Band of Brothers. Two volumes, paper cover. Price One Dollar; or bound in one volume, cloth, for $1.50.

The Reformed Gambler. Two vols., paper. Price One Dollar; or in one vol., cloth, for $1.50.

MRS. GREY'S NEW BOOKS.

Little Beauty. Two vols., paper cover. Price One Dollar; or in one volume, cloth, for $1.50.

Cousin Harry. Two vols., paper cover. Price One Dollar; or in one volume, cloth, for $1.50.

The Flirt. One vol. octavo, paper cover, 50 cents; or in cloth, for 75 cents.

MRS. GREY'S POPULAR NOVELS.
Price Twenty-Five Cents each.

Gipsy's Daughter.

Lena Cameron.

Belle of the Family.

Sybil Lennard.

Duke and Cousin.

The Little Wife.

Passion & Principle. 50 cents.

The Manœuvring Mother.

The Young Prima Donna

Alice Seymour.

Baronet's Daughters.

Old Dower House.

Hyacinthe.

Mary Seaham. Price 50 cents.

G. P. R. JAMES'S NEW BOOKS.

The Cavalier. An Historical Romance. With a steel portrait of the author. Two vols., paper cover. Price $1.00; or in one vol., cloth, for $1.50.

The Man in Black. Price 50 cts.

Arrah Neil. Price 50 cents.

Lord Montagu's Page. Two volumes, paper cover. Price One Dollar; or in one vol., cloth, $1.50.

Mary of Burgundy. Price 50 cts.

Eva St. Clair; and other Tales. Price 25 cents.

MISS ELLEN PICKERING'S WORKS.
Price Thirty-Eight Cents each.

Who Shall be Heir?

Merchant's Daughter.

The Secret Foe.

The Expectant.

The Fright.

Quiet Husband.

Ellen Wareham.

Nan Darrel.

Prince and Pedlar.

The Squire.

The Grumbler. 50 cents

Orphan Niece. 50 cents

COINS OF THE WORLD.

Petersons' Complete Coin Book, containing Perfect Fac-Similes of all the various Gold, Silver, and other Metallic Coins, throughout the World, near Two Thousand in all, being the most complete Coin Book in the World, with the United States Mint Value of each Coin under it. Price $1.00

MISS PARDOE'S WORKS.

The Jealous Wife. By Miss Pardoe. Complete in one large octavo volume. Price Fifty cents.

The Wife's Trials. By Miss Pardoe. Complete in one large octavo volume. Price Fifty cents.

The Rival Beauties. By Miss Pardoe. Complete in one large octavo volume. Price Fifty cents.

Romance of the Harem. By Miss Pardoe. Complete in one large octavo volume. Price Fifty cents.

Confessions of a Pretty Woman. By Miss Pardoe. Complete in one large octavo volume. Price Fifty cents.

Miss Pardoe's Complete Works. This comprises the whole of the above Five works, and are bound in cloth, gilt, in one large octavo volume. Price $2.50.

The Adopted Heir. By Miss Pardoe. Two vols., paper. Price $1.00; or in one vol., cloth, for $1.50.

W. H. MAXWELL'S WORKS.

Stories of Waterloo. One of the best books in the English language. One vol. Price Fifty cents.

Brian O'Lynn; or, Luck is Everything. Price 50 cents.

Wild Sports in West. 50 cents.

SAMUEL C. WARREN'S BOOKS.

Ten Thousand a Year. Complete in two volumes, paper cover. Price One Dollar; or a finer edition, in one volume, cloth, for $1.50.

Diary of a Medical Student. By author of "Ten Thousand a Year." Complete in one octavo volume, paper cover. Price 50 cents.

EMERSON BENNETT'S WORKS.

The Border Rover. Fine edition bound in cloth, for $1.50; or Railroad Edition for One Dollar.

Clara Moreland. Fine edition bound in cloth, for $1.50; or Railroad Edition for One Dollar.

The Forged Will. Fine edition bound in cloth, for $1.50; or Railroad Edition for One Dollar.

Ellen Norbury. Fine edition bound in cloth, for $1.50; or Railroad Edition for One Dollar.

Bride of the Wilderness. Fine edition bound in cloth, for $1.50; or Railroad Edition for $1.00.

Kate Clarendon. Fine edition bound in cloth, for $1.50; or Railroad Edition for One Dollar.

Viola. Fine edition, cloth, for $1.50; or Railroad Edition for One Dollar.

Heiress of Bellefonte and Walde-Warren. Price 50 cents.

Pioneer's Daughter; and the Unknown Countess. 50 cents.

DOESTICKS' BOOKS.

Doesticks' Letters. Complete in two vols., paper cover. Price One Dollar; or in one vol., cloth, $1.50.

Plu-ri-bus-tah. Complete in two vols., paper cover. Price One Dollar; or in one vol., cloth, $1.50.

The Elephant Club. Complete in two vols., paper cover. Price $1.00; or in one vol., cloth, $1.50.

Witches of New York. Complete in two vols., paper cover. Price $1.00; or in one vol., cloth, $1.50.

Nothing to Say. Illustrated. Price 50 cents.

DR. HOLLICK'S WORKS.

Dr. Hollick's Anatomy and Physiology; with a large Dissected Plate of the Human Figure. Price $1.25, bound.

Dr. Hollick's Family Physician. A Pocket-Guide for Everybody. Complete in one volume, paper cover. Price 25 cents.

SMOLLETT'S AND FIELDING'S GREAT WORKS.

Peregrine Pickle; and His Adventures. Two vols., octavo. $1.00.

Humphrey Clinker. 50 cents.

Tom Jones. Two volumes. $1.00.

Amelia. One volume. Fifty cents.

Joseph Andrews. Fifty cents.

MILITARY NOVELS.

By Lever, Dumas and other Authors.

With Illuminated Military Covers, in Colors.

Published and for sale at wholesale, by the single copy, or by the dozen, hundred, or thousand, at very low rates.

Their Names are as Follows:

Charles O'Malley,........*Price*	50	Valentine Vox..............*Price*	50
Jack Hinton, the Guardsman..	50	Twin Lieutenants................	50
The Knight of Gwynne......	50	Stories of Waterloo............	50
Harry Lorrequer................	50	The Soldier's Wife.............	50
Tom Burke of Ours.............	50	Guerilla Chief.................	50
Arthur O'Leary..................	50	The Three Guardsmen......	75
Con Cregan's Adventures	50	Twenty Years After...........	75
Kate O'Donoghue................	50	Bragelonne, the Son of Athos...	75
Horace Templeton..............	50	Wallace, Hero of Scotland	75
Davenport Dunn.................	50	Forty-five Guardsmen.......	75
Following the Drum.........	50	The Quaker Soldier, Two	
The Conscript. 2 vols., each	50	volumes, each	50

Sutlers in the Army, Booksellers, Pedlars and Canvassers, can sell thousands of the above works, all of which are published with Illuminated Military covers n colors, making them the most attractive and saleable books ever printed.

REYNOLDS' GREAT WORKS.

Mysteries of the Court of London. Complete in one large volume, bound in cloth, for $1.50; or in two volumes, paper cover, price One Dollar.

Rose Foster; or, "The Second Series of the Mysteries of the Court of London." 1 vol., cloth, $2.00; or in three volumes, paper cover, price $1.50.

Caroline of Brunswick; or, the "Third Series of the Mysteries of the Court of London." Complete in one large vol., bound in cloth, for $1.50; or in two vols., paper cover, for $1.00.

Venetia Trelawney; being the "Fourth Series, or final conclusion of the Mysteries of the Court of London." Complete in one volume, in cloth, for $1.50; or in two volumes, paper cover. Price One Dollar.

Lord Saxondale; or, The Court of Queen Victoria. Complete in one large vol., cloth, for $1.50; or in two vols., paper cover, price One Dollar.

Count Christoval. The "Sequel to Lord Saxondale." Complete in one vol., bound in cloth, for $1.50; or in two vols., paper cover, price $1.00.

The Necromancer. A Romance of the Times of Henry the Eighth. One vol., bound in cloth, for $1.50; or in two vols., paper cover, price $1.00.

Rosa Lambert; or, The Memoirs of an Unfortunate Woman. One vol., bound in cloth, for $1.50; or in two volumes, paper cover, price $1.00.

Mary Price; or, The Adventures of a Servant-Maid. Complete in one vol., bound in cloth, for $1.50; or in two vols., paper cover, price $1.00.

Eustace Quentin. A "Sequel to Mary Price." Complete in one large vol., bound in cloth, for $1.50; or in two volumes, paper cover, price $1.00.

Joseph Wilmot; or, The Memoirs of a Man-Servant. Complete in one vol., bound in cloth, for $1.50; or in two volumes, paper cover, price $1.00.

The Banker's Daughter. A Sequel to "Joseph Wilmot." Complete in one vol., cloth, for $1.50; or in two volumes, paper cover, price $1.00.

Kenneth. A Romance of the Highlands. Complete in one large volume, bound in cloth, for $1.50; or in two volumes, paper cover, price $1.00.

The Rye-House Plot; or, Ruth, the Conspirator's Daughter. One vol., bound in cloth, for $1.50; or in two vols., paper cover, price One Dollar.

Mary Stuart, Queen of Scots. Complete in one large 8vo. vol 50 cts.

May Middleton; or, The History of a Fortune. Price 50 cents.

REYNOLDS' GREAT WORKS.

The Opera Dancer; or, The Mysteries of London Life. Complete in one vol. Price 50 cents.

The Ruined Gamester. With Illustrations. Complete in one large octavo vol. Price Fifty cents.

Wallace: the Hero of Scotland. Illustrated with Thirty-eight plates. Price 75 cents.

The Child of Waterloo; or, The Horrors of the Battle Field. Complete in one vol. Price 50 cents.

The Countess and the Page. Complete in one large vol. Price 50 cts.

Ciprina; or, The Secrets of a **Picture Gallery.** Complete in one vol. Price 50 cents.

Robert Bruce: the Hero King of Scotland, with his Portrait. One vol. Price 50 cents.

Isabella Vincent; or, The Two Orphans. One vol., paper cover. 50 cts.

Vivian Bertram; or, A Wife's Honor. A Sequel to "Isabella Vincent." One vol. Price 50 cents.

The Countess of Lascelles. The Continuation to "Vivian Bertram." One vol. Price 50 cents.

Duke of Marchmont. Being the Conclusion of "The Countess of Lascelles." Price Fifty cents.

Gipsy Chief. Beautifully Illustrated Complete in one large 8vo. vol. 75 cts.

Pickwick Abroad. A Companion to the "Pickwick Papers," by "Boz." One vol. Price 50 cents.

Queen Joanna; or, the Mysteries of the Court of Naples. Price 50 cents.

The Loves of the Harem. 50 cts.

The Discarded Queen. One vol 50 cents.

Ellen Percy; or, Memoirs of an Actress. Price 50 cts.

Massacre of Glencoe. 50 cents.

Agnes Evelyn; or, Beauty and Pleasure. 50 cents.

The Parricide. Beautifully Illustrated. 50 cents.

Life in Paris. Handsomely Illustrated. 50 cents.

The Soldier's Wife. Illustrated. 50 cents.

Clifford and the Actress. 50 cts

Edgar Montrose. One vol. 25 cts

T. S. ARTHUR'S BEST WORKS.

Price Twenty-Five Cents each.

The Lady at Home.
Year after Marriage.
Cecilia Howard.
Orphan Children.
Love in High Life.
Debtor's Daughter.
Agnes; or, The Possessed.
Love in a Cottage.
Mary Moreton.

The Divorced Wife.
The Two Brides.
Lucy Sandford.
The Banker's Wife.
The Two Merchants.
Insubordination.
Trial and Triumph.
The Iron Rule.
Pride and Prudence.

Lizzie Glenn; or, The Trials of a Seamstress. By T. S. Arthur. One vol., cloth, gilt. Price $1.50, or in two vols., paper cover, for $1.00.

CHARLES J. PETERSON'S WORKS.

Kate Aylesford. A Love Story. Two vols., paper. Price $1.00; or in one vol., cloth, for $1.50.

The Old Stone Mansion. By Charles J. Peterson. Two vols., paper. Price $1.00; or in cloth, for $1.50.

Cruising in the Last War. By Charles J. Peterson. Complete in one volume. Price 50 cents.

The Valley Farm; or, The Autobiography of an Orphan. A Companion to Jane Eyre. Price 25 cents.

Grace Dudley; or, Arnold at Saratoga. Complete in one octavo volume. Price 25 cents.

Mabel; or, Darkness and Dawn. Two vols., paper cover. Price $1.00; or in cloth, $1.50. (*In Press.*)

J. F. SMITH'S WORKS.

The Usurer's Victim; or Thomas Balscombe. One volume, octavo. Price 50 cents.

Adelaide Waldgrave; or the Trials of a Governess. One volume octavo. Price 50 cents.

WAVERLEY NOVELS.

The Waverley Novels. By Sir Walter Scott. With a magnificent Portrait of Sir Walter Scott, engraved from the last Portrait for which he ever sat, at Abbottsford, with his Autograph under it. This edition is complete in Five large octavo volumes, with handsomely engraved steel Title Pages to each volume, the whole being neatly and handsomely bound in cloth. This is the cheapest and most complete and perfect edition of the Waverley Novels published in the world as it contains all the Author's last additions and corrections. Price Ten Dollars for a complete and entire set bound in cloth.

CHEAP EDITION IN PAPER COVER.

This edition is published in Twenty-Six volumes, paper cover, price thirty-eight cents each, or the whole twenty-six volumes, will be sold or sent to any one, free of postage, for Eight Dollars.

The following are their names.

The Heart of Mid Lothian,	Count Robert of Paris,
Guy Mannering,	The Pirate,
The Antiquary,	The Abbot,
Old Mortality,	Red Gauntlet,
St. Ronan's Well,	The Talisman,
The Bride of Lammermoor,	Quentin Durward,
Highland Widow,	The Monastery,
Ivanhoe,	Woodstock,
Rob Roy,	Anne of Geierstein,
Waverley,	The Betrothed,
Tales of a Grandfather,	Castle Dangerous, and Surgeon's Daughter,
Kenilworth,	
Fair Maid Perth,	Black Dwarf and Legend of Montrose.
Fortunes of Nigel,	
Peveril of the Peak,	Moredun. Price 50 cents.

Lockhart's Life of Scott. Complete in one volume. cloth. Price $1.50.

WALTER SCOTT'S PROSE AND POETICAL WORKS.

We also publish Sir Walter Scott's complete Prose and Poetical Works, in ten large octavo volumes, bound in cloth. This edition contains every thing ever written by Sir Walter Scott Price Twenty Dollars for a complete set.

EUGENE SUE'S GREAT NOVELS.

Illustrated Wandering Jew. With Eighty-seven large Illustrations. Complete in two vols., paper cover. Price One Dollar; or in one volume, cloth, for $1.50.

Mysteries of Paris; and Gerolstein, the Sequel to it. Complete in two volumes, paper cover. Price One Dollar; or in one volume, cloth, for $1.50.

Martin the Foundling. Beautifully-Illustrated. Two volumes, paper cover. Price One Dollar; or in one vol., cloth, for $1.50.

First Love. Price 25 cents.

Woman's Love. Illustrated. 25 cts.

The Man-of-War's-Man. 25 cts.

The Female Bluebeard. 25 cts.

Raoul De Surville. Price 25 cts.

SIR E. L. BULWER'S NOVELS.

Falkland. A Novel. One volume, octavo. Price 25 cents.

The Roue; or, The Hazards of Women. Price 25 cents

The Oxonians. A Sequel to "The Roue." Price 25 cents.

Calderon, the Courtier By By Sir E. L. Bulwer. Price 12 cents.

HUMOROUS AMERICAN WORKS.

With Original Illustrations by Darley and Others.

Done up in Illuminated Covers.

Being the most Humorous and Laughable Books ever printed in the English Language.

Major Jones' Courtship. With Thirteen Illustrations, from designs by Darley. Price 50 cents.

Drama in Pokerville. By J. M. Field. With Illustrations by Darley. Price Fifty cents.

Louisiana Swamp Doctor. By author of "Cupping on the Sternum." Illustrated by Darley. Price 50 cents.

Charcoal Sketches. By Joseph C. Neal. With Illustrations. 50 cents.

Yankee Amongst the Mermaids. By W. E. Burton. With Illustrations by Darley. 50 cents.

Misfortunes of Peter Faber. By Joseph C. Neal. With Illustrations by Darley. Price 50 cents.

Major Jones' Sketches of Travel. With Illustrations, from designs by Darley. 50 cents.

Quarter Race in Kentucky. By W. T. Porter, Esq. With Illustrations by Darley. 50 cents.

Sol. Smith's Theatrical Apprenticeship. Illustrated by Darley. Price Fifty Cents.

Yankee Yarns and Yankee Letters. By Sam Slick, alias Judge Haliburton. Price 50 cts.

Life and Adventures of Col. Vanderbomb. By the author of "Wild Western Scenes." 50 cents.

Big Bear of Arkansas. Edited by Wm. T. Porter. With Illustrations by Darley. Price Fifty cents.

Major Jones' Chronicles of Pineville. With Illustrations by Darley. Price Fifty cents.

Life and Adventures of Percival Maberry. By J. H. Ingraham. Price Fifty cents.

Frank Forester's Quorndon Hounds. By H. W. Herbert. With Illustrations. Price 50 cents.

Pickings from the "Picayune." With Illustrations by Darley. Price Fifty cents.

Frank Forester's Shooting Box. With Illustrations by Darley. Price Fifty cents.

Peter Ploddy. By author of "Charcoal Sketches." With Illustrations by Darley. Price Fifty cents.

Western Scenes; or, Life on the Prairie. Illustrated by Darley. Price 50 cents.

Streaks of Squatter Life. By author of "Major Jones' Courtship." Illustrated by Darley. 50 cents.

Simon Suggs.— Adventures of Captain Simon Suggs. Illustrated by Darley. 50 cents.

Stray Subjects Arrested and Bound Over. With Illustrations by Darley. Fifty cents.

Frank Forester's Deer Stalkers. With Illustrations. 50 cents.

Adventures of Captain Farrago. By Hon. H. H. Brackenridge. Illustrated. Price 50 cents.

Widow Rugby's Husband. By author of "Simon Suggs." With Illustrations. Fifty cents.

Major O'Regan's Adventures. By Hon. H. H. Brackenridge. With Illustrations by Darley. Fifty cents.

Theatrical Journey - Work and Anecdotal Recollections of Sol. Smith, Esq. Price 50 cents.

Polly Peablossom's Wedding. By the author of "Major Jones' Courtship." Fifty cents.

Frank Forester's Warwick Woodlands. With beautiful Illustrations. Price 50 cents.

New Orleans Sketch Book. By "Stahl." With Illustrations by Darley. Price Fifty cents.

The Love Scrapes of Fudge Fumble. By author of "Arkansaw Doctor." Price Fifty cents.

American Joe Miller. With 100 Illustrations. Price Twenty-five cents.

Judge Haliburton's Yankee Stories. Two vols., paper cover. Price $1.00; or cloth, $1.50.

Humors of Falconbridge. Two vols., paper cover. Price One Dollar or in one vol., cloth, $1.50.

GUSTAVE AIMARD'S WORKS.

The Prairie Flower. One vol., octavo, paper cover, price 50 cents, or bound in cloth for 75 cents.

The Indian Scout. One volume, octavo, paper cover, price fifty cents, or bound in cloth for 75 cts.

The Trail Hunter. One volume, octavo, paper cover, price fifty cents, or bound in cloth for 75 cts.

The Pirates of the Prairies. One vol., paper cover, price 50 cents or bound in cloth, for 75 cents.

The Trapper's Daughter. One volume, paper cover. Price 50 cents.

The Tiger Slayer. One volume, octavo, paper cover. Price 50 cents.

The Gold Seekers. One volume, octavo, paper cover. Price 50 cents.

All of Aimard's other books are in press by us.

GEORGE SAND'S WORKS.

Consuelo. By George Sand. Translated from the French, by Fayette Robinson. Complete and unabridged. One volume. Price Fifty cents.

Countess of Rudolstadt. The Sequel to "Consuelo." Translated from the original French. Complete and unabridged edition. Price 50 cents.

First and True Love. By author of "Consuelo," "Indiana," etc. Illustrated. Price 50 cents.

The Corsair. Price 50 cents.

Indiana. By author of "Consuelo," etc. A very bewitching and interesting work. Two vols., paper cover $1.00 ; or in one vol., cloth, for $1.50.

LIEBIG'S WORKS ON CHEMISTRY.

Agricultural Chemistry. By Baron Justus Liebig. Complete and unabridged. Price 50 cents.

Animal Chemistry. Complete and unabridged. Price 25 cents.

Familiar Letters on Chemistry.

Chemistry and Physics in relation to Physiology and Pathology.

The Potato Disease.

The whole of the above Five works of Professor Liebig are also published complete in one large octavo volume, bound. Price $2.00. The three last works are only published in the bound volume.

HUMOROUS ILLUSTRATED WORKS.

High Life in New York. By Jonathan Slick. Beautifully Illustrated. Two vols., paper cover. One Dollar ; or bound in one vol., cloth, $1.50.

Sam Slick, the Clockmaker. By Judge Haliburton. Illustrated. One volume, cloth, $1.50 ; or in two volumes, paper cover, for $1.00.

Major Jones' Courtship and Travels. Beautifully illustrated. One vol., cloth. Price $1.50.

Major Jones' Scenes in Georgia. Full of beautiful illustrations. One vol., cloth. Price $1.50.

Simon Suggs' Adventures and Travels. Illustrated. One volume, cloth. Price $1.50.

Major Thorpe's Scenes in Arkansaw: containing the whole of the "Quarter Race in Kentucky," and "Bob Herring, the Arkansas Bear Hunter," to which is added the "Drama in Pokerville." With Sixteen illustrations from Designs by Darley. Complete in one vol., cloth. $1.50.

Humors of Falconbridge. Two vols., paper cover. Price One Dollar or in one vol., cloth, for $1.50.

Piney Woods Tavern; or, Sam Slick in Texas. Cloth, $1.50 ; or 2 vols., paper cover, $1.00.

Yankee Stories. By Judge Haliburton. Two vols., paper cover. Price $1.00 ; or bound in cloth, for $1.50.

The Swamp Doctor's Adventures in the South-West. Containing the whole of the Louisiana Swamp Doctor ; Streaks of Squatter Life ; and Far-Western Scenes. With 14 Illustrations from designs by Darley. Cloth. Price $1.50.

The Big Bear's Adventure and Travels: containing all of the Adventures and Travels of the "Big Bear of Arkansaw," and "Stray Subjects." With Eighteen Illustrations from Original Designs by Darley. One vol., bound. Price $1.50.

Frank Forester's Sporting Scenes and Characters. Illustrated. Two vols., cloth, $3.00.

CAPTAIN MARRYATT'S WORKS.
Price Twenty-Five Cents each.

Japhet in Search of a Father.
Snarleyow.
King's Own.
Newton Forster.
Pirate and Three Cutters.
Phantom Ship.
Jacob Faithful.
The Naval Officer.

Pacha of many Tales.
Midshipman Easy.
Rattlin, the Reefer.
Percival Keene. Price 50 cents
Peter Simple. 50 cents.
Sea King. 50 cents.
Poor Jack. 50 cents.
Valerie. 50 cents.

GEORGE LIPPARD'S WORKS.

Legends of the American Revolution; or, Washington and his Generals. Two volumes, paper cover. Price One Dollar.

The Quaker City; or, The Monks of Monk Hall. Two volumes, paper cover. Price One Dollar.

Paul Ardenheim; the Monk of Wissahikon. Two vols., paper cover. Price One Dollar.

Blanche of Brandywine. A Revolutionary Romance. Two vols., paper cover. Price One Dollar.

The Lady of Albarone; or, The Poison Goblet. One vol., paper cover. Price 75 cents.

The Nazarene. One vol. 50 cents.

Legends of Mexico. One volume. Price 25 cents.

DOW'S PATENT SERMONS.

Each volume, or series, is complete in itself, and either of the volumes are sold separately to any one, or in sets.

Dow's Short Patent Sermons. First Series. By Dow, Jr. Containing 128 Sermons. Complete in one vol., bound in cloth, for $1.00; or in one vol., paper, for 75 cents.

Dow's Short Patent Sermons. Second Series. By Dow, Jr. Containing 144 Sermons. Complete in one vol., bound in cloth, for $1.00; or in one vol., paper, for 75 cents.

Dow's Short Patent Sermons. Third Series. By Dow, Jr. Containing 116 Sermons. Complete in one vol., bound in cloth, for $1.00; or in one vol., paper, for 75 cents.

Dow's Short Patent Sermons. Fourth Series. By Dow, Jr. Containing 152 Sermons. Complete in one vol., bound in cloth, for $1.00; or in one vol., paper, for 75 cents.

ADVENTURES AND TRAVELS.

What I Saw; and Where I Went. Being the private daily Journal and Letters of an educated Gentleman of Leisure and Fortune, who went abroad to see the Sights, and saw them. Price 75 cents in paper; or in cloth, for One Dollar.

Life & Adventures of Paul Periwinkle. Price 50 cents.

Adventures in Africa. By Major Cornwallis Harris. This book is a rich treat. Two vols., paper, $1.00; or in cloth, $1.50.

Don Quixotte.—Life and Adventures of Don Quixotte; and his Squire, Sancho Panza. Two vols, paper cover. Price $1.00; or in one volume, cloth, for $1.50.

MILITARY WORKS.

The Soldier's Guide. A Complete Manual and Drill Book, for the use of Soldiers and Volunteers. Price 25 cents in paper, or forty cents in cloth.

The Soldier's Companion.— With valuable information from the "Army Regulations," for the use of all Officers and Volunteers. Price 25 cts. in paper cover, or 40 cts. in cloth.

Ellsworth's "Zouave Drill" and Biography. Price 25 cents in paper, or forty cents in cloth.

The Volunteers' Text Book. This Work contains the whole of "The Soldier's Guide," as well as the whole of "The Soldier's Companion." Price 50 cents in paper, or 75 cents in cloth.

The United States' Light Infantry Drill. Price 25 cents in paper cover, or forty cents in cloth.

United States' Government Infantry and Rifle Tactics, full of engravings. Price 25 cents

REVOLUTIONARY TALES.
Price Twenty-Five Cents each.

The Seven Brothers of Wy-oming; or, The Brigands of the American Revolution.

The Brigand; or, The Mountain Chief.

The Rebel Bride. A Revolutionary Romance.

Ralph Runnion; or, The Outlaw's Doom.

The Flying Artillerist, or Mexican Treachery.

Lippard's Legends of Mexico.

Old Put; or, The Days of '76. A Revolutionary Tale.

Wau-nan-gee; or, The Massacre at Chicago.

Grace Dudley; or Arnold at Saratoga.

The Guerilla Chief. Price 50 cents.

Red Sleeve, the Apache Chief. Price 50 cents.

The Quaker Soldier. One volume, paper, $1.00; or cloth, $1.50.

SEA AND PIRATICAL TALES.

Life and Adventures of Jack Adams, the celebrated Sailor and Mutineer. Price 50 cents.

Life and Adventures of Ben Brace, the Sailor. Price 50 cents.

Jack Ariel; or, Life on Board an East Indiaman. One vol. Fifty cents.

Life and Adventures of Tom Bowling, the Sailor. Fifty cents.

The Petrel; or, Love on the Ocean. A Sea Novel. By Admiral Fisher. One volume. Price 50 cents.

Cruising in Last War. 50 cents.

Percy Effingham. Price 50 cents.

Percival Keene. Price 50 cents.

The Sea King. Price 50 cents.

Peter Simple. Price 50 cents.

Poor Jack. Price 50 cents.

SEA TALES, AT 25 CENTS EACH.

The Doomed Ship; or, Wreck in the Arctic Regions.

The Pirate's Son. Illustrated.

The Three Pirates; or, Cruise of the Tornado.

The Flying Dutchman.

Life of Alexander Tardy, the Pirate.

The Flying Yankee. By Harry Hazel.

The Yankee Middy; or, The Two Frigates.

The Gold Seekers; or, Cruise of the Lively Sally.

The River Pirates. A Tale of New York.

Dark Shades of City Life.

Rats of the Seine; or, River Thieves of Paris.

Yankees in Japan; or, Adventures of a Sailor.

Red King; or, the Corsair Chieftain.

Morgan, the Buccaneer; or, The Freebooters.

Jack Junk; or, The Tar for all Weathers.

Davis, the Pirate; or, the Freebooter of the Pacific.

Valdez, the Pirate; His Life and Adventures.

Gallant Tom; or, Perils of Ocean.

Yankee Jack; or, The Perils of a Privateersman.

Harry Helm; or, The Cruise of the Bloodhound.

Harry Tempest; or, The Pirate's Protege.

The King's Cruisers. By Harry Hazel.

Charles Ransford; or, Love on Board a Cruiser.

Red Wing; or, Cruiser of Van Dieman's Land.

The Pacha of Many Tales.

Pirate and Three Cutters.

The Man-of-War's-Man.

Rebel and the Rover.

Jacob Faithful.

Midshipman Easy.

Newton Forster.

King's Own.

The Naval Officer.

Phantom Ship.

Snarleyow.

Our Mess.

Wreck of the Golden Mary.

Wild Oats Sown Abroad; or, On and Off Soundings. 50 cents in paper; or in cloth, gilt, 75 cents.

AINSWORTH'S BEST WORKS.

Life of Jack Sheppard, the most noted burglar, robber, and jail breaker, that ever lived. Illustrated. 50 cents.

The Tower of London. With over One Hundred splendid Engravings. Two vols. Price $1.00.

The Miser's Daughter. Complete in two large vols. Price $1.00.

Pictorial Life and Adventures of Guy Fawkes. The Bloody Tower, &c. Price 50 cents.

The Pictorial Old St. Pauls'. A Tale of the Plague and the Fire. Illustrated. Price 50 cents.

The Star Chamber. Beautifully Illustrated. Price 50 cents.

Mysteries of the Court of Queen Anne. Price 50 cents.

Windsor Castle. One volume. Price 50 cents.

Mysteries of the Court of the Stuarts. Price 50 cents.

Life of Henry Thomas, the Western Burglar and Murderer. Full of Plates. Price 25 cents.

Pictorial Life and Adventures of Dick Turpin, the Burglar, Murderer, etc. Price 25 cents.

The Desperadoes of the New World. Price 25 cents.

Life of Ninon De L'Enclos. With her Letters on Love, Courtship, and Marriage. Price 25 cents.

Pictorial Life and Adventures of Davy Crockett. One volume. Price 50 cents.

Grace O'Malley—Her Life and Adventures. Price 50 cents.

Life of Arthur Spring. Price 25 cents.

HARRY COCKTON'S WORKS.

Valentine Vox, the Ventriloquist. One volume, paper cover. Price 50 cents; or a finer edition in cloth, for $1.50.

Sylvester Sound, the Somnambulist. Illustrated. One volume. Price 50 cents.

The Sisters. By Harry Cockton, author of "Valentine Vox, the Ventriloquist." Price 50 cents.

The Steward. By Harry Cockton. Price 50 cents.

Percy Effingham. By Harry Cockton. Price 50 cents.

BY VARIOUS GOOD AUTHORS.

Somebody's Luggage. By Chas. Dickens. Price 25 cents.

The Two Prima Donnas. By George Augustus Sala. Price 25 cents.

The Haunted House. By Chas. Dickens. Price 25 cents.

The Deformed. By Mrs. Marsh. Price 25 cents.

The Iron Cross. By Sylvanus Cobb, Jr. Price 25 cents.

The Nobleman's Daughter. Price 25 cents.

Robert Oaklands; or, The Outcast Orphan. By Leigh Ritchie, author of "Robber of the Rhine." Price 25 cts.

Webster and Hayne's Speeches in the United States Senate, on **Mr. Foot's** Resolution of January, 1830. Also, Daniel Webster's Speech in the Senate of the United States, March 7, 1850, on the Slavery Compromise. Price 50 cents.

Train's Union Speeches. Complete in two volumes. 25 cents each.

Father Tom and the Pope. Price 25 cents.

Rifle Shots at the Great Men. Price 25 cents.

Tom Tiddler's Ground. By Charles Dickens. Price 25 cents.

REV. CHARLES WADSWORTH'S SERMONS.

America's Mission. A Thanksgiving Discourse. By Rev. Charles Wadsworth. Price 25 cents.

Thankfulness and Character. Two Discourses. By Rev. Charles Wadsworth. Price 25 cents.

Politics in Religion. A Thanksgiving Sermon. By Rev. Charles Wadsworth. Price 12 cents.

Thanksgiving. A Sermon. By Rev. Charles Wadsworth. Price 12 cents.

WORKS BY POPULAR AUTHORS.

Lady Maud, the Wonder of Kingswood Chase. By Pierce Egan. Price 75 cents in paper; or a finer edition, bound, for $1.50.

Mysteries of Three Cities: Boston, New York, and Philadelphia. By A. J. H. Duganne. Price 50 cents.

Red Indians of Newfoundland. A beautifully Illustrated Indian Story. By author of "Prairie Bird." Price 50 cents.

Whitehall; or, The Times of Oliver Cromwell. Illustrated. Price 50 cents.

The Greatest Plague of Life; or, The Adventures of a Lady in Search of a Good Servant. By one who has been "worried to death." 50 cents.

Corinne; or, Italy. By Madame De Stael. The poetical passages by L. E. L. Only unabridged edition. 50 cents in paper, or 75 cents in cloth.

Moredun. A Tale of 1210. By Sir Walter Scott, Bart., author of "Ivanhoe," etc. Price 50 cents.

Flirtations in America; or, High Life in New York. Complete in one volume. Price 50 cents.

Life in the South. With Illustrations by Darley. Price 50 cents.

Llorente's History of the Inquisition in Spain. Complete in one volume. Price 50 cents.

Genevra. By Miss Fairfield. 50 cts.

Aristocracy; or, Life among the Upper Ten. By Joseph A. Nunes, Esq. Price 50 cents.

Tom Racquet; and His Three Maiden Aunts. Full of Illustrative engravings. Price 50 cents.

The Two Lovers; or a Sister's Devotion. A Domestic Story. By author of Twin Sisters. Price 50 cts.

Thackeray's Irish Sketch Book. By W. M. Thackeray, author of "Vanity Fair." Price 50 cents.

Salathiel. By Rev. George Croly. 50 cents in paper, or in cloth, 75 cents.

The Coquette. By the author of "Misserimus." One of the best books ever written. Price 50 cents.

The Fortune Hunter. By Mrs. Anna Cora Mowatt. Price Fifty cents.

Ned Musgrave; or, the Most Unfortunate Man in the World. By Theodore Hook. Price 50 cents.

Clifford and the Actress; or the Reigning Favorite. By Margaret Blount. Price Fifty cents.

The Jesuit's Daughter. By Ned Buntline. Price 50 cents.

Ryan's Mysteries of Marriage. Full of Illustrations. 50 cts.

The Orphan Sisters. By Mrs. Marsh, author of "The Deformed." Price 50 cents.

Romish Confessional. By M Michelet. Price 50 cents.

Abbey of Innismoyle. By Grace Kennedy, author of "Father Clement." Price 25 cents.

Father Clement. By author of "Dunallen." Price 50 cents in paper, or 75 cents in cloth.

Wilfred Montressor; or, the Secret Order of the Seven. A Romance of Life in the New York Metropolis. Illustrated with 87 Illustrative Engravings. Two vols., paper cover. $1.00.

The Cabin and Parlor. By J. Thornton Randolph. 50 cents in paper; or in cloth for $1.00.

Henry Clay's Portrait. By Nagle. Size 22 by 30 inches. Price $1.00 a copy. Originally sold at $5.00.

The Miser's Heir. By P. H. Myers. Price 50 cents in paper cover; or 75 cents in cloth, gilt.

Victims of Amusements. By Martha Clark. Suitable for Sunday-Schools. One vol., cloth. 38 cents.

CHRISTY & WOOD'S SONG BOOKS.

No music is so generally esteemed, or songs so frequently sung and listened to with so much delight, as is the music and the songs of the Ethiopian Minstrels. They have commenced a new epoch in Music, and the best works relating to them are those mentioned below. Each Book contains near Seventy Songs.

Christy & Wood's New Song Book. Illustrated. Price 12 cents.

The Melodeon Song Book. Price 12 cents.

The Plantation Melodies. Price 12 cents.

The Ethiopian Song Book. Price 12 cents.

The Serenaders' Song Book. Price 12 cents.

Budsworth's Songs. 12 cents.

Christy and White's Complete Ethiopian Melodies, containing 291 songs, and beautifully bound in one volume, cloth, gilt. Price $1.00.

www.ingramcontent.com/pod-product-compliance
Lightning Source LLC
Chambersburg PA
CBHW030556040726
47497CB00008B/2747